PRAISE FOR JUDITH O'BRIEN'S *ONCE UPON A ROSE*

"A richly detailed backdrop of food, clothing, and manners heightens the drama and provides a touch of humor as Deanie's twentieth-century sensibilities encounter sixteenth-century reality. . . . A sweet love story unfolds amidst deadly intrigue. This beautifully realized romance by the talented Judith O'Brien uses the magic and mystery of time-travel to full effect."

—*Publishers Weekly*

"Ms. O'Brien's ability to richly depict Henry the VIII's court is mesmerizing. She gives her reader a clear and vivid portrait of Henry as a cruel, spoiled king who rules by his moods. She adds a singular twist on time-travel and a powerful love story to ensure us of a glorious tale to add to our collection."

—*Rendezvous*

"Judith O'Brien joins the ranks of master storytellers with a delicious, hilarious story of a Nashville star taking sixteenth-century London, and the royal duke who joins her magical adventure, by storm."

—Maria C. Ferrer, *Romantic Times*

PRAISE FOR
ASHTON'S BRIDE

"Quite simply, a must-read. . . . "

—*Publishers Weekly*

"This is more than just a time-travel, it's about finding out where you belong. Lush descriptions, vivid characters, and strong emotional writing combine to make this an unforgettable novel."

—*Rendezvous*

"I was captivated from the very first page. *Ashton's Bride* is fabulous! Poignant, powerful, utterly compelling and so very heartwarming. Judy O'Brien is the most exciting—and most original—new voice to hit the romance scene in years!"

—Brenda Joyce, author of *The Game*

"This tender, funny love story will haunt me for a long time. . . . I feel as if I've discovered a rare and charming new treasure to add to my list of favorite authors. Ms. O'Brien's fresh and witty style tickled both my funny bone and my heartstrings."

—Teresa Medeiros, author of *A Whisper of Roses*

"Judith O'Brien makes you cry and she makes you laugh. *Ashton's Bride* is an utterly heartwarming love story with characters who will captivate you and leave you basking in a warm, magical glow."

—Dorothy Cannell, author of *Femmes Fatal*

"This is one new writer who has a whole new light on the art of writing. I enjoyed this book, and it was with real regret that I had to stop when the story ended. 5 Bells, NOT TO BE MISSED!"

—Bell, Book and Candle book dealer

"This is a rare and delightful book. . . . Judith O'Brien has a wonderful sense of humor and she knows how to combine it with the kind of drama, fantasy, and romance readers cherish. I was utterly caught up in the lives of Margaret and Ashton—laughing with them, crying with them, and rooting for them to triumph."

—Deborah Smith, author of *Silk & Stone*

PRAISE FOR

RHAPSODY IN TIME

"Ms. O'Brien takes you on a journey into the Roaring Twenties you'll never forget. The storyline takes many exciting and dangerous twists and turns to a stunning conclusion. This one is a must-read. Excellent."

—*Rendezvous*

"*Rhapsody in Time* is an exciting time-travel romance that pays homage to the New York City of the Roaring Twenties. Judith O'Brien has gifted the audience with two dynamic lead characters and a fast-paced romance."

—Harriet Klausner, *Affaire de Coeur*

"Her characters are wonderful and so believable that readers can't help but cheer them on. Time-travel has a new voice, and her name is Judith O'Brien."

—Maria C. Ferrer, *Romantic Times*

Books by Judith O'Brien

Rhapsody in Time
Ashton's Bride
Once Upon a Rose
Maiden Voyage

Published by POCKET BOOKS

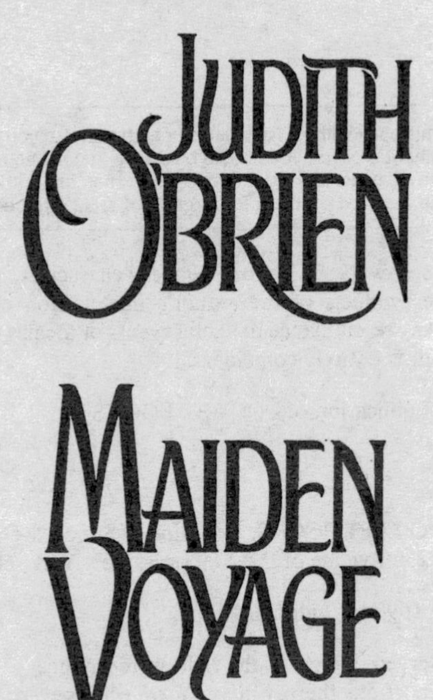

POCKET BOOKS
New York London Toronto Sydney Tokyo Singapore

An *Original* Publication of POCKET BOOKS

POCKET BOOKS, a division of Simon & Schuster Inc.
1230 Avenue of the Americas, New York, NY 10020

ISBN: 0-671-50219-0

First Pocket Books printing January 1997

10 9 8 7 6 5 4 3 2 1

Cover art by Mitzura Salgian

Printed in the U.S.A.

For Gary Estes Gale (1958–1995)

Carla's husband, Merritt's preferred relative, Seth's favorite grown-up, and forever our cabana boy . . . you are missed everywhere but in our hearts.

And thank you to everyone in Ireland—all of you—but especially Mary, Jeffrey, and dear Stan. You showed me a world I could never have imagined!

Finally, thank you, Ed.

MAIDEN
VOYAGE

PROLOGUE

A gray-green shaft of light cast uncertain shadows over Charles MacGuire's cluttered desk. Early evening always made the room seem sinister, the sun's final rays flickering about the dusty furniture, swirling in the corners.

The bustling noises of modern Dublin, the high-pitched garda sirens, the buses and car horns, even the voices of children—all were muffled by the thick glass windows of his office.

The wall clock pinged a vague announcement of the time. The clock was well over a hundred years old, and as far as Charles could tell, it had never struck the correct hour. There was a mathematical formula that had to be calculated with every chime. It had just struck three times, with a humming quiver, followed by a creaking moan and a final ding.

"Ah," Charles said to himself. "'Tis half seven."

It had been his father's clock, and his father's

father's. They all worked as solicitors—calm, reliable men, specializing in the more mundane aspects of the law.

One last glance at his papers and he could safely flee the office for a nice glass of whiskey at the Shelbourne. The tortoiseshell bifocals dipped off the bridge of his nose as he squinted. Reaching up to scratch his head, he was surprised by the bald spot there. It always took him by surprise, the lack of hair that crept so suddenly over his scalp, and he just past fifty. Shame.

One last look at Old Man Finnegan's papers, and the Jameson was as good as swallowed.

This had been one of the more ridiculous cases of his career. Delbert Finnegan had left his entire estate to a relative who might not even exist. What made the case particularly vexing was the nature of the estate. It consisted of a failing furniture factory and a rather tatty town house in one of Dublin's poshest neighborhoods, Merrion Square.

The select few who had managed to grab one of Merrion Square's brick Georgian beauties could usually afford the best real estate in the world. Merrion Square dated from 1760, as did the town houses and the magnificent park in the center of the square. And of all the homes and embassies and fashion designer shops that surrounded the park, there was only one acknowledged disgrace.

Number eighty-nine and a half Merrion Square South, home of the lately departed Delbert Finnegan, was a bona fide eyesore. The masking tape on the windows and the iron bars propping up the arched doorway only hinted at the mayhem within.

Yet architects and university students were always

peering at the tumbledown town house with glazed, reverent expressions. The National Trust and the Royal Georgian Society had made repeated and impassioned pleas to Old Delbert to leave the house to them. They could restore it to its former glory, transform the eyesore into a museum.

Still, the house remained empty and decaying, although it was in no worse condition than it had been when Old Delbert was alive and puttering about the ground floor in his paisley robe and tasseled cap.

The Maiden Works Furniture Company was in no better shape than the house that went along with it. Located on Maiden Lane, a dirty little alley just off the Wicklow Road, the furniture produced there was said to be fine indeed, but too dear for most people to afford. Occasionally there were scattered rumors of an actual piece of furniture being purchased, although Charles had yet to procure solid evidence on the matter. According to his guess, the factory would fold about the same time the Merrion Square town house would finally tumble into the street. In other words, at any moment.

The final and apparently unintentional joke had been played by Old Delbert himself. The ninety-seven-year-old bachelor who, even as death beckoned had held a nebulous conviction of meeting the "right girl," left his considerable estate to any relative who could be located.

Charles sighed. There were no relations in Ireland, that was for sure. He had exhausted the list of possibilities in England and Scotland and Australia and even New Zealand. There was one final place he had to search for an heir: America.

Not today, he thought to himself. He would begin again on Monday. He would . . .

Then he saw it.

A pile of memos next to the morning tea mug. His assistant, Miss Regan, must have placed them on his desk. With an annoyed sigh, he dragged them forward, dreading the tangled trail he would be forced to decipher.

According to the information gathered by Miss Regan, who had been spending her afternoons at the National Library with musty genealogical papers, there was a possibility that a line of the Finnegan family was living in America's Middle West.

"Good Lord," he said aloud. "Miss Regan is going to have to ring up a place called Whitefish Bay, Wisconsin."

With that he straightened his tie and clicked off the lamps. As usual, Charles whistled a jaunty tune as he walked the three blocks to the Shelbourne.

Chapter 1

Maura Finnegan cleared her throat, indicating to the rest of the board that the meeting was about to begin. Conversations were hastily concluded, papers were shuffled. A secretary silently refilled coffee and water cups. All eyes were now focused on Maura Finnegan.

To the casual observer, she seemed too young to be seated in the oversize chair at the head of the oblong table. Her complexion was fresh as a child's, luminous and free of obvious cosmetics. Her long red hair was pulled back into a severe French twist, and she wore no jewelry other than a plain watch. Although her teal suit was expertly cut, it, too, was simple.

"Good morning." She smiled, glancing around the table at the faces of men and women old enough to be her parents. There was a general murmur of greeting, brief return smiles before she looked down at the agenda before her.

Maura was exhausted, far too tired to lead the

meeting. She had passed the entire night in a fruitless quest for sleep, paging through paperback novels, flicking past television channels, listening to the radio. Nothing seemed to soothe her. It had been that way for over a month now, ever since Roger had dumped her.

Someone was speaking.

Maura blinked and focused in the direction of the voice.

And again she thought of Roger.

He had seemed so perfect. Everyone who met him had invariably pulled her aside.

"What a great guy!"

When they first met, she had been intimidated by his overpowering air of success. He arrived in Milwaukee like a bolt of lightning, fresh and clean and wonderful. If not exactly handsome, he was indeed well-groomed, with an exceptionally fine set of teeth. She had noticed his teeth when they first met.

It had been at a Christmas party, a dull affair hosted by the advertising agency that handled her father's company. Later no one could remember why he was at the party, since no one could recall meeting him before the event, much less inviting him to the party.

With his blond hair combed straight back and wearing a black overcoat, he had walked directly to where she was seated, a handful of peanuts cupped in his hands. To her astonishment, he siphoned the peanuts into her lap.

"I wish they were emeralds," he whispered. "They would match your eyes."

She could not respond for two reasons. One was that everyone in the tinsel-festooned lobby was staring at them. The other was that she had seen a PBS special the week before, and a variation of the "wish they were emeralds" line had been uttered over seventy years before by playwright Charles MacArthur to Helen Hayes. She did not mention that she had seen the same show, for it was the meaning of his words that was so important. The line had worked on Helen Hayes, and it sure worked on Maura.

Their romance began at that moment, a whirlwind affair full of flowers and red wine and evenings spent by the roaring fireplace of her parents' home. She had felt so alone after the death of her father, following less than two years after her mother's death. In one fell swoop she had been robbed of her remaining family and forced into the uncomfortable position of running the family business.

And then came Roger. With little hesitation, she had allowed herself to be swept into his capable arms. Clever, strong Roger seemed a godsend.

Then an odd thing happened: People stopped commenting on what a great guy he was. She attributed it to jealousy. On the part of the women it was because their own mates could never hope to compare to Roger. With men, it was because Roger was effortlessly all they longed to be. Of course, that had to be the reason, simple and understandable jealousy.

Roger seemed to know everything, from the best restaurants to the finest wine. The waiters had even been impressed, she could tell, when he sipped a glass of burgundy and proclaimed it "a pretty little wine."

It didn't matter that she no longer saw most of her friends or that they spent more and more time alone, isolated from the rest of the world. Nor did it matter that he never introduced her to his own family or friends.

"I'm jealous of the time you spend with other people," he had said, and she, of course, felt the same way. Although he wanted her to meet his family, a large brood that seemed to have come straight from an idealistic sitcom, his brothers, all lawyers or doctors or architects, were always jetting around the world. His parents, old-fashioned—his father was a retired judge, his mother president of the garden club—stayed back east, but he had told them all about her, and they eagerly awaited meeting their boy's girlfriend.

Someone was still speaking at the meeting. Maura made all of the practiced motions of appearing to pay attention. Her green eyes seemed to flash with intelligence every few moments, but the reaction was to her own tortured thoughts, not to the actual speaker.

Although he was a man's man in every way, Roger had been free to show his soft side to women. Once she even saw a tear in the corner of his eye when they were watching *The Pride of the Yankees.* Later he claimed the moisture had been the result of new contact lenses, but Maura knew better. He was sensitive and tender, her Roger. The kind of man she had always dreamed of meeting. The kind of man she had always dreamed of marrying. Someone to help her with the company.

For in reality, Finnegan's Freeze-Dried Cabbage

was not the moneymaker it once had been. By the time of his death, her own father, sidelined for the last six months, had no idea how bad things had become. Maura had seen all of the books, the black-and-white balance sheets that added up to a company on the brink of collapse, and hid the truth from her father.

He had established the company twenty years before, convinced that Finnegan's Freeze-Dried Cabbage would pave the way to a freeze-dried vegetable empire.

But freeze-dried cabbage had never really caught on. As a side dish it tasted like salty wood shavings. Their biggest clients now were dry soup and sauce manufacturers, who buried the product safely under other ingredients. Unless a new use for Finnegan's Freeze-Dried Cabbage could be found, it was only a matter of time before the business went under.

The company had inched forward with her father at the helm, but with Maura it had stalled. It had been her dad's forceful personality that had propelled Finnegan's Freeze-Dried, not the product.

Maura, at the age of twenty-seven, did not have that winning personality. Instead, she had a business degree from Notre Dame and, for the past year and a half, Roger.

Without Roger, she was absolutely nothing.

Her hand clenched, and she squeezed her eyes shut for a moment, forcing the tears to go away. Not now. She couldn't cry now. Later, back home, she could again close the door and give way to her grief. But not at a business meeting.

The small slip of paper in her hand was damp from

her moist grasp. It didn't matter that the ink had been smeared. She knew the sum total penned by her secretary, knew the numbers with a scalding accuracy.

In a neat, precise hand, it said "Final Account—Overdraft $98,872."

Only five weeks before, Maura had confided in Roger, showing him the company books, allowing him to go over the figures at his leisure. He was a financial adviser, a term etched on his business card. If anyone was in need of financial advice, it was Maura and Finnegan's Freeze-Dried.

Roger had an idea. He would save the company. But in order to do so, he would have to be given complete autonomy. No one should be told of their plans, of his authority. Otherwise, the mere hint of financial distress would destroy the company. Creditors who had been polite would become demanding, and the law was on the creditor's side.

"Let me handle this," he had said, chucking her under her chin.

It had been so easy, such a relief.

As the days passed, Roger seemed less and less available. His four daily phone calls dwindled to three, then two, then one every other day until finally they stopped altogether. It had only then become clear—Roger left her as soon as he realized the company was on the verge of collapse. He had not wanted Maura. He had wanted her company.

Unfortunately, both the company and Maura were utter failures.

And now he was gone. Not only had Roger left Maura, he had left Milwaukee and the state of Wisconsin as well. He had vanished into thin air, taking with him the remaining balance of the company accounts—including the overdraft of nearly one hundred thousand dollars.

Earlier that morning she had called Harvard in hopes of tracking him down through their alumni office. Nobody going by the name of Roger Parker had been in the class he had claimed as his own. Indeed, nobody with his name and major from his alleged hometown had ever attended Harvard.

It was only after the woman at the alumni office had commented on the name of Roger's hometown that Maura realized why it had seemed so familiar. He had claimed to be from Grovers Mill, New Jersey.

"Isn't that where Orson Welles set *War of the Worlds?*"

Of course, it was. For whatever Roger claimed to have done or been or lived could invariably be traced to a scene in a movie or play. His was a life of pure fiction, and Maura had been all too willing to believe every line.

She jumped, aware that the boardroom had been quiet. They were staring at her again, all of the executives of Finnegan's Freeze-Dried. Soon they would all know what had happened, what she had done.

With a forced smile she looked at the man standing at the head of the table. He was the marketing director of Finnegan's Freeze-Dried Cabbage, ready to present the results of his newest project. It was yet another effort in their never-ending search for new uses for dried cabbage flakes.

". . . and the testers were also quite thrilled with the range and variety of our product," he concluded.

Who cares, she almost shouted. In another week there would be no product, there would be no company. Instead she took a deep breath and nodded for him to continue.

Peter Jones had no idea that his job of twenty years was in jeopardy. He had two kids in college and a big mortgage. Like everyone else at the table, he had not been shown the complete financial report.

She recalled that when she was a child, Peter Jones used to laugh out loud at the outfit her parents made her wear every St. Patrick's Day, the green-and-white shamrock number still moldering in the suburban Whitefish Bay house, awaiting a Finnegan granddaughter to commence a second generation of torment.

Concentrate, she told herself. *Make everyone think you have a grip on the situation. Act interested in Peter Jones's report.*

"Excuse me," she interrupted.

Peter Jones paused. He still viewed her as the carrot-topped kid in the green step dancing getup.

"Peter? Could you please clarify that last statement?" Maura tried to curb the edge to her voice.

"Of course, Maura."

Poor guy, she thought. She had to think of something. She had to come up with a way to save the company, to save these people's jobs.

Roger had left after betraying her, but the truth was that by believing Roger when she had so desperately wanted to, she herself had betrayed the employees. In the end she alone was accountable.

Peter Jones continued. "You see, we have hired the very best recipe testers in the nation. They have created several dozen delightful items, all using liberal amounts of Finnegan's Freeze-Dried, of course. We will create an entire advertising campaign employing my new recipes."

"May we hear a sample of the menu?" Maura was pleased with herself. She had been paying attention. She sounded interested.

"Of course, Maura. We have managed to employ cabbage in every aspect of this menu, from drinks to dessert. To begin with, there will be a new cocktail this fall—sure to be a rage among all the upwardly mobile individuals in the nation. Forget the margarita, throw away the Beaujolais. The new drink of choice will be Absolut Finnegan's."

"Pardon?"

"We have contacted the vodka company, and they are a bit reluctant to join forces at this precise moment. But I assure you, once they taste the sophisticated blend of pureed Finnegan's Freeze-Dried Cabbage and their vodka, they will be absolutely . . ."

"Cabbage and vodka?" Maura's exhausted panic suddenly gave way to a manic urge to giggle. She felt like a mourner at a funeral who recalls the most riotous joke ever told. The rest of her life was a shambles. She eventually had to tell everyone assembled that she had single-handedly destroyed the company, that they would all soon be jobless, yet all she could do was think of how funny freeze-dried cabbage seemed. "Equal parts cabbage and vodka? Just like that?"

Peter Jones straightened his spine. "We serve it in a hurricane glass with a sliver of raw potato on the rim."

Maura managed to transform her guffaw into a sneeze. "Bless yous" rounded the table.

She averted her eyes as she spoke. "How does it taste, Peter?"

"Well." He took a fortifying breath. "It is rather sophisticated. One of the kitchen testers who created the recipe likened it to some of the great but unlikely combinations in culinary history. Who would ever imagine pate—made from duck and goose livers—could taste so sublime? Or that sauerkraut and corned beef could make a Reuben?"

He pressed forward. "Our first idea was to ignite the cocktail. A flaming drink is always impressive. But the whole kitchen smelled like a tenement."

"I see." Maura bit her lip and noticed other board members were suddenly staring directly ahead. It was often hard to discuss Finnegan's Freeze-Dried Cabbage with a straight face.

"So we serve it chilled over shaved ice. It is a bracing drink with a nice kick to it." Jones began paging through his notebook. "Let's see, we have brunch dishes, such as Creamed Cabbage on Toast Points and Eggs Benedict Finnegan. Then there are your piquant dishes, perfect for every occasion—the Homestyle Cabbage Dijon, Crepes à la Cabbage, and so forth. Desserts include Chocolate-Dipped Cabbage Fondue and Emerald Cabbage Sorbet."

At that moment Maura was startled, and relieved, by a tap on her shoulder. Her secretary, with a concerned look on her face, passed a typed message.

"Maura—sorry to interrupt. There is an overseas call from Dublin on the line with urgent legal information. Will you take it now or return the call?"

Legal information. Her heart sank. Had word spread already of their disaster? Were the sharks circling—from Dublin, no less?

Maura smiled as she stood. Whatever the call was about, it couldn't really make much of a difference. Unless a sudden miracle occurred, everyone would soon know Maura Finnegan had managed to destroy everything that had been entrusted to her.

She simply didn't care anymore, about cabbage or recipes or presiding over the meeting or the crumbled slip of paper she left behind on the table. "I'm sorry, Peter. There is a matter of great urgency I must attend to. But could you please continue?"

The expressions on the other board members' faces were of repressed mirth mingled with tedium. *Thank God they don't know,* she thought as she left. *Please—let me think of something.*

The miracle arrived in the form of an echoing long-distance phone call.

Within a matter of hours, Maura was informed that she was sole heir to a town house and furniture factory in Dublin. More calls, confirmations, and frantic cross-Atlantic faxes arrived from a solicitor's office, from two Irish banks and a government official.

The estimated worth of the estate allowed her to take out an emergency loan to keep Finnegan's Freeze-Dried afloat for at least another month. It was, indeed, a miracle, a brief reprieve. Although this wasn't really the best time to fly to Ireland to claim her inheritance, it would be worth it if the sale of the properties provided enough money to save Finnegan's Freeze-Dried.

By the following week, Maura Finnegan had sent an interoffice memo to the staff concerning her departure. Peter Jones was informed that he would be temporary head of Finnegan's Freeze-Dried, and he was clearly delighted.

Luggage was brought up from her parents' basement. Telephone calls were made to friends and business associates. Everything had been arranged swiftly and efficiently, handled with the dispassionate care of a well-oiled assembly line.

Maura saw the journey as a final stab at redemption. Her round-trip ticket had been paid for by the bank. It was an Aer Lingus standby, the modern day equivalent of steerage. Just as her ancestors had traveled to a New World, she, too, was on a voyage—her maiden voyage—to a new world—a new life.

But she was not returning to the land of her ancestors in triumph. The irony was not lost on Maura that in venturing to Ireland she was attempting to win the exact thing millions of immigrants had sought in the New World.

She was seeking a second chance.

Chapter 2

Maura refused to be seduced by Ireland.

The moment she boarded her flight, when the attendant greeted her in Irish and pointed to a "cozy seat with a grand view," Maura set her chin in defiance.

This was not a journey to be enjoyed. She did not deserve enjoyment or even mild pleasure. This was a trip of salvation, not a vacation.

She learned long ago that Americans were embarrassingly quick to fall in love with all things Irish. She watched tourist after tourist board the plane and fall prey to the intoxicating Celtic charm.

"This is not a holiday," she muttered to herself as she cinched the seat belt a little too tight.

But a euphoric sense of anticipation swept over the passengers, Irish and American, as they settled into their seats. Maura had been on dozens of flights, including trips to Paris and the Caribbean, and there had always been a business-as-usual routine about boarding.

This was different. Even as the plane waited on the tarmac for an extra forty-five minutes before takeoff, everyone behaved as if on a giddy holiday.

Perhaps she could simply enjoy the flight. Maybe leaving all of the angst of the past few weeks behind would clear her mind.

Maura tapped a foot and paged through the in-flight magazine, wondering if the couple sitting across the aisle would actually develop full-blown brogues by the time they landed. She couldn't help but wonder how a country as small as Ireland had managed to culturally entrance so much of America.

Her own life was a perfect example, with a childhood that had been punctuated by step dancing lessons and watching her mother decorate their home in shamrock-themed splendor. She had felt the weight of her own Irishness in Wisconsin, distant though it was in years and miles from Ireland.

In spite of her pure colleen looks, the emerald eyes, and thick red hair, Maura was less than half Irish. Indeed, the red hair had been a legacy of her German grandmother. But her German grandmother had never carried the last name Finnegan, nor had she graduated from Notre Dame, home of the Fighting Irish.

Her entire life had been spent trudging unwillingly through an Irish heritage of dubious authenticity. Now the last laugh was on her, Maura Finnegan, new and temporary heir to number eighty-nine and a half Merrion Square.

Another thought was lurking darkly in the back of her mind. As a child, she'd had nightmares about Ireland. It was a strange place to have nightmares about—not Transylvania or some eerie moonscape but green and friendly Ireland had haunted her dreams.

She could trace it back to a flutter of activity when she was in third grade. A girl from England had enrolled in her school, and Maura had told her mother that she wished she, too, could speak with such a lovely accent.

Her parents had exchanged glances. Then her father told her that perhaps she could, indeed, speak with an accent. Finnegan's Freeze-Dried was seriously considering an offer from the Irish government to move its headquarters to Ireland.

Odd, how just a mere sentence had turned her world upside down. Her parents never realized the rampaging fear that had enveloped her with the suggestion. She remained silent, but all she could think about was leaving Whitefish Bay and all of her friends, her home, all that was familiar and taken for granted.

At night she would lay awake, eyes wide in the darkness, and imagine being the new girl with the funny accent. No one would want to play with her, and if they did, she would always be different, not like the rest of the kids.

What were kids like in Ireland? Did they ride bikes and play with dolls? Did they watch the same TV shows? Would the teachers at her new school be mean?

Night after night she had remained awake, clenching the sheets in her hands, wondering and worrying until tears would inevitably roll from her unblinking eyes, trickling into her ears until she rubbed them away. But the thoughts remained, always there just beneath the surface, even during the day.

Her parents never mentioned the move again, and it wasn't until she was in the fifth grade that she finally had the nerve to bring the subject up at the table.

"Move to Ireland?" Her father paused as he dished mashed potatoes next to his meat loaf. "Oh, that! Honey, that deal fell through years ago. No, baby. We're staying right here in Wisconsin. Pass the salt, please."

So that was that. She had been tormenting herself for almost two years over nothing.

Maura had forgotten all about that old fear until she began making preparations for this trip. Then it had returned with a vengeance, new and far more powerful, as if laying dormant for almost two decades had endowed it with supernatural strength.

Her childhood nightmare was becoming a reality.

"First time?" asked a chipper woman to her left.

Maura glanced around before realizing the woman had been speaking to her. "Pardon?"

The woman spoke slowly. "Is this your first time in Ireland?" She was wearing a jumpsuit made from purple parachute material. Maura wondered if it was a fashion or safety statement.

She almost pointed out that they were not, in fact, in Ireland yet, but somewhere over Bangor, Maine. Yet on the movie screen was a video about Gaelic football, the attendants were passing out tea with Kerry Gold cream, and someone in the back of the plane was singing "Paddy's Green Shamrock Shore." This was not the time to quibble about technicalities.

"Yes, it is," Maura managed to return the woman's smile.

"I've been eight times," the woman announced with pride, chest out as if ready to receive a medal. Maura had long ago noticed that Irish Americans rate their Celticness with the number of trips they've made to Ireland. One was acceptable, two was better, and three or more journeys lifted the traveler from the realm of tourist to the lofty circle of native Celts on a pilgrimage home.

The woman then leaned toward Maura, a wink flashing from her oversize bifocals. "You'll fit right in, dear. You have the map of Ireland right on your face."

And if Maura had a penny for every time someone told her she bore the map of Ireland on her face, she could have retired years ago.

"Thank you," Maura replied automatically. Why was she expected to take every reference to her Irishness as a compliment? Did other nationalities have the same problem? Did people say "You have the map of Bulgaria on your face" or "You certainly look French Canadian," and expect to be repaid with lavish thanks?

Maura clenched her fists and tried to calm herself, aware that she was managing to make a perfectly pleasant flight into an emotional nightmare.

This was an opportunity, she reminded herself, a golden chance to try something new. She could save the business, secure a future for herself as well as the employees. Why was she trying to sabotage the inheritance before she even set foot in Ireland?

The answer was simple. Maura Finnegan was afraid.

Never before had she undertaken such a terrifyingly unfamiliar task. Her life had thus far been dictated by her parents and by circumstance, then by Roger. There was never serious consideration of any college other than Notre Dame, never any doubt that her first few months working at the family company would eventually stretch into years. There was a comforting sameness to her life that had been not at all unpleasant.

Her father's death following so soon after her mother's had been a stunning blow, of course. The only uncertain moments had come in the realm of romance, where relationships were volatile, where she didn't know exactly how to act or how to feel. Before Roger, before her father's sickness, her future had seemed as predictable as St. Patrick's Day arriving on March 17.

Now she was traveling to a foreign country in order to right a terrible wrong. And she had to do it all alone.

With a shuddering sigh Maura closed her eyes and tried in vain to sleep. And as had been usual lately, even that small task was unsuccessful.

The airplane passed through a gentle puff of clouds, the final approach before landing in Dublin.

Maura rubbed her eyes, not willing to blink for fear she would miss her very first glimpse of Ireland. At first there were hazy, indistinct patches of earth cloaked in a gauzy mist.

Then the mist cleared, and in spite of the self-imposed cynicism that had consumed her for the past few weeks, she gasped.

The land below her was the most beautiful sight she had ever viewed. There was an ethereal splendor to the countryside, a vivid weave of colors and shades and brilliant sunshine that seemed impossible, even mythical. The browns of the earth were rich as chocolate, the greens were overlaid with yellows and blues. It did not seem real, more like a painting rendered with a magical pallet and a brush kissed by fairy dust.

Before she could scoff at her own imagination, more beauty streamed in through the plastic window. The green of the hills was a hue she had never before imagined, lush and intense, as if layer upon layer of clover and grass were meshed in a single color. Crisscrossing the fields were rugged stone walls, luminous gray and white, and small cottages, some with thatched roofs. A shaft of sunlight burst through the clouds, and as the plane banked, a rainbow, pastel colors glowing over the early morning dew, arched over a hill.

Then she saw Dublin, shimmering just beyond the countryside. Something passed through her, a strange jolt of fear and excitement, and a single, absurd thought.

"Home," she breathed. "I'm coming home."

Later, after she'd checked into her hotel, she remembered how she had felt as the plane landed. It had been a silly thought, the product of an overwrought mind in need of a good night's sleep. After all, how could someone come home to a place they'd never been before?

There was a message waiting for her at the front desk of the Mont Clare Hotel. Charles MacGuire would call at the hotel for afternoon tea, and he hoped she had a pleasant journey from America.

Her first urge was to rush out and find her new home, but she forced herself to wait. She had been warned that the place was "rather tatty," and she needed to rest before facing the grim reality.

As she began to unpack before settling in for a nap, she realized there were no drawers in her room. She had two suitcases and one hanging bag full of clothes and nowhere to put them. With resignation she telephoned the front desk.

"Excuse me," she sighed. "Sorry to bother you, but I have no drawers in my room."

The young man on the other end of the line issued a sharp intake of breath. "Just a moment, ma'am," he said in a rush, as if in a hurry to hand the phone to someone else.

A woman answered. "Hello," she said in a professional tone. "How may we help you?"

Maura stated her name and room number, and mentioned her lack of drawers. The woman at the desk seemed taken aback.

"No drawers?" the clerk whispered. "My goodness."

The distinct sounds of giggling could be heard on the other end. "Brian, be still." The clerk's voice was muffled, as if she had been holding a hand over the mouthpiece. "Forgive us, ma'am. We have a new boy down here and he's rather cheeky. So, you would like us to send you up some drawers?"

"Yes, please."

"And how many would you like?"

"Oh, I don't know. Whatever is standard, I guess."

There was a silence from the desk. She seemed at a loss for words. "How about ten for starters," she suggested. "If you need more, we'll be happy to oblige."

"Great. Thank you," Maura began to hang up, but the clerk was still talking.

"And when shall we deliver them?"

Maura looked at the clock. It was ten in the morning, and Charles MacGuire would come at four that afternoon. "I'm going to sleep for a few hours, but I'll be down in the lobby for tea at four. How about then?"

"Of course, Miss Finnegan."

Even as she drifted off the sleep, Maura wondered at the strained tone of the clerk's voice. It was really rather odd.

Charles MacGuire, Maura decided, was what her father would have called a character.

He was tall, about fifty years old, with round spectacles and a thatch of graying chestnut-colored hair over his forehead. There was something youthful about him, a happiness that was infectious.

"So wonderful to meet you," he exclaimed, bounding through the polished brass front doors. Maura was delighted he had finally arrived—it was almost four-thirty, and the desk staff had been giving her peculiar looks.

"Please forgive me," he begged, pumping her hand in greeting. "I forget how punctual Americans are. In Ireland meeting at four usually means thinking about that meeting at four, pulling on your jacket twenty minutes later, and not arriving until just before five."

Although she'd felt uncomfortable alone in the lobby, all those feelings evaporated in the company of Charles MacGuire. He motioned for tea and pulled up a chair next to the one she'd been sitting in.

"My, Miss Finnegan, you certainly are young. And, if I might add, lovely as well." He gave her a quizzical look. "Indeed . . ."

Maura folded her hands in her lap, waiting for the inevitable "map of Ireland on your face" comment.

"Indeed, Miss Finnegan," MacGuire said, tapping an index finger against his chin in thought. "You have such a fresh, American look."

Maura grinned. She was about to say something else, when a prim-looking clerk approached carrying a large bundle wrapped in brown paper. "As you requested, ma'am," she bobbed, her eyes not meeting Maura's.

"Huh?" Maura questioned and began to untie the parcel.

"Goodness, gifts already." Charles MacGuire smiled.

She unwrapped the package just as the tea tray and small crustless sandwiches arrived.

"What on earth?" Maura mumbled, pulling out a very large pair of ladies' underwear. She pulled back the paper, and there were several more pairs of massive white briefs.

Charles MacGuire choked on a cucumber and cress sandwich. "You asked for those drawers?"

Maura glanced at him, her eyes wide with confusion. Then it dawned on her. She began to laugh, tears filling her eyes.

"I asked for drawers, you know—a piece of furniture." Her hand rattled the brown paper, drawing even more attention to the contents of the package.

"You mean a press? You meant to ask for a press?"

She nodded, and he, too, began to laugh, his own eyes becoming moist with hilarity. Other people in the lobby paused and stared at the two of them, the well-dressed gentleman and the young woman holding up an enormous pair of ladies' briefs, both doubled over with laughter.

"Miss Finnegan, if I may be so bold—let's go for more appropriate refreshments. My favorite spot, the bar at the Shelbourne Hotel, is just around the corner. Shall we leave?"

She could only nod, and not knowing what to do with the underwear, took it up to the desk. The young boy Brian was alone there, and his ears flushed red.

"I'll pick these up later," she managed to say. Brian quickly pulled them under the desk. Together, Charles MacGuire and the heir to Delbert's Disgrace walked to the Shelbourne.

"And when she opened the parcel, there were no less than ten dozen pair of tremendous knickers! At least ten dozen . . ."

Maura stifled a yawn and smiled as the tale was retold for the seventh time by a man named Ray who had joined them three rounds ago. She was surrounded by nodding faces, indistinct to her exhausted eyes.

Charles MacGuire had produced the papers she needed to sign, documents verifying her identity and that she fully understood the stipulations of the will. The swift shuffle of papers seemed to be the last event of the evening in Maura's control.

The bar at the Shelbourne Hotel was bright and airy, with a more casual, friendly feel than the lavishly decorated lobby. Floor-to-ceiling windows allowed sunlight to flood the room, and the patrons seemed to be drinking pints of ale and stout rather than the martinis and whiskey next door.

The walnut bar was a long and amiable place. Everyone glanced up—although not at once—when she had entered with Charles.

"She's younger than I imagined, isn't she, Bart?"

"Aye, she is at that, Seamus. What would you guess, twenty-one or two?"

"Nah. She must be at least twenty-six. She's already graduated from university and worked at her family company these past seven years."

Maura spun to face the conversing men, who seemed slightly put out by her intrusion. They were leaning on the bar with comfortable familiarity, the way you'd prop stocking feet on an old coffee table.

"Gentlemen"—she smiled—"I'll be twenty-eight next September."

"I don't believe it!" The one named Bart gestured to the bartender for a drink, pointing to his own empty pint of stout and his friends. "Miss Finnegan, Charlie, what will you be having?"

Maura was momentarily puzzled. "Um, a white wine, I suppose." She had just made a rather bold point of letting them know she had overheard them discussing her, and they seemed pleased.

"Seamus, check her teeth." Bart motioned to Maura. "Don't be alarmed, my girl. Seamus is a doctor of veterinary medicine. I believe you may have been misled as to the date of your birth, and Seamus can tell by looking at your teeth how old you really are."

Seamus smirked, set down his drink, and began to approach Maura with a set of appallingly filthy fingers, swiping them once across the front of his worn tweed jacket. "I'm more accurate when it comes to horses, Miss Finnegan, but I can assure you of your correct age within eighteen months."

"No!" She ducked under his arm. Charles laughed and introduced three more people who had just entered the bar.

Now it was approaching eleven o'clock and Maura leaned with her elbow on the bar. Before her were five untouched white wines, all gifts from the crowd surrounding her. They had not allowed her to buy drinks in return, and instead made her promise to invite them all to her new home once she was settled.

It was still light outside, the streetlamps had just switched on. Charles mentioned that in the summer, dusk lingered until just before midnight.

"Unfortunately, we must pay the price in the winter, when the sun sets at four in the afternoon," he said sadly, and his animated face crumpled at the thought.

"Charles," Maura mumbled. "When can I see my

new home? You have the keys, and I've been here for over six hours."

"Ah! Why didn't you say so!"

It was difficult to convince everyone at the bar to remain there, not to follow Charles and his client to the town house. There was much protesting and wailing until Charles offered to buy them all a round of drinks if they would simply stay put and allow him to do his job as a solicitor. He was beginning to slur his words, and Maura wondered if he knew exactly where they were going.

A thought crossed her mind: She was in a foreign country, with a drunken lawyer and no idea of their destination.

Yet as soon as they waved good-bye, he seemed sober as, if not a judge, at least a juror.

"Are you sure you know where we're going?"

He laughed. "I reckon everyone in Dublin knows where we're going. Should I forget or be mowed down by a passing lorry, just ask the next passerby, and they will be more than happy to escort you there."

The earlier numbness and exhaustion seemed to lift. She no longer felt as if she were in a dream, her body detached from her thoughts. Everything was clear now, the traffic noises that were more shrill than at home, the cars buzzing fearlessly on the wrong side of the street, large green double-decker buses tilting as they rounded the corners.

She was really there in Dublin about to face her new home.

CHAPTER 3

❦

Masking tape.

Maura's first impression of her town house was that it held an excess of masking tape. The windows were covered with tape tracing the cracks in the glass. Brown tape was all over the front door and seemed to be holding the center doorknob in place. There was tape on the broken bootscrape, tape on the wood pillars bracing the front door. Even the house's identity, eighty-nine and a half, was proclaimed on the fan window over the door with discolored, inexpertly placed masking tape.

"The glass broke ages ago," Charles explained. "Over the door, where the numbers are, there used to be a grand design, grandest on the square. Now it's just plain glass and tape."

She swallowed.

The structure was the shabbiest on the block, perhaps in all of Dublin. Although the basic design of the house was the same as the others, its appearance was vastly different. It was sad, mournful, stripped of all pride. Had the building been a person, someone would be in jail for unspecified crimes of abuse and neglect.

Gone were all of the architectural details that made the rest of the square so elegant. Instead of a small garden or carefully trimmed hedges, there were two square plots of dirt and weeds and trash. There were no richly painted doors with shiny brass knockers and knobs, no cared-for iron fence, no lovingly restored brickwork. It was a four-story building that would have been equally unattractive in Brooklyn or Indianapolis as it was in Dublin.

"Well," said Maura when she had at last found her voice. "It sure looks solid."

"That it is!" Charles vaulted up the two front steps, careful to miss the top step which seemed to be crumbling into a gravelly mound. He tapped at one of the columns bordering the door, proving how sturdy the building was.

A chunk of the column fell to the ground.

"Ah, well." He cleared his throat. "This is just cosmetic, you see. Not a weight-bearing, um, thing."

Maura moved closer, where she could see an iron rod placed across the two columns just below the masking tape numbers. The pole ran the entire length of the entrance. "What's that for?"

"Oh, just a little bit of propping to keep the door in place."

"I see."

She hadn't expected much, never dreamed of owning one of the magnificent homes on the square. But from the outside, this house seemed uninhabitable.

"Shall we go inside?"

Maura blinked as if in a daze. "Sure. Why not?"

Already she was wondering how she could explain her swift return to Wisconsin. As Charles struggled with the key, a long piece of pierced metal that looked more ceremonial than functional, Maura had an unwelcome vision of Roger. If not for him, she could be enjoying this adventure, free of the panic that had threatened to choke her. Try as she might, it was impossible for her to completely forget her mission.

Her thoughts returned to her town house. The exterior may not be attractive, but perhaps the interior was in better shape. Some people actually cultivated a tumbledown appearance to their homes to better protect the riches within. Number eighty-nine and a half could very well be one of those unassuming homes that conceal their beauty from the outside world, saving their lavish splendor for the owners.

Maura stepped forward at the thought.

"Now the inside is a little less polished than the outside," Charles warned as he pushed with his left shoulder to open the door. It didn't budge. He took a step back and threw his full weight against the door. With a shuddering creak it opened.

There was a moldering scent that immediately prickled her nostrils and caused her eyes to water. Charles sneezed. He held the door open with one hand and fumbled for the light switch with the other.

The entrance was at once bathed in a gentle yellow light. A single bulb hung from what should have been a magnificent chandelier. The wire holding the bulb was black and naked except for a few splices of masking tape. On the ceiling were the faint tracings of circular molding, where plaster once ornamented the chandelier.

She was standing on an old black-and-white marble floor, and before her was a gentle arch that echoed the doorway, all plaster and fragments of ornate design. Just beyond the archway was a grand staircase sweeping upward to the next floor. Without waiting for Charles, she began to climb the steps.

"Just a moment, Maura," she heard him mumble. "Let me latch the door. Hold on. Don't you want to see the rooms down here? Wait, Maura. The steps may not be entirely safe."

She didn't listen. Instead she felt herself gliding up the steps, unaware of any other sensation than a need to reach the next floor. Dust and plaster swirled about her legs, and where her hand touched the banister, puffs of dirt became unsettled. Maura paid no attention to the filth.

She knew exactly where to go. Her eyes were focused not on the hazardous stairs but on where she wanted to be.

She stumbled on one of the broken steps but kept climbing.

"Maura!" Charles seemed very far away now, a tiny voice in the distance.

At the top of the stairs she walked past the first door and went directly to the second, toward the front of the house. The light was indistinct, a streetlamp outside threw flickering shadows through a hall window. Dark patches spotted the wall where tape and flecks of dirt speckled the old glass.

Glancing at the doorknob, she grasped it firmly and pushed the door open.

"I'm coming with a torch. It was right at the foot of the steps." Charles said behind her.

Maura ignored him and stepped into the room.

At once she felt the sensation of air rushing from her lungs. She stumbled backward against a wall, as if tossed by some unseen force, her heart pounding wildly in her ears. Charles was speaking, but she heard another voice, deeper and richer.

"Be quiet," she cried, wanting Charles to hush so she could hear the other voice. But nothing seemed to come from her mouth, no sound other than a gasp.

"It must be the fumes." Charles was prattling on as he swung the flashlight. "This place has been closed for so long. Isn't there a switch? Let me see here . . ."

Alone. She wanted Charles to leave so that she could be alone, by herself in her own house.

She closed her eyes and tried to catch her breath. There was too much noise. Charles should be quiet. Her own heart beat unsteadily in her ears, almost drowning out the other voice.

It was soft, the other voice. A beautiful masculine voice.

"Ah, here we go," she heard Charles say from across the room. And with that, he turned on the light.

The room was unfurnished, bare but for the yellow wallpaper that was hanging in shreds. Where was he? The man with the voice. He was in the room just a moment ago. She had felt his presence as powerfully as her own.

He was gone now. She could feel it, the sudden emptiness of the place.

Charles was speaking, pacing around the room, pointing to the boarded-up fireplace and the carvings on the mantel. Nothing he said seemed to make any sense to her jumbled mind.

"And the paper alone is quite valuable," he droned, touching a wall. Some of the paper crumbled off like burned ash, floating gently to the dusty bare floor. "It's the original Georgian paper. Think of it—hand-printed by some artist over two and a half centuries ago."

Charles straightened, holding the red flashlight in both hands. "Do you want it, Maura?"

For a moment she was confused. "The wallpaper?"

He gave a brief, uncertain smile. "The wallpaper and the house it's attached to. Tomorrow afternoon I'll take you to the factory. It's just a few miles down the Wicklow road. Will you give it a try?"

There was no other answer she could give. "Of course, I will." The answer was so emphatic she surprised herself.

"Grand! That is simply grand!" Charles seemed to bounce across the room. "I'll walk you back to the hotel, then."

"Can't I stay here?" She meant it. The thought of leaving now was almost painful, like leaving a sick friend.

He seemed momentarily startled. "Your clothes and everything are back at the Mont Clare, and you're booked through Tuesday week."

"But I can leave whenever I want, right?" She was suddenly desperate. "I don't have to stay there, do I? I can leave tomorrow morning and come over here?"

"Of course you can, Maura." Charles stopped smiling. "You're not in prison. I just assumed you'd be staying at the Mont Clare for a few more days until this place can be made more comfortable."

"It's fine just the way it is."

He gave her a dubious look.

"I want to move in as soon as possible," she explained, wringing her hands. They both looked at her anxious movement, and she stopped.

"Very well. I'll instruct one of the porters at the hotel to bring your luggage over here in the morning." He began to leave the room and paused as she seemed hesitant to follow.

"Maura? Are you coming?" Charles held the door for her.

"Oh, sure." She cast one last glance at the room with the yellow wallpaper before he turned off the light. "Charles, what would this room be called?"

He thought for a moment. "I suppose it was originally the front parlor. The downstairs held the formal dining room and salon, where entertaining was done. This would have been a more casual place, a family room."

She mulled the thought over as they descended the stairs. "The front parlor," she muttered. "There, beneath the landscape. Between the two windows. It is there."

"Excuse me?" There was an eager grin on his face, as if he expected the punch line of a joke.

"What?"

He held the front door as they emerged onto the street. The evening was comfortably warm, just a trace of a chill. A light breeze blew the aroma of flowers and leaves from the park across the street, a gentle, green fragrance.

"You said something," Charles prompted. "About a landscape between the two front windows."

"Did I?" Maura was genuinely perplexed as she looked back at the house. "Well, I don't remember. I guess I was just thinking that between the windows would be as good a place as any for a painting."

As they began walking away, she turned once more toward number eighty-nine and a half. "Good night," she whispered.

Charles shook his head and wondered, not for the first time, why Americans were such a fanciful lot.

By noon the next day, all of Maura's bags were arranged in a third-floor bedroom of her new house. Now she had plenty of drawers, four chests and a highboy in her bedroom alone. The furniture was so dusty and dirty that she simply kept the clothes in the suitcases.

The entire house seemed to be lifted from the late eighteen hundreds. In the light of day she could wander each floor, stunned at the remnants of bygone lives that seemed to inhabit each room. It was like strolling through an accidental time capsule.

There were shreds of modern life, but they seemed unwelcome intruders. A telephone in the kitchen was at least fifty years old. There was an empty coffee can filled with dried paint, although she could not find a spot in the house that had been painted in recent decades. In front of the house, down a flight of rickety iron steps just behind the dirt patch where a garden would have been, was the old servants' entrance. It was cluttered with several feet of trash and a lone workman's glove—parched stiff by the weather with a finger pointing upward—lay atop the heap.

Maura explored the inside of the house, overwhelmed by the task of even cleaning up the exterior. Her new home was indeed a mess, but an enchanting mess. There was an intrinsic nobility to the house, as if a little dirt and trash were only temporary aberrations, momentary damage that Maura alone could heal.

For this was a house that had been lived in and loved. The corners were rounded smooth, the steps sagged in the middle where centuries of feet had made a permanent indentation. There were marks and chips on the walls where heavy furniture had bumped. In the upstairs rooms there were more marks, and Maura imagined children playing, relegated to the nursery when the weather prohibited running in the park across the street.

She reached the room with the yellow wallpaper, the front parlor. Unlike the other rooms, it was free of furniture and wall hangings, as bare as the rest of the house was cluttered. In spite of the lack of furnishings, there was a heavy feeling to the room, a sense of weight and presence that was absent from the others.

Adjoining the yellow parlor was a drawing room jammed with dark furniture and richly colored Persian carpets. Some of the furniture must have come from the yellow room, for she could envision a certain heavy chair being perfectly placed between the two front windows, and a painting leaning against the wall would fit the empty space over the fireplace. Blowing off the surface dust, she tilted the landscape painting toward the light for a better view. It wasn't exactly brilliant, more competent than inspired. She looked closer and saw a tiny horse on a hill that in fact looked more like an enlarged dachshund. Someone in the distance, perhaps a shepherd, although there were no sheep, was equally distorted, a tiny pinheaded creature waving a crook.

Yet from the size of the painting, it would indeed fit exactly between the two windows, right where a dark outline indicated a picture had once been hanging.

How had she guessed that before she even saw the painting?

There was a small writing desk, a lady's desk, at an angle. That, too, belonged in the front parlor. A matching chair, gentle lines upholstered the same shade of yellow as the wallpaper, stood a few feet away. Maura pulled the chair to the desk, pleased as if she had reunited a pair of lost lovers.

She stared at the desk and chair for what seemed to be a long time. After a moment's hesitation she sat in the chair and scooted her legs beneath the desk.

The fit was exact, as if the desk and chair had been built to her own measurements. Her hands hovered just above the blotting paper before she rested them atop the desk.

A tingling hum seemed to jolt up her arms, as if she had tried to silence a tuning fork. It wasn't an unpleasant sensation, just peculiar and unexpected.

She remained at the table, hands pressed to the blotting paper, as the feeling ebbed.

Slowly she raised her hands. There was nothing unusual now, and she clenched her fingers as if testing to see if anything else would happen. Nothing did.

There was a small drawer just above her legs. She pulled the brass knob, and the drawer slid open onto her lap. There were old pens inside, the kind that had to be dipped into ink before they would write. There were also bottles of dried ink, the corks crumbling, in colors of black and deep blue.

Fine stationery was carefully stacked to the side, and she ran a finger over the paper, savoring the richness of the smooth texture. Some other papers were crumpled in the back of the drawer, and she reached back and yanked them forward.

As she left the room, brushing her hands on her jeans to shake off the dust, she caught a glimpse of herself in a mirror. For a brief moment Maura seemed different to her own eyes, an elegant figure in a graceful ivory dress. Her hair was loosely caught at the top of her head, gently framing a face that radiated a gentle beauty. At her waist, tucked into a wide pink satin belt, was a dainty sprig of flowers, pastel colors of delicate wild blooms.

Yet when she stepped forward for a closer look, all she saw was her own image in old jeans and a flannel work shirt. Her hair was hanging in ragged tendrils about a face too pale for today's robust fashion. There were dark smudges under her eyes, testimony to the sleepless nights that proceeded the trip to Dublin. She looked awful. But contrary to her appearance, she was beginning to feel alive and vital, a simmering excitement that seemed more potent than the after effects of traveling to a new place, meeting new people and moving into a strange house.

She peered closer at her own image and touched her face, frowning at the smoothness of her skin. Her fingertips glided to her hair, soft and thick.

No one had ever called Maura pretty. She was always cute or attractive, with a nice figure and appealing eyes. But for some reason, she was beginning to *feel* pretty.

With a smile she went to her luggage to pull out some clean clothes that wouldn't look out of place in either Merrion Square or a solicitor's office. She might be a newcomer, but she felt a sudden, bewildering urge to belong. Not just for a while but forever.

CHAPTER 4

❦

Charles appeared just before noon, his tie askew, hair in disarray, wearing the same clothes from the day before. Maura was certain they were the same, for the elongated drop of Guinness was still decorating his shirt, and the grease stain from where he wiped his fingers after eating the bag of potato chips, or crisps as he had called them, was still on his trouser leg.

"Grand morning, isn't it?" His voice was enthusiastic, but he winced as a bit of sunlight crossed his face.

"It is." She grinned, holding the door wide for him. "I can't wait to see the factory, Charles."

"Ah. Maiden Works Furniture." He stepped into the hallway, craning his neck to see into the first-floor parlor and the dining room just beyond. "Why, I do believe the place is already looking in the rights."

"All I've done is rearrange some of the dust."

"And a fine job you've done." He nodded. "Now,

about the factory. I had a very interesting telephone call this morning."

"Really?" Maura paused before reaching for her purse. She was all ready to see the factory, the rest of her inheritance.

"The factory, unfortunately, hasn't turned a profit for the past three years. In fact, the history of that place is spotty at best."

"How do you mean spotty?" She placed her purse back on the hall table, realizing they were not leaving until Charles had completed what he wanted to say.

He raised his eyebrows, and they seemed to peek above his glasses like a tangle of untrimmed hedges. "You know about the history of this place, do you?"

"No. As a matter of fact, I don't. You only got in touch with me a few weeks ago, Charles."

"Right. Of course. Well, you see, this town house was built by Fitzwilliam Connolly, a very distant relation of yours. So distant, in fact, that Miss Regan was unable to find any proof of its existence at all."

"Oh. Then why am I here?"

"Because you may not be a close relation of Fitzwilliam Connolly, but you are more certainly a distant relation of Delbert Finnegan. That is all that matters in the case of this estate."

"Why is that name familiar?"

"Delbert Finnegan?" A brief frown of mild alarm crossed the solicitor's face. "Because he left you this house and the factory."

Maura laughed. "No, I mean Fitzwilliam Connolly. Why is that name familiar to me?"

He seemed relieved. "Ah, the man himself, is it! Connolly was something of a legend. He was in shipping, a business his brother took over after his murder."

"Murder?"

"Yes. Not to worry, though. It didn't happen in this house."

"Well, that's a relief."

"It happened on the front steps."

Maura crossed her arms. "When did this happen? Did they ever catch the guy?"

Charles smiled. "Ah, so you'll be bolting the doors and windows now, eh? It happened hundreds of years ago. Even if they didn't catch the fellow, I doubt he'd be bothering you much now. Although Delbert did claim he'd seen old Connolly himself every now and again. Of course it always seemed to happen after Delbert had enjoyed a few too many pints."

Maura scoffed. She didn't believe in ghosts. "But they did catch the murderer?"

"Most certainly. Poor Fitzwilliam Connolly was murdered by his closest friend. They even attended Trinity College together, this fellow Patrick Kildare. Seems Kildare didn't care much for Connolly's politics, which in Ireland back then was reason enough to jab a friend in the back."

"Yikes."

"Indeed. Here, grab your pocketbook, and I'll explain all of this on the way. Are you hungry?"

"A little," she confessed.

"I thought as much. Joe told me that you ate barely enough to keep a sparrow alive."

"Joe?"

"The chap over at the hotel who served your breakfast. Remember him? A slight man in a green jacket? He said you didn't use any butter on your bread. Shame. You shouldn't eat your bread dry in Ireland."

"I'll remember that."

"I tell you what. We'll have a quick look round the factory, then we'll grab some lunch and a spot of tea."

After locking up the house, a task that required several tries and a few kicks and jiggles, Charles led her to his car.

"Ah, a moment," he mumbled, tossing papers and magazines and what seemed to be a half-eaten sandwich from the passenger's seat to the back, where the refuse joined a similar pile of trash. "Here we go." He held the door open for her with the flourish of a Buckingham Palace coachman.

The car seemed to have originally been some light color, although now it was so caked with muck and mire that she really couldn't be certain. Charles bounced into the driver's seat and roared out of his parking place with all the gear-grinding of a Formula One starting line.

She patted the seats for seat belts.

"Ah, I took them out," he said when he noticed her movement. Just then they took a hard turn, and she was slammed against the door.

"Why did you take the seat belts out?" Maura asked when she finally caught her breath. It was disorienting to be on the wrong side of the road, sitting in what should have been the driver's seat.

"I used the seat belts as luggage straps last summer when I went on holiday in Spain. Have you ever been there? It's a brilliant place. All the sun in the world. Mind, here's a rather fierce turn . . ."

She clutched the bottom of the seat as they made an impossibly tight left, closing her eyes. Charles seemed undisturbed by the young man on the motorcycle who was gesturing wildly at the car.

"Now, about this morning's telephone call. It seems there is someone interested in buying the factory."

"The dog! Watch out for the dog!"

"Not to worry. Dublin dogs are clever beasts. See?"

Through the closed window she heard a yelp and craned her head to see the small terrier limping away.

"I think you hit that dog!" she gasped.

"Nah. I just taught him a lesson. May have saved his life. Anyway, this bloke I spoke to has foreign backing, German, I believe. And he is very interested in the factory."

She closed her eyes before speaking, blocking out all thoughts of the intersection they were approaching. "Um, why would anyone want to buy a factory that hasn't turned a profit in three years." Against her better judgment, she opened one eye slightly. "Oh my God! The bus! The bus!"

With both hands he pulled the steering wheel to the right, never lifting his foot from the gas. Her body flew against the stick shift, but Charles kept talking.

"It seems the prospective buyer wants to modernize the plant, put in all sorts of high technology machinery, and hire Irish engineers to run the place."

His voice had remained calm, and Maura stared at him with alarm. He had been completely unaffected by what she was beginning to realize was a near-death experience.

"How far are we from the factory?" She was unable to hide the frantic tone from her voice.

"Oh, a bit. Would you like to hear some music?" He let go of the wheel and began to fumble below the glove compartment for a tape. "I have Neil Diamond and your man Garth Brooks."

"NO!" She lowered her voice when he frowned. "I mean, no thank you. I'd rather talk than listen to music."

"Don't you like Garth Brooks?"

"He's fabulous. I love him, really I do. Can't get enough. I just would like to hear more about this offer."

He shrugged. "So in any case, Maura, I believe you should consider the offer very carefully."

"I'll keep that in mind," she whispered, mentally adding "if I survive."

"Ah, here we go."

He pulled up before a small, single-story white stucco building. "The roof was thatch until about twenty years ago."

There was a sign above the door, 'Maiden Works Furniture.'

"Before we go in, I'll give you a bit of the background. When Fitzwilliam and his father were alive, the company was strictly a shipping concern. But Andrew, the younger brother who took over after Fitzwilliam's untimely end, didn't have the knack. He even lost money in the slave trade."

"When was this?"

"Oh, I suppose about 1770 or so, just before you Yanks began causing all that trouble in the Colonies."

Now that the car had stopped, she was able to smile. "The Colonies, eh?"

"Not that I blame you. I'm all for stirring up the

empire a bit. So Andrew Connolly decided to go into brewing."

"Wait a minute. He went from shipping to brewing?"

"It makes sense if you think about it. He had all these barrels just lying about."

"Oh. So how did the brewery fare?"

"Not so well. The younger Connolly thought it best not to compete with Mr. Guinness, so he brewed instead a citrus-flavored and pineapple beer. Those were two fashionable flavors back then, you see, not that anyone had the faintest idea what they tasted like. So Andrew made a guess and came up with what he called a dessert ale. It was his firm conviction that Dublin specifically and the world in general was in desperate need of a change from regular stout."

"It sounds awful."

"From all accounts it was, although it was later discovered that the pineapple beer made a sturdy varnish. So he marketed the same formula as a varnish and had some success before his death. There was a bit of difficulty because the varnish was so very sweet that insects would become imbedded in the finish. Andrew's the one who expanded into furniture. After his unsuccessful attempt to export butter to the new world."

"He tried to export butter? Didn't it become rancid on the way over?"

"How clever you are! It did indeed. Your poor great-great distant uncle Andrew could have used your sense back then, but he was convinced that the Colonies needed Irish butter every bit as much as the world needed pineapple ale."

Maura was about to comment but remembered that her own father was responsible for the founding of a freeze-dried cabbage company. She, of all people, could not pass judgment on anyone's business. "Did they ever make anything else?"

They climbed from the car. It wasn't until she stood that she realized her knees were still trembling from the ride to the factory.

"Oh yes. But you should really ask Jimmy O'Neil about that. Ah, and here's himself. James!"

A short man clad in a worn black suit emerged from the front door. The most startling aspect was his hair, luxurious swirls of pure white, culminating in a stiff brush on the top of his head. The overall effect reminded Maura of a cockatoo.

The man waved and then said something in a strange, guttural language.

Charles MacGuire laughed and nodded. "Right you are! And this is Maura Finnegan."

He extended his hand and again said something. And again, Charles chuckled.

"I'm sorry," she apologized. "I don't speak Gaelic. But it's nice to meet you."

Both men stared at her in befuddlement. Charles leaned toward her. "What on earth are you talking about?"

"Didn't he just speak Gaelic?"

"No. He just addressed you in perfect English."

The man made another indecipherable comment, and again both men turned towards Maura.

She realized she was expected to say something. "Oh. How nice," she stammered.

The men exchanged glances, and Jimmy O'Neil shrugged before Charles spoke.

"What's gotten into you, Maura? He just said that Rosie Cahair up the road died. Granted, she was well into her nineties, but still . . ."

"I'm so terribly sorry! I'm just, well . . . I suppose my ears are still messed up from the flight over, and I didn't get much sleep."

The men nodded, Charles with the slightest of frowns, and then Jimmy O'Neil said something else. Maura followed Charles's cue, and together they all went into the factory.

It was a dark, low-ceilinged place, and as Maura walked she was aware of wood shavings beneath her feet. A few men were hunched over sawhorses, two were having a cup of tea from tin mugs. Hanging from the ceiling were seatless chairs, legless tables, and pieces of wood that could not be identified as any sort of furniture.

Jimmy kept up a running narration, during which she was torn between looking in the direction he pointed and staring at his face in the hope that a word or phrase might become understandable.

Whatever the problem was, she seemed to be the only person who had any difficulty understanding the man. And when the other workers were introduced, she was able to speak to them, to comprehend if not every word, then at least every other word.

Jimmy O'Neil said something, and Charles agreed. "What a grand idea! What do you think, Maura?"

"Oh, well, yes. I wish I'd thought of it myself."

"Then it's done! Shall we?"

She smiled as they left the factory. Jimmy O'Neil

seemed to be in a state of great excitement, and he made a dash for Charles MacGuire's car and dived in the backseat. He didn't seem to mind the trash and refuse, his face beaming with anticipation.

Maura reluctantly slid into the passenger's seat, stopping herself before she began the futile search for a seat belt.

"So will tomorrow do then, Maura?" Charles asked as he threw the emergency brake.

"Tomorrow? For what?"

He didn't look over his shoulder before roaring into the street. "To meet the fellow who's interested in the factory. Blast, what's his name again, Jimmy?"

Jimmy O'Neil said something that sounded like "Blafferbonner."

"Of course." Charles nodded. "His name is Donal Byrne. A young, bright fellow from what I can tell."

"Um, where are we going, Charles?"

"Now weren't you listening?"

Jimmy made a comment that was apparently hilarious. The men began to discuss where they were going, but Maura could only understand Charles's half of the conversation. She gathered their destination was but a few feet from Merrion Square, and she could be home in two shakes. The official name of where they were going was Doheny and Nesbitt, but everyone simply called it Nesbitt's. Charles described the place with the sonorous tone of a tour guide, the historical and literary significance as well as the fine architecture of the building.

Jimmy added his own thoughts, and Charles seemed to heartily agree.

"Ha! So it's a building!" Maura exclaimed. They ignored her.

There seemed to be a brief exchange about the value of the splendid sign, the exact sapphire hue of the Bay of Dublin. Although it had been founded in 1867, making it new by Irish standards, it was most certainly considered one of the most monumental sites in the country by those in the know.

But what they failed to mention to her was that Nesbitt's was a pub.

It didn't seem possible that so many people could fit into such a small place.

By early evening many of the patrons had spilled onto Lower Baggot Street, clutching their pints and chatting with amiable abandon as they used the scuffed hoods of cars as sofas. Maura recognized many of the people from the night before at the Shelbourne, others merely looked familiar. She managed a counterfeit smile of recognition to all of those who seemed to know her.

The pub became a sea of faces, bobbing with a crushing tide of affability. She noticed several partitions dividing the bar, frosted glass and wood trapdoors with round knobs, and was informed that they were called snugs, providing patrons at the turn of the century with a way to avoid their wives when the unfortunate women would peek through the door to check on their spouses.

Other bits of information free-floated into her mind. Everyone there professed to be writing a book, although a gentleman with a somber voice warned that the Irish tended to talk their books rather than actually commit them to paper.

Again they would not allow Maura to buy drinks, until she realized she should simply buy them without consulting the patron first. The publican knew exactly who was drinking what and managed to tally a half-dozen bills accurately in his head, all while pouring additional pints and singing a rousing interpretation of "The Foggy Dew."

After a while, a remarkable thing happened. Someone tapped her arm and said, "Mind your purse."

She turned, and it was Jimmy O'Neil. She understood what he had said!

"Thank you!"

He nodded. "This can be a rough bunch," he added.

This reminded her of the language lab in high school, where you would plug into a dialogue in French, and after a while it all made sense. Suddenly she could understand every word Jimmy O'Neal was saying, as he began a poetic description of a swivel dowel versus a regular hinge on a settle table. She had no idea what he meant, but it sounded lovely just the same.

Perhaps it was the stout he had consumed or her own wine but the man was a natural born conversationalist.

Later she would wonder what time she finally got home. Although she was escorted home by eleven men, including Jimmy O'Neil, no one seemed certain of the precise hour. It was late, it was dark, and Maura had never been more exhausted in her life.

That was her last thought before she fell into a deep, dreamless sleep.

Then something woke her up.

She felt the slow wave of alertness creep over her limbs with languor. The last thing she wanted to do was leave her sleepy sanctuary. It was too comfortable, too wonderfully soothing to relinquish. She had waited so long for such a perfect slumber, and now something was forcing her eyes open.

With reluctance she took a deep breath and struggled to rouse herself, rubbing a weak hand over her eyes. She recalled falling into bed fully dressed and gave a smile at the evening in Nesbitt's. Straitlaced, stick-in-the-mud Maura had actually closed down a pub! For those blissful moments, with everyone laughing and telling outrageous tales, she had become one of the crowd. She had managed to forget her own problems for the evening, allowing herself nothing more grave to ponder than enjoying the company.

There was a noise downstairs.

All remnants of sleep evaporated. The lights were blazing throughout the house. She had forgotten to turn them off. Whoever it was seemed undeterred by the thought of running into her.

Her heart flipped and began pounding as if she had just run a mile. Had she locked the door properly? She remembered flicking the latch, but she may not have clicked it all the way. Old locks are temperamental and . . .

He was climbing the stairs. She could tell the intruder was a man. Although he was careful enough to be quiet, the steps were creaking louder than they did with her weight.

Oh God, she thought. Oh God.

As in a bad dream, she was unable to find her voice. Her throat felt as dry as sandpaper. She was alone; there was no one to turn to.

This was just like her old nightmare, all by herself in a strange country. Yet this was worse, far worse than her childish imaginings had been.

Now she could hear him just beyond the bedroom door. Why hadn't she bolted the bedroom door shut or at least closed it? It was wide open, inviting anyone to enter.

He paused, for the creaking stopped for a moment before it resumed.

"Please," her small voice cracked. It was a soft plea, barely audible. She clutched the bedcovers, knuckles white with futile strength, her gaze darting frantically about the room. There was nowhere to hide.

She was about to squeeze her eyes shut, not wanting to see the intruder. Another part of her forced her eyes to remain open, wide and alert. If these were going to be her last few minutes of life, she wanted to be fully cognizant.

And then he entered the room.

He was a stranger, a man she had never seen before. She knew that the instant she saw him. And he was wearing a peculiar outfit—a loose white shirt, tightly fitted breeches, and knee-high leather boots. His hair fell just below his shoulders, thick and dark, tied into a ponytail with what appeared to be leather, perhaps a piece of brown cloth.

His features were obscured by his stance as he

turned away, distracted. From his commanding presence alone she would have recognized him, had she ever seen him before. His back was toward her, a broad, muscular back. He did not seem aware of her presence.

Her thoughts tumbled with a detached lucidity. He didn't know she lived there now. The place had been vacant for so long.

The intruder bent down. She watched his movements. Graceful, he was so graceful for such a strong man. She looked at his boots. They seemed to gleam even in muted light.

He turned, and at last she would have been able to see his profile, at least part of his face. But he raked his fingers through his hair, loosening a lock from the fastening.

And then he turned to her, hands clenched in anxious frustration. His eyes were startling. Although she couldn't tell what color they were, they were bright and animated. Keen intelligence seemed to glow even from across the room. His features were strong and masculine without being harsh, his forehead broad and free of lines, straight eyebrows a shade or two darker than the sun-lightened hair. His nose was classically handsome, not the pert nose of a boy but the defined, slightly irregular nose of someone who had led an active, perhaps even reckless life. His bit his lip, and for a moment she saw a flash of very white teeth.

Amazingly, he still failed to see her. Although his eyes searched in her direction, there was no startle of discovery, no hint that he saw her cowering in the bed.

The intruder's apparel seemed strange for a burglar. He looked as if he had just been riding, and she even imagined a far-away fragrance of horses. With swift movements he walked across the room toward her. She almost called out for him to be careful. Her two bulky suitcases were directly in his path.

Instead of stumbling, he moved right through her bags, his legs translucent until he reached the other side.

At that moment Maura Finnegan realized her intruder was a ghost.

Her hand clamped over her mouth to prevent herself from screaming. After a few shuddering breaths, her eyes still following him, she could see a blurry view of a chair through his torso. He paused, his shoulders moving as if he had just taken a great swallow of air, and again pushed his hair back with his hand.

Maura removed her hand from over her mouth. "Hello," she whispered.

He did not hear her. She repeated herself, her voice surprisingly strong and steady, but again there was no indication that he could hear her.

"May I help you with anything?" Maura asked with the polite tone of a shopkeeper.

Suddenly he left the bedroom.

Without thinking, she hopped off the bed and followed him. His movements were so fast she nearly tumbled down the stairs. Only her desperate grasp of the banister saved her from falling.

She did not take her eyes off him as he entered the yellow parlor.

"Hello," she repeated as she followed him into the

empty room. Her voice seemed louder and more confident now that she knew he couldn't possibly hear her.

The ghost began to touch the wallpaper, searching and probing with his strong fingers. His hands were large and well formed, but she noticed the little finger on his left hand was slightly bent and crooked.

"Did you break that finger?" she asked. Out of sheer nervousness she began to giggle. "Get a grip, Finnegan," she muttered, folding her arms across her chest. The room suddenly felt terribly cold, a damp, full chill.

As he moved she watched him, powerful features betraying urgency. He seemed to be breathing hard. She couldn't hear a sound, even though she was now close enough to touch him, to be aware of his every expression, every subtle change on the exquisite face, every sound he would have made.

If only he were alive.

She reached out a finger, slowly, tentatively.

"I'm not afraid of you," she said, surprised because the moment the words had escaped her lips, she realized they were true. "I want to help you."

At that he froze, all movement ceased. For a startling second she thought he had heard her. A thrill rushed through her at the thought, and she was about to speak again when he winced and ran from the room.

Maura blinked and after a moment followed him down the stairs. The front door flew open, and again she wondered if she had locked it. He ran down the outside steps and paused for a few moments. Then he seemed to relax, glancing to the left, then to the right. His hair was slightly curly, she noticed, at least at the ends, where it rested against his back.

He turned to go back up the steps and stopped, his gaze directly on her.

"Hello," she said, stepping back.

A vague smile formed on his lips. "Well, I'll be damned." His voice was low, and later she wasn't sure if she had actually heard him or if she had simply read his lips.

Suddenly he jerked forward, as if hit in the back by a powerful whack. On his face was an expression of surprise and anger and then pain, a terrible agony.

"Are you hurt?" Her voice was tight.

He stumbled forward on the steps, arm outstretched, and she ran toward him. A crimson stain spread on the back of his white shirt, just below the ends of his hair. Yet she saw no one else, heard no other sounds. She took another step forward, grasping at her ghost as he crumpled to the ground.

And then he was gone.

She whirled around, frantically searching, but there was nothing on the steps but a few dried leaves.

Nothing.

Her ghost was gone.

She sniffed. There was a distinct odor, a mingling of smells. One was of a fireplace, and she glanced up at the rooftops of Merrion Square, the old-fashioned stacks upon each house. Across the street was the walled-in park, the center of Merrion Square, with trees and flowers and benches.

The other aroma was pungent and metallic. It was a

fragrance she recognized from an awful day of duck hunting a few years earlier.

It was the smell of blood.

She walked back into the house in a daze, carefully locking the front door, bolting it firmly. Then she wandered through the home, methodically flicking off the light switches as she progressed. The sun was just beginning to lighten the sky and the rooms. Soon it would be time to get up.

Her watch read four-thirty in the morning. How long had the entire episode taken? It couldn't have been more than thirty minutes from the time she first heard her ghost to the time he disappeared.

Her ghost.

Funny, she thought, stepping over the luggage he had so easily glided through, she was thinking of him as "her ghost." She sank back onto the bed, thoughts rioting. And somehow, even after witnessing a long-ago homicide, she fell into a restless sleep.

Chapter 5

The only logical explanation Maura could think of the next morning was that the ghost had been a hallucination. It made sense that after her first full day in Ireland, which ended, not incidentally, in a pub, she would have imagined seeing a ghost. And not just any ghost but the spirit of Fitzwilliam Connolly.

This sort of thing had happened once before in college. It had been during final exams in her junior year, when she had pulled two consecutive all-nighters studying for a statistics exam. As she walked across the campus for the test, she passed the statue of the Virgin Mary. And the statue gave her a high-five sign, veil waving in the wind, with all of the sideline ebullience of Vince Lombardi.

When Maura gave a second glance, the statue was again motionless stone, the veil stiff and unyielding. Whether it had really happened, if the old piece of stone had actually waved encouragement or if too little sleep and too much caffeine had caused her to snap she never knew. What she did know was that she aced the final, much to her own surprise, not to mention that of her professor. In the end it didn't really matter what had prompted the success, her studying or the statue. It had been miraculous in any case. All she had been certain of was the result.

Perhaps seeing Fitzwilliam Connolly was the same sort of thing. It was almost laughable. And she did indeed giggle a few times as she dressed, her hair still wet from the shower.

Clearly she was falling under the spell of the house, and her imagination couldn't help but be sparked by her new surroundings. There was something enchanting about the place, about the uneven walls and sagging steps, the thickly painted windowpanes, the lopsided doorways and old, broken bits of hardware worn down to a smooth sheen of such softness it seemed more like gentle, aging flesh than lifeless brass. It was a house that had seen so much life, the very walls itself seemed to have absorbed a very real sense of mortality.

One thing she was convinced of was the importance of keeping the dream to herself. As whimsical as Charles MacGuire seemed to be, he was still a lawyer. Should he view her as mentally ill or in any way incompetent, it would be his primary duty to ensure the safety of the estate. She had no doubt she would lose the house and the factory in the stroke of a pen.

Just as she began to descend the steps, the telephone in the kitchen rang. It was a peculiar sound, a metallic jingling unlike the pulsing beeps of Touch-Tone phones.

She picked up on the third ring. "Maura! So it works then—grand!"

Charles and his voice of unrelenting cheerfulness assaulted her ear, and she held the receiver at arm's length.

"Hello, Charles," she whispered, hoping he would take the cue and speak in a softer tone. He did not.

"I had the phone switched on this morning. Hope you don't mind. Do you have a cold? Your voice sounds a bit weak."

"No. I'm fine."

"Brilliant! Now I did hear from this chap Donal Byrne, and you're to have lunch with him this afternoon."

"Oh. All right." For some reason she was nervous about meeting the businessman. "Will you be there?"

"No. I think it would be best if you two discussed the matter alone first. I've discovered that the presence of a solicitor seems to put people on edge. Just have a lovely meal—I'm sure he'll grab the check."

Her finger twirled the telephone cord. "Where am I meeting him? And how will I know him?"

"I can't help you there—I've never met the bloke. I assume since he's Irish, he must have the same devastating attractiveness which we all modestly claim."

An involuntary laugh escaped from her end of the conversation.

"I'll make another assumption and suppose that you just thought of a rather humorous joke that is too bawdy for mixed company. Now, let me see here, I wrote down the time and place somewhere. Here we go, right where it should be, under the tea mug. You're to meet him at half one this afternoon. And he's making it easy on you—you're to meet at the Shelbourne. Can you find it again by yourself?"

"Yes, that won't be a problem. But is there anything I should know about this guy?"

"Not that I can think of. Just have a jolly good lunch. And you might try the salmon—they do a fine job of the salmon at the Shelbourne. And don't forget the Dublin Bay prawns if they're on the menu. Oh, and this lovely soup . . ."

"Would you like to come and order for me?"

"Grand idea entirely!" Charles chuckled. "Now ring me this afternoon and let me know how it goes off, what you think of his offer. Don't dismiss him until you've really weighed the options."

"Thank you." She smiled. "I really appreciate everything you've done."

"Not at all, my dear, not at all. Now off you go."

After hanging up the receiver, and with over three hours until her lunch, she decided to explore the neighborhood. It was a beautiful day with just a trace of hazy fog, the sun casting a purplish hue over the city.

There was a fresh scent that seemed to linger with each breeze, and she paused in Merrion Square Park and later in Phoenix Park. She strolled over the Half Penny Bridge, walked down O'Connell Street past the General Post Office that still bore the bullet holes from the Easter Uprising of 1916. There were department stores, bookstores, shops that carried nothing but woolens and lace.

She did check her watch just before noon and wandered some more. There were bronze statues positioned all over the city. One, just at the foot of Grafton Street, was of Molly Malone, although a woman with two small children said that it was usually called "the Tart with the Cart." Next to the Half Penny Bridge was another set of statues, two women on a bench called "the Hags with the Bags," and finally a river with a woman's face in the center. The artist meant it to be Mother Ireland, but it had been unofficially renamed "the Floozie in the Jaccoozie."

Again she checked her watch. And blinked in surprise. It was one forty five—she was already late.

"I'm never late," she muttered to herself, trying to get her bearings. She was all turned around, mistaking the corner of Phoenix Park for St. Stephen's Green, asking directions and receiving conflicting answers, each guide convinced that his or her route was indeed a shortcut.

By the time she made it to the Shelbourne, it was just after two in the afternoon. The lobby was lavish but welcoming, Georgian splendor at its most comfortable. She could see it better now than two nights before, when jet lag and simple confusion made everything run together. Now, even in her haste, she noticed how plush sofas and chairs contrasted with the stiffly ornate molding on the walls and ceiling.

Slightly out of breath, she patted her hair and straightened her shoulders.

"Hello," she said to the host, who greeted her from his podium in the restaurant doorway. "I'm here to meet Donal Byrne. Is he here yet?"

"Heavens, yes. He's been here since a quarter past one."

Great, she thought. The one punctual Irishman, and she's late.

The dining room was full of tourists and businessmen and bustling waiters. She was led to a table by a window, where the solitary figure of a man sat reading a book.

His back, the first glimpse she had of Donal Byrne, was broad, and he shifted as he turned a page. Even in the natural light, his hair was very dark, if not black. Leaning against the foot of his chair was an expensive-looking briefcase.

"Mr. Byrne? Miss Finnegan has arrived," the host said before bowing slightly and leaving.

She saw his hand clench, such a small movement, and then he rose to his feet.

"Miss Finnegan?"

Whatever she had expected, it most certainly was not the man who now faced her. He somehow looked familiar to her.

Donal Byrne looked down at her, his eyes—an astonishing shade of blue—betraying nothing.

"Please sit down." He gestured to the empty chair, and mutely she nodded and sat, very nearly flipping backward when she tried to scoot the chair forward.

Without a word he stepped behind her and eased her into place. She felt the warmth of his hands on the back of her chair.

"I'm sorry I'm so late. I lost track of the time."

He didn't say anything as he returned to his own chair.

Donal Byrne was a very handsome man. His face was almost boyish, but that was simply a matter of his coloring, a fresh vitality over the vaguest of tans. He looked like a man who spent time outdoors, not in a gym, or perhaps playing some sort of sport. What would he play, she wondered. Tennis? No, that wasn't right. Soccer? Maybe. Just maybe.

"I do hope you're enjoying Dublin so far, Miss Finnegan." And the way he spoke was glorious. His accent was different from the others she had heard, from Charles or the people at Nesbitts and, thank goodness, from Jimmy O'Neil. It was more pronounced than the Dublin accent of Charles, more of what she had imagined an Irish accent to be.

"Oh, it's just wonderful!" She giggled nervously. Her voice had reached an embarrassingly high pitch. Several other diners glanced at her.

A waiter handed her a menu, but she didn't want to look at it, not yet.

Donal Byrne closed the book he had been reading. Maura smiled at him. His eyes were truly remarkable. Any woman would love to have eyes that blue. Yet he was utterly masculine. Everything about him was masculine, almost ridiculously so, from the squarish cut of his jaw to the black eyebrows, straight and severe, to his mouth.

It was hard to look away from the mouth, from his lips. He had yet to smile, but Maura had no doubt it would be a glorious smile.

He leaned down and slipped his book into his briefcase.

"What are you reading, Mr. Byrne?"

Why did she say that?

For a moment he did not respond. He simply stared at her.

Without taking his eyes off her, he reached down

and pulled out the book. It was then that she noticed the little finger of his left hand, the slight bend at the joint that made the entire finger slightly crooked.

Where had she seen that before?

Brusquely, he pushed the book across the table to her.

She smiled, and read the title. "Let's see. *Microeconomics and the European Common Market.* Sounds like a real gripper." She handed the book back across the table, and he slipped it back into his briefcase. "I'm personally waiting for the movie to come out. I hear Mel Gibson's been signed."

"Miss Finnegan, would you please look at the menu and order? I was here on time, and I am starving."

She felt her cheeks turn hot. "Please call me Maura."

The menu was thankfully large enough to hide her face. She stared without comprehension, meaningless words clustered in strange clumps. The selections merged together like a chalk drawing in the rain, as her eyes began to ache.

It was ridiculous. What was wrong with her? Why was she so intimidated by him?

The waiter was at their side, pencil poised.

Donal Byrne cleared his throat before speaking. His fingers drummed on the table, the noise muffled by the thick linen tablecloth. From the safety behind her menu fort she watched his hands, the dark hairs on the back of his strong hands, the crooked finger.

"Miss Finnegan, do you know what you'd like?" His voice was still harsh, annoyed.

Yes, she thought to herself, glancing up at Byrne. *I would like you to be civil to me.*

Instead she said, "Why don't you go first, Mr. Byrne?" He hadn't asked her to call him Donal. That she had noticed.

"Fine. I'll start out with the Dublin Bay prawn salad, and then I'll have the grilled salmon."

"Very good, sir. And you, ma'am?"

"I'll have the same thing." She folded the menu and gave it back to the waiter.

"Excellent. And would you like some wine, sir?"

Maura paused. Maybe if he had some wine, he'd lighten up. Maybe he wouldn't seem to dislike her so very much.

"No. Just water. Miss Finnegan, would you like anything?"

Part of her wanted to order a double martini. In fact, most of her wanted the double martini. "Water will be fine, thank you."

When the waiter left, they lapsed into silence. She made another attempt at conversation. "I'm rather surprised you were here on time, Mr. Byrne." Why on earth was she beginning to speak with a British accent? She was clenching her jaw so tight it ached. "Yes, I am indeed surprised you were here so promptly."

"You are?" It was the first time his voice was free of that peculiar edge.

"It's just that I understand that in Ireland, having a one-thirty appointment means thinking about it at one-thirty, pulling on your jacket at one forty-five, and arriving sometime after two."

There. Wasn't that what Charles MacGuire had said when he arrived late at the Mont Clare?

"I see." The edge was back in his voice. "A picture

postcard view of Ireland, where all the wee happy folk frolic away in shamrock-colored top hats. Well, let me tell you something, Miss Finnegan. I was raised in a small town in the west, what you Yanks would call picturesque. We had tour buses pass through every day, and your blue-haired American ladies with their plastic cameras would snap our photos to send off to their friends in, in—where are you from again?"

"Wisconsin," she whispered.

He nodded once. "To send to their friends in Wisconsin."

She wouldn't cry. She refused to give him the satisfaction. She would not cry.

Just then the waiter slid a parfait glass filled with hideous faces before her. There were pinchers and beady eyes and scorpion tails.

And she screamed.

The waiter paused and glanced at Donal Byrne. "Your prawns, miss."

The restaurant seemed to have grown silent as everyone stared at her.

"Oh, of course." She tried to maintain some sort of dignity. "I wasn't expecting . . ." What could she possibly say? That she wasn't expecting a tall glass filled with science fiction monsters? That she was expecting shrimp cocktail, not something from a Godzilla film? "Thank you," she said at last.

She was so mortified, she didn't notice the brief smile that flitted across Donal Byrne's mouth. If she had, she would have realized her guess had been correct.

His smile was indeed glorious.

* * *

Maura Finnegan was not what he had expected.

Donal Byrne poured himself a stiff tumbler of Jameson and settled into a worn chair, his favorite. It did not match the rest of his flat, not in the least, but he loved the lumpy comfort of the old chair, the upholstery worn thin on the armrests and the back, the hideous shade of orange and olive tweed. It reminded him of home.

Once the thought of home had made him feel safe, but that was before, when he was still in Munich. Since returning to Dublin the dreams had started again, vague as they had always been, now with a new sense of terror. When he was a university student he had always assumed the dreams were simply a product of his overworked mind. Yet now they brought with them a real fear, not for himself but for someone else. His mother? No. Not these dreams, Not anymore.

He took a sip, and then another. Maura Finnegan. For some reason, Charles MacGuire had given Donal the clear impression that she was a rather plain American, young but plain. When she finally arrived at the Shelbourne, Donal had been taken aback.

She was beautiful.

Not in a traditional way, at least she wasn't beautiful the way other Yanks were. Instead, she did seem more like an Irish beauty, an idealized one, with translucent skin and green eyes and hair that would seem too red on anyone else. On her it was perfect.

Of course, she also had those good American teeth. What was it about American teeth? Were they all straight and white and flawless?

If Charles MacGuire had possessed an ounce of

professional integrity, he would have warned him about her appearance. Then again, what could he have said?

"Mind the heiress, bucko. She's a looker."

All MacGuire had said was that she was delightful and had a wonderful personality. That's where Donal had been misled. In his experience, any woman described as having a "wonderful personality" usually suffered from some sort of physical affliction. Most often, she had a full mustache, perhaps mismatched limbs, or a squinty eye.

Not Maura Finnegan.

He wanted this factory, Maiden Works Furniture. No, more than wanted. He *needed* it to complete his dream. His future was linked to Maiden Works. The factory would be modernized, new machinery made, if possible, in Ireland and manned, most certainly, by Irish men and women.

It would give them an option so many others had not had, an option he himself had not had: to stay in Ireland. To remain at home and work at a good job instead of going to England or Australia or, God forbid, America.

Donal had very nearly been forced to move to the Bronx when he first graduated from university. His cousin, with a doctorate in physics, was already there, illegally working as a bartender. There were thousands of Irish in America without green cards, working as nannies or bartenders or waiters. More often than not they held at least university degrees.

Donal had been lucky. Just as he was about to pack up for the Bronx, he was called to interview for a job in Munich. After three more interviews he landed the job with a German pharmaceutical company. He remained there for nearly ten years, nose to the grindstone, working long hours and weekends.

It had paid off. The firm had honed enough faith in him to back his business ventures in Ireland.

Maiden Works was perfect for his needs. On the threshold of bankruptcy, it was ripe for the picking. The building itself was not too large, but hopelessly outdated. With new equipment and personnel, it would be easily modernized. All it needed was guidance and vision and, of course, more than a little cash. These were things he had. Now all he needed was the factory itself, what should be the easiest item on his list.

And at last Donal could stay in Ireland. Perhaps one day marry an Irish girl with Irish values.

Then came this American.

Unlike many of his friends, he had never been fond of Americans, especially Irish Americans. They were by far the worst of the lot, grimacing and complaining about warm bitter beer, always asking for ice cubes in their drinks, always taking blasted photographs. They spoke in loud voices, as if the Irish were deaf. The men all wore trousers hitched with low-hanging belts, the women wore bright-colored sweaters and seemed enchanted with simple woolens and ashtrays and scarves printed with artificial Celtic patterns.

They went into restaurants and asked for their style of food, they checked into hotels and expected American-style accommodations. Many times he had heard tales of bed-and-breakfast hosts tormented by these visitors.

If they wanted everything to be American, why didn't they just stay at home?

They seemed to view the world as their own personal theme park. Everything was for them, to have at their leisure and pleasure. Everything was disposable, a throwaway mentality he had never understood, nor had he ever wanted to understand.

Poor Maura Finnegan, the expression on her face when the Dublin Bay prawns were set before her. She had clearly been expecting shrimp, not the six-inch crustaceans that were more like crawfish than peeled shrimp.

He had to grudgingly admire the way she overcame her initial shock and watched him, gamely imitating his method of pulling them apart. Donal did notice that she kept turning their faces away from her own.

Never mind. Soon she would be back in Wisconsin, and the company would be his. She would again run her father's freeze-dried cabbage concern.

Perhaps he should have mentioned her father's death, a polite acknowledgment of his passing the previous year. From what he had learned from MacGuire, she had been devastated. But he couldn't be overly concerned with niceties, certainly not to someone who stood in his path. It would muddy the water. He couldn't afford to let emotions, anyone's emotions, get in the way.

He would put out of his mind the way he treated her at lunch. If he thought about it, he would most certainly be ashamed. By the end of the meal she had answered his questions in monosyllables, asking him to put his offer in writing for her later perusal.

One thing he could not afford was to think of her as a woman. She was an American, a businesswoman. She was his adversary, his opponent.

That's why he had allowed her to pick up lunch. He thought that would even the playing field, so to speak, but she had seemed bewildered. Later, when he recalled how she had surreptitiously checked her wallet, he realized that she might have been worried about having enough money.

It didn't matter. Women were always complaining about not being treated as equals. He was just giving her a dose of what they wanted.

But if she had been a man, he knew he would have paid. Of course he would have. He was the one with the offer, he was the one who had requested the meeting. He should have taken the bill.

"Damn it," he mumbled.

He would have to make it up to her now. Probably take her for another meal, maybe to a show, and this time be on his best behavior.

"Damn it!"

And somehow, in spite of his irritation with himself and the situation, he couldn't help but smile.

"I don't care, Charles. I refuse to take his offer. He's a jerk."

Maura was putting away groceries in the kitchen, wrapping the telephone cord around her arms as she moved. With an impatient shake she disentangled herself and waited for his response.

"He may very well be a jerk. But he's a well-funded jerk, my dear and you may not get any other offers.

Never overlook the importance of a solid cash backing. It can make the most unappealing person suddenly seem marvelous."

She would rather keep the company than sell it to him. She would just have to come up with the money to save her father's company some other way.

"Did I tell you he made me pay for lunch? For God's sake, Charles, I was barely able at cover the bill. As it is I have to go back to the Shelbourne to give the waiter a decent tip."

"I'll admit, I'm rather surprised that he didn't take the check. Perhaps he was trying to prove a point."

"That he's a jerk?" Just then the carton of milk she had unpacked was knocked to the floor by the telephone cord, spilling all over the yellowed linoleum.

Charles laughed, and before they hung up he again urged her to consider the offer. She said she would, but she had really made up her mind. There was no use even contemplating the issue any further. The less she had to do with Donal Byrne, the better. She would just have to think of something else.

Back home in Wisconsin, she would have felt silly about going to bed so early. But in spite of four cups of tea with dinner, Maura was simply unable to keep her eyes open past nine-fifteen. She was physically and, above all, emotionally exhausted.

Her flannel nightgown embraced her, the fresh, new sheets and blankets she had bought welcomed her, and with a sigh she flicked off the lights without even reading a single page of the paperback novel she had yet to begin.

And then she was awake.

She wasn't disoriented this time. The sound of footsteps on the staircase wasn't frightening. If anything she was mildly surprised. It hadn't occurred to her that he would come again.

By the time he entered her bedroom she was fully awake. Just to make sure, she tried to remember which nightgown she had unpacked. Without glancing down, she remembered the red-and-blue flannel one.

A quick peek under the covers confirmed that was exactly what she was wearing. Perhaps this was real, not a dream.

His strides were every bit as sure, his gestures seemed the same as the night before. Yet there was something different about him.

"Hello," she said, her voice even and firm. "Nice to see you again."

He paused for a moment and then walked across the room in the identical path as the previous night. She couldn't remember if he paused before.

Either he seemed more solid or she was simply noticing more details. His loose white shirt had drawstrings on the cuffs. The stitching on his trousers was visible, and his boots seemed so shiny, they flashed darts of reflective light as he moved.

Again he paused, and for the briefest of moments he seemed to look right at her, and she realized his eyes were brown, so deep they seemed pitch-black.

Maura was already out of bed when he left the room. As she scurried after him, she wondered why she wasn't afraid of the ghost. She had been frightened the night before, when she thought he might be a burglar.

For some odd reason, the notion of an encounter with a ghost was far less frightening than the thought of meeting with a flesh-and-blood live person, particularly a man.

This time she stopped to put on a pair of slippers. "Hey, wait a minute," she called.

Did she hear him halt on the staircase?

When she caught up with him he was in the yellow parlor, the empty room. He frowned, as if surprised there was no furniture there, and then turned to leave, brushing right past her. His arm touched her shoulder, and she gasped—it felt like a cold breeze.

She was directly behind him as they descended to the first floor.

"Don't go outside," she whispered.

But he walked straight toward the front door.

"No, please." She ran to the door, reaching it before he could.

Using her body as a barricade, she pressed herself against the door. "You can't go out there."

His face remained resolute, oblivious to her plea, and his hand began to grasp the doorknob.

"No! You can't leave!"

He jumped back, dark eyes now wide with perplexed shock.

"What the—" he began.

"You can't leave!"

Slowly, a smile spread over his face, and he crossed his arms with deliberate languor.

"Who the devil are you, my sweet?"

Maura leaned forward just slightly. "Can you see me?" She kept her voice soft, not really expecting a response.

The smile broadened, and he, too, leaned closer, so close she could see the beginnings of five o'clock shadow on his jaw. "Yes, I can," he whispered. "Not only can I see you but I would very much appreciate knowing what the bloody hell you are doing in my house."

Chapter 6

Maura stared at the man, unable to speak.

"Well? You were chattering up a storm, and now you have gone mute."

This was not happening. It was absolutely impossible, beyond the maddest of dreams.

Then why could she feel him, a frigid air that seemed to course about his body? And his voice, so firm and commanding.

"I . . . I . . ." she stammered.

"Yes?" He seemed almost amused and settled back on the heels of his boots.

The absurdity of the situation suddenly hit her—she was talking to a ghost, and he was awaiting an answer. She finally returned his smile. "You will never believe me," she shook her head in wonderment.

"Where are you from? You have a most puzzling accent."

Just as she was about to reply, she realized that he

seemed to have no idea he was dead. For all he knew, this was still 1767, and this was indeed his house. Should she try to tell him the truth—that he had been dead for over two centuries?

No. How could she?

And then another thought crossed her mind: Perhaps she, Maura Finnegan, was the ghost. Perhaps if they should open the front door, she would be faced with Dublin in 1767.

"I'm from the Colonies," she said at last.

"Are you now? Whereabout in the Colonies?" The skepticism was thick.

"Um," she hesitated. What would have made sense in 1767? She certainly couldn't mention Wisconsin. Struggling to remember the books she had read about Colonial America, all she could come up with was *Johnny Tremain,* a novel she had read in fifth grade. "Boston," she said at last. "I'm from Boston."

"Boston, is it? I myself am familiar with that town. Perhaps we share acquaintances."

"Well, I don't know. I haven't been there for quite some time." It crossed her mind to mention Johnny Tremain. It was a name, at least, and she could elaborate that he was an apprentice silversmith.

But it didn't seem likely that the only name an adult from Boston could recall from home was a fictitious adolescent boy with a crippled hand.

"I see." He said nothing for a while, but slowly glanced over her from head to toe.

"Is that the latest fashion in Boston?"

"Oh." Without hesitation her hand flew to her throat, where the plaid flannel nightgown buttoned.

The hem didn't quite reach her ankles, revealing her slippers—an old pair of moccasins.

Just as she was racking her brain for something clever to say, he began to laugh. The small chuckle exploded into an all-out guffaw. "Very well played, miss! Very well played indeed!"

Still clutching the nightgown at the throat, she smiled and nodded. "Thank you," she said uncertainly.

"Well, where is she then?"

"Where is who?"

"Kitty! I know she put you up to this, my Katherine! This is the best jest she has done yet."

"Oh. Kitty." Maura pretended to look for her. "I don't know where she went. Isn't it just like Kitty to run away like this?"

The ghost paused, the smile fading from his face. "You have no idea who I am speaking of, do you?"

"Why do you say that?"

"Because you, miss, are a terrible liar. Have you ever even been to Boston? Or the Colonies?"

"Of course I have!"

"I'll wager you've never been five miles from Dublin. That is an atrocious attempt at an accent." He crossed his powerful arms, appraising her. "Now what are you really doing in my home? You don't seem to be a regular sort of thief."

"I am not a thief."

"Excellent! That is the first sentence you have uttered that has the faintest tinge of sincerity. So you are not a thief. What is your name, if I may be so bold?"

"I'm Maura Finnegan." She was about to reach out her hand to shake his when she realized he was probably composed of nothing but vapor. She quickly withdrew her hand, and he raised an eyebrow.

"I am Fitzwilliam Connolly." He bowed slightly. "But I presume you knew that already."

She nodded. "I took a wild guess."

"Ah. So, Miss Finnegan. It is 'miss,' is it not?"

"Yes, but please call me Maura."

"Christian names, is it? Our friendship is progressing at an alarming rate. So before any misconceptions can spring between us and kill our mutual fondness before it has a chance to flower, please tell me what you are doing in my home at this outrageous hour."

A thousand thoughts crossed her mind, reasons that could explain her presence, but nothing would work. She could claim to be a distant relative or perhaps a lost traveler, which was feeling more accurate by the moment, but ultimately that would fail to explain the situation.

Nothing would make sense to Fitzwilliam Connolly.

"Do you really want the truth?"

"My dear lady," he sighed. "I believe I have all but begged you for the truth. Please."

"You're not going to like it."

"I have already prepared myself for that eventuality. Indeed, at this moment I can think of no explanation I could possibly find pleasurable."

"Would you like to sit down first?"

An incredulous expression crossed his face, his eyes suddenly even darker than before. "You are asking me if I would like to sit down in my own house? Nay, I will stand. And I am losing patience swiftly, Miss Finnegan."

"Maura."

"Maura, then. Would you tell me? Now?"

She cleared her throat.

"Well, I hate to be the one to tell you this . . . How do you feel, by the way? I mean, are you feeling light-headed or strange?"

"I am indeed beginning to feel strange," he admitted.

"Really? How so?"

"Never in my entire life have I ever entertained the slightest desire to strike a woman or to wrap my hands about her neck. Yet at this moment in my life, I can think of little else."

Taking a step back, just out of his reach, she spoke as evenly as possible. "All right—here it goes. You are dead. You are a ghost. It is 1996 and I own this house as well as the factory. You are haunting this place because you were murdered right on the front steps—"

His composed features suddenly exploded into enraged passion, and he lunged for her arm. "You devil! I will . . ."

His hand passed right through her sleeve.

They both remained very still, and he again reached for her arm. This time she moved toward him, and his hand went through her torso.

"I'm sorry," she whispered, as he stared at his hand, an expression of betrayal, confusion on his face.

"It must be you," he growled. "You are the one who does not exist. I recall I have seen you in my dreams—you are the one who haunts."

But as he spoke he began to look around the house, his voice losing the anger with every lightbulb and electrical outlet, every modern touch.

"What has happened?" he said softly. "I can see furnishings from my own time. They are shadows, overlaid shadows."

"I'm so sorry," she repeated.

The look on his face was heartbreaking, an expression of loss and sorrow she would remember for the rest of her life. "This cannot be so." And then he closed his eyes. "Who murdered me?"

"I don't remember his name. I believe it was a friend of yours."

He opened his eyes. "A friend?" A glimmer of black humor was there. "Remind me to cross him off my Boxing Day assembly list."

She could see the staircase through his body. "You're beginning to fade."

And he simply nodded, becoming fainter with each passing moment until she could barely make out his form.

"Good-bye," she said. There was no response, and she was alone.

It was very nearly dawn. As she went back up to the bedroom, her legs heavy with each step, she wondered if he had vanished forever. If not, when would he return?

It was just before nine in the morning when the telephone rang.

"Hello, Miss Finnegan?" The voice on the other end was vaguely familiar.

"Yes?"

"This is Donal Byrne. I hope you don't mind my ringing you—Charles gave me your number."

When she did not respond, he made some sort of noise. Could it have been a laugh?

"Are you still there? I wouldn't blame you if you simply slammed down the receiver altogether. I wouldn't blame you if you threw the phone out of the window, hoping I'm attached."

"How can I help you, Mr. Byrne?" Maura barely recognized the cold voice as her own.

"I owe you an apology. Could you please forgive my appalling behavior yesterday?"

"Okay, consider yourself forgiven. Listen, Mr. Byrne, I really have nothing to say to you. Thank you for calling. Good-bye."

She began to hang up.

"No, wait a minute!"

Reluctantly, she put the receiver back to her ear. "Yes?"

This time the sound he made was, indeed, a laugh. Maura struggled to remain stern, but the laughter was so winning, so utterly captivating, that she was forced to smile.

"Please, let me make it up to you. I was a sorry example of Irish hospitality."

"If you'll recall, Mr. Byrne, I paid the bill. Therefore, I was the one placed in the position of offering hospitality."

"I deserved that, surely. Will you please have dinner with me tonight?"

"I don't know, Mr. Byrne. I'm not sure if I have enough cash on me."

"Ouch. I deserved that one as well. I promise, this

time it will all be on me. Oh, and are you at all interested in theater?"

"Maybe," she said noncommittally.

"I managed to get two tickets to the Abbey for tonight—they're doing *Playboy of the Western World* by—"

"By John M. Synge! I'd love to see that!" She straightened, toning down her enthusiasm. "And how much will I be charged for the tickets?"

"The fee will be dining beforehand with me and absolutely no talk of business. Will you come?"

"What will you do if I say no?"

"I'll hang my head in shame every day for the rest of my life."

"Hum. That's a tempting thought."

Again he laughed.

"Oh, all right, I'll go."

"Thank you. I'll come by round five, if that's not too early. I thought I could show you a few sights." He seemed reluctant to end the conversation, and Maura couldn't help but enjoy his discomfort. "What will you be doing today?"

"Well, I'm going to visit the factory again, then do a little research."

"Research? On what . . . no. Let me guess. You're going to look up your Irish heritage, your genealogical roots."

"Sort of. I'm going to find out all I can about Fitzwilliam Connolly."

"Are you now?" He paused for a moment. "I wrote several papers on him while I was at university. I still have some books and probably the papers as well. Shall I bring them by?"

Maura was taken aback. This actually demonstrated kindness, even a modicum of unforced consideration. He was clearly bent on pulling out his company manners.

"That would be great. Thank you."

"Not at all. Oh, and you might want to stop in at the National Gallery. It's right near you. They have a large portrait of Connolly hanging in the main room. It's rather like coming face-to-face with the man himself. Well, I'll see you at five, then."

"Fine. I'll be ready."

"And do you think I'd have any right to scold you if you weren't? Good-bye."

The line was dead before she could come up with a snappy response. In a way she was relieved. Donal Byrne, in a light mood, was far more difficult to keep up with the angry Donal Byrne.

Maura paid the taxi driver, her eyes fixed on the factory.

On a second viewing, with her vision growing ever clearer, the structure bearing the tattered Maiden Works Furniture sign seemed more dilapidated and hopeless than before.

Again she arrived at tea time, although it was a different hour than the previous day. There were only a handful of employees sipping from their tin mugs.

Jimmy O'Neil greeted her with a wave. At least she assumed his gesture had been a greeting, for he had again lapsed into his incomprehensible tongue. She turned to another man, one with a tweed cap so worn it was shiny.

"Excuse me, why are there so few people at the factory today?"

He seemed reluctant to answer. "Well, miss, there must be some sort of illness going about. Yes. I believe that is the root of our trouble."

"What sort of illness?"

"Well, it seems to vary with the individual. Some get it in the middle, some on top. It all depends." With a tip of his hat he walked away, leaving Maura to wonder what sort of mysterious illness could possibly decimate the work force.

It wasn't until she spoke to some of the other employees that she discovered the truth. One particular man, a worker by the name of Kermit MacGee, had called in sick. It turned out that he was the main reason many of them showed up at work so regularly. When word spread that Kermit MacGee was absent, there was a sudden outbreak of the mystery illness.

An entire factory had been halted because he had called in sick.

As outrageous as it seemed, as absolutely irresponsible as it was on the part of the employees, Maura couldn't help but be both amused and somehow touched. These were men who had worked together for a long time and had forged relationships beyond the walls of Maiden Works.

The reality was that there was not enough for the employees to do, not enough work to keep them all busy, thus the frequent, lengthy tea breaks.

Something had to be done.

She asked about getting a taxi back to Merrion Square, and Jimmy O'Neil shook his head and said something.

"Drith to methelp," he grinned.

"Good man," someone chimed, and the rest agreed.

"The best." She nodded. He may have just offered to vivisect a cat, but everyone seemed pleased just the same.

So she was somewhat surprised when he took her by the arm and lead her to a small red car. The front and back fenders were held on with string, and the rear windshield was missing. He held the door for her, and it was at that point she realized he intended to drive her home.

At least, she hoped that was his intention.

He started the car, smiling and pointing to the left, then the right. Obediently, she looked to the left and the right, an expression of wonder on her face as she pretended to understand what he was saying.

This time she didn't even attempt to locate seat belts. In a vehicle bereft of windshields, proper fenders, and—she noticed with alarm—functioning latches on the doors, the mere notion of a seat belt seemed hopelessly optimistic.

Jimmy O'Neil was a far better driver than Charles MacGuire, and soon she was able to relax and even catch a word or fleeting phrase of his conversation.

Suddenly he pointed to two hitchhikers, both with overloaded backpacks, a Nordic-looking couple. She realized he intended to give them a ride, and she smiled.

He was a kind old man, she thought.

The hitchhikers were grateful. In broken English they told her they were from Sweden and had been traveling for six weeks. Jimmy O'Neil spoke some apparently friendly words, but they obviously couldn't understand.

After a while they gestured to the side of the road, where they clearly wished to be let off. Jimmy grinned, nodding with comprehension, his brushy white hair remaining stiff and upright throughout. He leaned over Maura, and she pressed her back against the car seat in mild alarm.

He punched a button on the glove compartment, and out swung a fully functioning taxi meter.

"Two pounds sixty," he said with the clarity of a college professor.

The two hitchhikers exchanged puzzled looks.

"You're charging them for the ride?" Maura asked incredulously.

"Thatha mot ther car!" Jimmy replied indignantly.

Maura reached into her purse and handed him three pounds. He chuckled and released a lever on the dashboard. It was for the back door, unlocking it for the passengers. It occurred to her that had she not paid, or if they hadn't been able to come up with the fare, he might not have unlocked the doors.

By the expression on the hitchhikers' faces, the same thought had also occurred to them. They thanked her and scrambled out of the car as quickly as their backpacks would allow.

"Do you always do that? Pick up foreigners and charge them for the ride?"

Jimmy O'Neil stared at her mouth as if he couldn't understand her, and drove away. They rode in silence, and when they reached Merrion Square, he winked.

"Thatha moth ter car," he said, or perhaps repeated, she wasn't sure.

"Next time, ix-nay on the ide-ray," she muttered struggling with the car door. It finally gave way under a fierce kick. As he drove away, she heard him laugh loud and hard.

The National Gallery was literally next door to Maura's home on Merrion Square. In the front yard was a statue of George Bernard Shaw, a patron of the museum who had spent many hours there in his youth.

She wasn't quite in the mood for an art gallery. At least, not until she stepped over the threshold. And then, that was the only place she could imagine being that afternoon. The place was remarkable, with stunning paintings and sculptures spanning centuries, all exquisitely displayed.

She followed a trio of monks in coarse brown robes and sandals, eavesdropping on their conversation.

"Ah, another by Jack Yeats . . ."

"Did you see this one, Brother Brendan? One of Moynan's best, I believe . . ."

"Is the American girl still following us?"

At that point she ducked into another room, right after a cluster of schoolchildren. And there, in the center of the grand gallery, was a full-length portrait of Fitzwilliam Connolly.

"Good Lord," she exclaimed out loud. No one seemed to take note of her, and slowly she approached the painting.

It looked a little like the man, just a little. The clothing was nicely drawn, satin breeches glinting impressively, and a striking velvet drape in the background was absolutely marvelous.

But his face was all wrong. Whoever executed the painting—and she peered at the brass plate to catch the artist's name—had made his nose too long and his chin too short. The eyes were almost there, dark enough, but without the flash of intelligence she had seen, the humor. And the artist had painted them so close together, they very nearly gave the impression of being crossed.

Perhaps it was the powdered wig, with the set curls, that irritated her the most. Or the foppish brocade jacket in a particularly galling shade of baby blue.

Fitzwilliam Connolly was not a fop, nor had he ever dressed as a fop. Of that she was certain. In fact, she couldn't imagine him sitting still long enough to be painted. He seemed to be in constant motion.

"I hope he didn't pay for this," she muttered to herself. Again she looked at the nameplate below the painting.

"Fitzwilliam Connolly. Artist, Katherine Burbridge Connolly, circa 1768."

Well, that explained it. The poor man was already dead by the time the work was done and had no control over the ridiculous clothes they dressed him in.

Was the Katherine who painted him the same one he had mentioned to her, the Kitty he thought had been behind her appearance in his home? If so, she had indeed been quite the prankster. The portrait was evidence enough of that.

It bothered her all afternoon, that silly painting. Even as she showered and dressed for the dinner with Donal Byrne, she kept on thinking of the simpering painted smile on the man's face. It was nothing like Connolly's real smile, the dangerous undertones that seemed to lurk just below the surface.

Once again, Donal was frighteningly punctual. If she had been watching the sweep hand of her Timex, she was sure that the rusty doorbell would have rang right as the hand clicked to the twelve.

This time Maura was ready, purse in hand. For some foolish reason, she had decided to wear her prettiest dress, one she had worn to a wedding the year before. It was an ankle-length cream silk with a pattern of soft roses. The sleeves were capped, the neckline scooped but not too low. With the hat she wore for the wedding, she had been told she looked like a character from an F. Scott Fitzgerald novel. Without the hat she felt less conspicuous, but she did wear the same towering shoes. By the end of the reception she had very nearly gotten the hang of walking in them, so she felt it safe to wear them for a second time.

Even if Donal Byrne didn't think she looked attractive, at least she felt attractive.

Donal Byrne stood on the crumbling front steps, looking impossibly handsome in a blue blazer, khaki trousers, a button-down shirt, and, of course, the obligatory red-and-blue striped tie. Yet somehow he managed to transcend the clean-cut cliché of his clothing. There was something almost wild about him, his black hair more unruly than she remembered, and his eyes—his eyes—that extraordinary shade of blue. In the brightness of the Dublin afternoon the pale blue was circled with a darker color.

Those same eyes widened as he saw what she was wearing. "Miss Finnegan"—there was the faintest hint of a smile—"now aren't you looking fit today?"

"So are you, Mr. Bryne."

He straightened his tie with one hand, and she realized there was a large manila envelope in the other. "I have the information on Connolly for you. I can't find all of the books. I'm afraid they are still boxed up from the move from Munich. I'll get them for you as soon as possible."

"Thank you." She put the envelope inside before closing the door.

Donal took a step back, his eyes focused on the door to the town house. "Are you sure you'll be warm enough?" He ran a hand through his hair, still staring at the door. He felt unsettled, uncomfortable at being so close to the home. Again he spoke. "The evenings can get pretty chilly in Dublin, even in the springtime."

"I'm fine. It gets well below zero back home in the winter." *Why would he care about winter in Wisconsin,* she asked herself.

"Well, I hope it won't get quite that cold tonight. Do you need a hand with the key?" He stepped to the doorway, his jaw set.

"No, thank you." After much struggling, she was finally able to close the door. "I think this needs a new lock."

"Nah," he said. "Just a bit of oil should fix it nicely. Americans are always wanting to throw away perfectly good things if they happen to be old."

"That's not true. How can you make a statement like that?" This was going from bad to worse. "Listen,

Mr. Byrne, maybe we should just forget tonight. This may be a disaster in the making." She began to pull out the keys again to go back inside.

"No, wait. Please. Forgive me."

It would have been easy to dismiss him had he not started to laugh. "I swear, I don't know what it is about you. I don't believe anyone has brought out worse behavior in me since Billy Connors in primary school."

Just out of curiosity, she turned to see what he looked like when he smiled. That was all. Simply human curiosity.

Very slowly she turned toward him, and the instant she saw his face, she tightened her hold on the key.

He was so handsome. And so familiar.

Again he laughed and reached for her hand. She didn't have the time or inclination to pull away.

"Come. Are you hungry?" There seemed to be no notion of canceling the date on his part. "We'll go to a place just around the corner. Can you walk in those shoes?"

He gave a dubious glance at her wobbling ankles. She had only worn them at that wedding reception, and she had been sitting down most of the time, so she herself wondered if walking was an actual option.

But the last thing she wanted to do was prove him right.

"Of course," she said lightly. As she stepped down the concrete stairs, grasping the shaky railing, she noticed a very faint smile on his face. Her hand-over-hand progress would have been more appropriate for rappelling down the side of a cliff, but it did get her onto the street.

Crooking his arm in her direction, which she accepted with a shrug, he began at a brisk pace. She took three steps for each one of his, struggling to keep up and listen to his running commentary on historic sites.

"Now that building, of course, is Leinster House, the Irish equivalent of Parliament. It used to be a private home, built by the earl of Kildare in the middle of the eighteenth century. And if it looks familiar, it may be because the man who designed your White House in Washington used this as his inspiration. Are you sure you can walk in those shoes?"

"Of course I can." She tried to take a larger step, but only succeeded in dipping to the left. "Is your car parked nearby?"

"I didn't drive tonight. I thought it was a grand night for a stroll. The restaurant is just a bit ahead. Now, the interesting thing about Leinster House is that it looks different from each side. From this angle, it resembles a sprawling country mansion. But from the Kildare Street side, it appears to be an unassuming town house . . ."

His voice had a magnetic, lilting quality, a soothing tone even as he spoke of houses and landmarks. It was a voice she could never imagine tiring of, a voice that would always be compelling.

Finally they reached the restaurant, a strange little place called The Griffin in a back alley. She hadn't thought it possible, but Donal Byrne had managed to find a Dublin restaurant devoid of all charm and warmth. The decor was straight out of a Sears catalog, from the red vinyl chairs to the black velvet matador painting displayed over a plastic fireplace. There was a large needlepoint of John F. Kennedy, a smaller one of the pope, and a laminated cardboard plaque that read "An Irish Prayer."

"Ah, we're in luck," Byrne winked. "We've beaten the crowd."

As far as she could tell, they were the only people within a two-block radius. She couldn't imagine throngs of diners pushing through the entrance, all eager for the ambiance of The Griffin.

"Here, take a seat." He pulled out a chair for her and picked up two menus.

"We seem to be alone. Does anyone work here?" Just as she spoke, her voice echoing off the hard plastic surfaces, there was a loud clatter from the kitchen, and the door swung open.

"Donal! A thousand welcomes!" A short, stocky man with a pencil-thin mustache approached their table, arms spread wide. His apron was stained with brownish splotches that suggested either dried blood or liberal splashes of Gravy Master.

"Hello, Nino." He extended his hand, and the two men shook furiously before turning their attention to Maura.

Nino's eyebrows shot toward his gleaming hairline.

"This is Maura Finnegan, an American."

"So you're the one who inherited Delbert's Disgrace and the factory. An Irish welcome to you!"

"Nino is not actually Irish, so he has absolutely no right to offer you an Irish welcome." Byrne announced. "He's from Italy."

"But I learn English in Clare," he said proudly.

His accent was, indeed, as peculiar as the restaurant.

"Wine, Donal?"

"Certainly, Nino. You know very well that no one can eat your food unless the wine comes first."

Instead of being offended, Nino laughed joyously and clapped Donal on the back before scurrying off for the wine.

"You won't get this on a tour bus," Donal said as he opened the menu.

"That's certainly a safe bet." She glanced at her own menu, removing a dried lettuce leaf from the beverage selection list, and realized it was an Italian-Irish restaurant. Stews and soda breads were listed alongside linguini and pesto dishes. The pizza column included toppings such as rashers, poached eggs, breakfast sausage, and grilled kidneys.

Nino returned with two wineglasses and an open bottle that wasn't completely full. A new stain was on the bib of his apron—a path of red wine. His chin had a small dribble of wine.

"Here we go." He grinned. "Would you like to taste it, Donal?"

"No thanks. I trust you've already done that. How is it?"

"Grand! I got a bit of cork in the first swallow, but the second and third were brilliant."

"Well, that's good enough for me. Maura?"

"Fine." He had called her by her first name. Did he even realize it?

"Nino," she said looking at the menu. "Are there any specials today?"

"Specials? Every day is special!"

Byrne took a sip of wine. "It really doesn't matter what you order. I'm afraid everything is awful."

Nino clapped in agreement. "He's right, of course. But if I were you I'd stay away from the cabbage frittata and the kidney pizza."

"And take a miss on the potatoes with pesto sauce," Byrne added. "The linguini with cod and bacon ravioli is pretty wretched as well. What kind of soup are you opening up tonight, Nino?"

"Ah, minestrone or chicken noodle."

"The soup comes straight from a can, so it's fairly consistent."

The front door opened, and three customers entered. "Nino," one of them called. "So the sanitary board hasn't closed you down yet?"

Nino beamed. "Not yet! You've come just in time—we're deciding which can of soup to open."

As the evening progressed, Maura realized they had not been kidding. The food was terrible. The soup was indeed canned. The meatball in her pasta—a shape she'd never seen before, Nino seemed to call it either "foot" or "fool," and she wasn't sure if he was referring to the shape, the main ingredient, or the person who ordered it—was made from lamb. The salad was a quartered head of iceberg lettuce served with a dollop of house dressing made, Nino confided, by blending equal parts mayonnaise and steak sauce.

But Donal had been right. By the time they were finished with dinner, there was a line snaking outside and down the alley. And in spite of the food and strange surroundings, she realized that she'd had a delightful time. Whether it had been because of Nino or Donal or just the quirky charm of the place, a quality that had nothing to do with the decor and everything to do with the people, she couldn't recall having a more wonderful meal.

"Just imagine how popular this place would be if the food was actually edible," he said as they left.

During dinner he had called her Maura several times, and she had used his first name once. She enjoyed the way he pronounced her name, the vowels seemed to take a longer time than usual to escape his lips.

She also learned that Donal Byrne had a marvelous sense of humor. He laughed easily, even at some of her comments, which she found an endearing trait.

And he was a good listener. She found herself telling him all about her parents, about growing up in Wisconsin, college. All too soon it was time to leave in order to make the curtain at the Abbey Theatre.

"It's not far," he said as they walked passed Trinity College to O'Connell Street and over the bridge.

It was difficult to determine what was more uncomfortable, her feet in the ridiculously high heels or the rest of her body in the light dress. It had become cold enough that she could see Donal's breath as he spoke.

As they waited for a crossing light to change, he took off his blazer and placed it on her shoulders. "I know that it isn't as cold as Wisconsin, Maura, but I don't recall your lips being this shade of blue before."

"Thank you." She slipped her arms into the jacket, enjoying the warmth from his body. There was something intimate about wearing his jacket, something wonderfully physical.

By now her feet hurt so much, she was almost numb to the pain.

"I can't believe I wore these shoes, my feet are killing me," she blurted out.

He laughed. "I'm afraid I can't help you there. While I don't mind lending you my jacket, I believe my shoes would be a bit too large. And I'm not sure if I could carry off your shoes with your panache."

She wore the jacket throughout the play, not only for warmth but simply to wear his coat. During the performance his arm rested next to hers, and when he whispered a comment he took hold of her wrist. His hand was large and warm, a wonderful hand. Although *The Playboy of the Western World* was one of her favorite plays, the only aspect of the performance she could recall with perfect clarity was the nearness of Donal, every shift and sigh and laugh.

It occurred to her when he was hailing a taxi to take her home that she could definitely fall for Donal Byrne, not just a little bit but in a major way.

She wanted him to kiss her at the door or take her up on the offer when she asked if he would like a cup of tea. But he did not kiss her, nor did he come in. He seemed all too eager to leave rather than enter the house. Instead he shook her hand, and promised to call her the next day.

That was something, she thought as she entered the house. At least he'd call.

She was about to go upstairs when she realized she was still wearing his jacket. He was already gone when she opened the door, already vanished round one of several corners he could have taken.

With a smile she slipped her hand into the jacket pocket. There was a piece of paper there, and she pulled it out. It was a memo with a company letterhead. The letterhead was in German, but the memo was in English. She was about to put it back when her own name caught her eye.

"Sirs," the memo read. "Acquisition of Maiden Works Furniture is imminent. The single obstacle, Maura Finnegan, will soon be removed by either persuasion or force. More funds needed to secure ownership. Respectfully, Donal Byrne."

For a stunned few minutes she simply reread the memo, her hands beginning to tremble with fury and something else, a crushing disappointment. This had all been a ploy, the charm, the laughter, the kindness. He pretended to actually care about her. It was all pretend, she realized, from the moment he called that morning until his departure from her steps.

"That bastard." The tears began to fill her eyes, hot and heavy and painful. "That bastard," she repeated, shouting it in the marble entranceway. It felt good to shout, to cry.

She walked over and slumped on the steps, her forehead resting on one hand, and sobbed louder, unable to stop. She was such a fool. Would she ever learn?

Suddenly a man's voice was behind her. "Good God. Don't tell me you wore that in public?"

And there, at the top of the steps, stood her ghost.

CHAPTER 7

"Please, could you go away?" Maura wanted to be alone. She needed to think, to sort things through. Above all, she needed more time to cry.

"I am not sure if I can go away." The ghost descended the staircase. "Besides, my dear, this is my home."

"Listen, I've had a really awful evening."

"It did not appear that way from the upstairs window. Indeed, I thought you were on the verge of assaulting, in the friendliest and most welcome sort of way, the gentleman with the red cloth about his neck."

"Red cloth? Oh, you mean the tie." She turned around, and slowly stood up from the steps. "You were *spying* on me? Don't you have anything better to do?"

"It appears not. I just learned that I am deceased,

and at the moment I have yet to find alternate employment."

"I'm sorry," she sighed. "It's just . . . why are you looking at me like that?"

"Good Lord, is this what women wear?" His dark eyes took in her form, from large blue blazer to the high heels and the filmy silk of her dress.

"Thank you very much." She clenched her teeth. "If I had known coming to Dublin would be such an ego-booster . . ." She stopped and glared at him, the peculiar set of his mouth. "Are you laughing?"

"No. Not at all."

"You are!"

"I apologize, my dear. You just became so indignant when I simply asked you about your clothing. It is all very strange to me, I meant no offense." He executed a graceful bow at the waist. "Please. I have little enough to laugh about."

She shoved her hands back into the jacket pockets. "I'm sorry, too. I'm just upset, that's all."

"With your seamstress?"

"My what?"

"Your cloak seems overly large, you have no petticoats, and your shoes are tall enough for a mast. I believe your seamstress has been rather negligent."

"Oh, this jacket isn't mine. It belongs to Donal, eh, Mr. Byrne. You know, the guy with the red cloth on his neck."

"Ah. So you exchanged clothing before he left?"

"No. He just gave me his jacket because he thought I would be cold." She took a deep breath. "Actually, he just wants to buy me out."

The ghost seemed shocked, but quickly recovered. "I see. So he wishes to give you money in exchange for the pleasure of an evening."

"No! He wants my company."

"That is precisely what I am referring to, madame. Call it whatever you wish. The fact remains he is paying for the pleasure of your company. Now whether you actually, well . . ."

"The business, the firm—not me." In exasperation she hit the banister with her palm. His only reaction was a faint smile. "It's the company you founded, Maiden Works. It's even at the same location, the same building you knew. For God's sake, there are probably the same employees. Do the names Jimmy O'Neil or Kermit MacGee ring a bell?"

A slow comprehension illuminated his features. "My company? He wants to purchase the shipping concern that I, Fitzwilliam Connolly, built from nothing?"

"It's no longer a shipping company. It's a furniture factory."

"Furniture? What ever do you mean?"

"Please, I don't want to get into this."

He ignored her. "And what right do you have to be here and to bandy about the name of my company? You are naught but a woman, a simple, weak woman of no apparent virtue or wit."

Her hands clenched into fists. "You are just like Donal, nothing but a bastard."

"I am not! I am the rightful heir, I am . . ."

"I don't mean literally. Gees, I've had enough. Please step aside so I can pass by."

"No."

"Fine. I'll walk right through you, then."

"No. Please, do not do that to me." Although he stood solid and motionless, stiff as an oak tree, there was a vulnerability to his voice. "Please."

She stopped, looking up at him from several steps away. "Mr. Connolly, I am exhausted. All I want to do is sleep. I'm tired of being insulted by Irishmen I do not even know. All in all, this has been a miserable evening."

"Then I hope you accept my apology not only for my behavior but for that of my countrymen. We Irish are known for our hospitality. Should anyone betray it, five more Irishmen will double their efforts to ensure your comfort."

"Why is it that ever since I arrived here, all I hear about is the famous Irish hospitality? But so far I've paid for lunch, been forced to walk around on cobblestones in high heels, and been driven in circles by madmen in motor vehicles." She took a breath to continue, but he interrupted.

"That brings us to another point. Where are you from? I do not believe your tale of Boston and the Colonies."

"Okay, I'll tell you the truth. I am Maura Finnegan from Whitefish Bay, Wisconsin. I'm from the United States of America, which is exactly what the Colonies became after we declared independence from England in 1776. I inherited my father's company, Finnegan's Freeze-Dried Cabbage, when he died last year, but it's on the brink of collapse. I thought I could save it, really I did. But I can't, it's simply impossible. Then this man I was seeing, his name is Roger—at least that's what he told me, it may have been a lie like everything else—left me when he discovered I wasn't rich and that the company was failing. In other words, he was a fortune hunter, and I was without a fortune. So then I discovered that I inherited this home and the furniture company, because I am some sort of distant relative of yours, I guess. Way distant, if that's any comfort. And then this guy Donal who wants to buy the company from me, which would solve all my financial problems, made me pay for lunch. Then he took me out and was kind and charming, but it turns out he is just like Roger. Better looking, of course, but just like him."

He reached for her, and dropped his hand midway, but she did not see him. She was talking to herself by now, absorbed in her own misery. Again she sank to the steps and sat down, kicking off her shoes. "Donal just wants the company. I'm an obstacle, nothing more or less. I found this memo." She pulled out the crumpled paper then put it back into the jacket pocket.

"Your name is Maura, is it not?"

For a moment she didn't answer. His tone was so soft, so gentle, and she felt a chill as he moved closer.

Instead of speaking, she didn't trust her own voice, she simply nodded.

"It is a beautiful name."

"Thank you."

"Were you named for your mother?"

Maura shook her head, staring down at her stocking-clad feet. There was a large run along the side of her leg, and she reached down and pulled it, causing the run to climb higher like a fireman's ladder. "I was supposed to be a boy. They were going to name me Peter. When I turned out to be a girl, they named me after a nurse who was working the night shift at the hospital where I was born."

"I see." She wasn't sure if he really understood or not, but he was being kind just the same. "I believe it is a good thing they were not stubborn and decided to name you Peter even though you were a girl. Or that a Bertha or Gertrude was not in attendance that evening."

In spite of her distress, she looked up and smiled at him. And he returned the smile, his face transformed. It was a smile of warmth and friendship.

"May I ask you another question?"

She nodded. He seemed to have difficulty phrasing his words and attempted to begin a few times before stopping. At last he looked her directly in the eye. "I believe it will be best if I just make this question plain. All that you said before, about the Colonies and where you are from, I believe you. With everything else I have learned, your explanation is the least fantastic. There is just one facet of your history I fail to comprehend. And upon this single item may hinge the whole of your story, I cannot be sure."

She tilted her head slightly, and he gazed at her for a few moments, his eyes tracing the path of a curl that fell over her shoulder. He returned again to her face, and his expression softened.

"Could you please tell me"—he struggled for the words—"what in the name of Jesus is frizzed and dried cabbage?"

And when she finally stopped laughing, and when he finally stopped laughing, she explained the whole industry to a man who had been dead for nearly two and a half centuries.

It wasn't her idea to pull the stitches out of Donal's jacket. At least, not at first.

The ghost had thought of it, recalling a time when his Kitty, in a pique of justified anger—he had flirted shamelessly with her own cousin—carefully snapped the threads of his jacket with her fingernails. The garment remained intact for several days, until, while conferring with a gentleman who wished to ship a good quantity of linen using his shipping line, the left sleeve glided off his arm and onto the gentleman's boot. When Fitzwilliam leaned down to collect the sleeve, the other one descended gracefully to the floor.

"I deserved it, I did." He laughed, coaxing a smile from Maura. He was sitting on the steps, his elbows resting on the stairs above. "I wonder what happened to her, to dear Kitty."

"Oh, I almost forgot—I saw a painting of you in the National Gallery."

"What in the name of the devil is the National Gallery?"

"It's an art museum. Anyway, your picture was painted by a woman named Katherine Burbridge. Was that your Kitty?"

"Yes! Indeed it is!" He shifted forward. "But I never sat for a portrait by her. I told her I would after we were married, but that never happened."

"Yes it did. You must have forgotten, Fitz. The nameplate said Katherine Burbridge Connolly, so you must have married her."

"I never would forget our marriage," he said quietly. "Well, perhaps . . ."

"Perhaps what?"

"I may have forgotten the wedding ceremony, but never the wedding night."

"Men. All the same." Then she straightened. "Wait a minute—Donal gave me some information on you."

"Donal? You mean the young man with the unfortunate jacket?"

She was already across the hallway. The manila envelope was still there, and she returned to her place on the steps, opening the metal twist. "Let's see. These are papers he wrote while he was at the university."

"Trinity?" Fitzwilliam peered over her shoulder. "He writes a fine hand, remarkably fine."

"Hum? Oh, he didn't write that. It was done with a typewriter, a little machine that makes your words look printed. And no, Donal attended University College. Okay, here we go . . ."

"What's that?" He pointed, his arm just over her shoulder.

"A paper clip. Now here it says—" She paused.

"Go on."

"Do you really want to hear this? Let me skip to stuff about your life. There's no need to hear all of this."

"I already know about my life, madame. I wish to know about my death and what transpired with Kitty."

"Here. You read it." She began to hand him the papers, and he leaned back from it.

"I cannot."

"You can't read?"

"Of course I can read. I do not know if I can hold anything. I have not tried."

They both looked down at the papers, and slowly she began to hand them in his direction. At first he made no movement, then he reached out, his palm upwards.

She carefully placed them on the outstretched hand. They floated to the steps, scattering across the stairs, some flitting to the marble floor as if there had been nothing at all to stop them.

His hand clenched, and he made a single short punch with his fist before he spoke. "I thought not."

"Then I'll read this to you," she bent over and gathered the papers, intent on putting them in order. With her head lowered, she was unaware of the expression on his face, of the sadness, the intensity with which he followed her movements.

By the time she was finished, he was again relaxing languidly on the steps, an ascendancy gentleman in carefree leisure.

"All right. I'll just skim through and give you all of the facts."

"Don't you wish to read Mr. Byrne's editorial comments?"

"Not particularly."

She did not see his brief smile.

"It says here that Katherine was, indeed, your fiancée."

"So my memory does serve me well."

"You were planning a large wedding when you were murdered by . . ."

"Who?"

"You were murdered by your best friend, Patrick Kildare. I'm sorry."

"Kildare? Never! There must be some mistake. Was there a trial? By God, I'll not believe it. What happened at the trial?"

"Just a moment." Her finger traced down the paragraph. "There was no trial."

"No trial?"

"It seems it was clear to all that your friend Kildare murdered you right on the front steps. He apparently wanted it to look like a random mugging."

"Mugging?"

"Sorry, a street robbery. It was assumed that he was angry about you and the Catholics."

"The Catholics?"

"Let me go a little further." Flipping the page, she continued reading. "Oh, Fitz. This was so nice of you!"

"What? Tell me what the hell happened!"

"That you used to hold leases for your Catholic neighbors because it was illegal for Catholics to own property. So you held their titles and gave them all of the money." She bit her lip. "That was really wonderful."

"Then what happened?"

"Do you know that I'm a Catholic?"

"Maura, I am very happy for you. Could you please tell me more?"

"It's just that you did this with so little fanfare. I mean, you were genuinely concerned about your neighbors, about the injustice of it all. So many people make noise about being charitable, about trying to change the world, but you actually . . ."

"God damn it, madame! Would you just tell me what happened?"

She jumped when he shouted. "Sorry. Apparently Kildare did not approve of your sentiments. He tried to talk to you about it. He was afraid that the Catholics would take over and drive all of you ascendancy folks from the land. You guys were badly outnumbered. Oh, this is interesting."

"What? What happened?"

"No, it's just that Donal compares the ascendancy government and its treatment of Catholics with the United States and its treatment a hundred years later of Native Americans. The difference was that in America there was more land and fewer Indians. Here in Ireland, everyone was packed more closely together. Acre per acre . . ."

"I don't give a bloody hell about acreage. Tell me what happened with Kildare."

"Oh. Anyway, it seems a Catholic lynch mob . . . oh. This is terrible, Fitz. Before Patrick came to trial, he was lynched by a mob. And in retaliation, Dublin Castle randomly hanged over three dozen men. Only it wasn't so random. They hanged the Catholic men you had helped, since they assumed they were the ones guilty of lynching Kildare."

"No. This is impossible."

"And then . . ." She hesitated.

"Continue."

"Did you have a younger brother named Andrew?"

"Yes, I do, I did." Fitzwilliam glared at her. "Pray

God, nothing happened to him. We were the only two who survived, my mother died giving him to the world. Pray God, was he spared?"

"Oh, Fitz. Yes. Andrew lived to an old age, well into the next century."

He let out an explosive sigh. "One gift. One to be thankful for." Then his eyes peered closely at her face. "Tell me. What is amiss."

"Your brother married Kitty."

At first he gave no indication of hearing. She began to repeat the words. "I said, he . . ."

"Never. I will not believe it." He stood so swiftly she gasped. "He was but a child, younger even than Kitty. We teased him to distraction. Kitty would never have married Andrew."

Before she could say anything else, he began to fade.

"Fitz, are you all right?"

"Never. Never. Never."

And then he was gone.

The sunlight was just beginning to streak through the filmy windows. She collected the papers, pulled a few more threads from Donal Byrne's blazer, and went into the kitchen for a strong cup of tea.

Maura was just finishing the last page of Donal's papers when someone knocked on the front door. She had slipped into an old pair of jeans and a green sweater, both of which offered warmth against the chilly, damp morning.

It was something of a surprise that Donal Byrne, the coldly calculating businessman, could write with such passion. For long stretches she even forgot who the author was, that he considered her an "obstacle," that every kindness had been part of an overall battle plan.

Had she read his papers without knowing him, she would have wanted to meet him.

The second knock was louder than the first, and she reached the front door before the third.

It was Donal Byrne.

"I hope I didn't wake you," he said charmingly.

Her stomach flip-flopped, and she crossed her arms.

"No. I was awake, reading your papers."

"Were you?" The smile dropped from his face. He seemed so fresh, so clean. "What did you think? I wrote them years ago, of course. Were they of any help?"

"Yes. Thank you. They were very interesting." She shifted, aware that she should probably ask him in for tea or coffee. But she was unable to get the memo out of her mind. However wonderful he seemed, that one slip of paper held his real thoughts about her, all she needed to know.

"Are you sure all of your information was accurate?"

"Why, yes. I didn't vary from the basic historical facts. I simply elaborated on the possible reasoning behind them." He ducked, as if trying to get a better view of her face. "Are you angry with me?"

"No. Why would I be angry with you? I hardly know you."

"You just seem, well, distant."

A car horn honked as it turned a corner, and she glanced over at it. Anything to avoid looking into his face.

"I suppose you want your blazer back."

"Well, yes."

"I'll get it for you."

It was rude to leave him standing on the steps, but she had to get away, to put some space between them. The house seemed a warm comfort, refuge from the world, folding her into its safe walls.

When she picked up the jacket, she made sure the memo was still in the same pocket. And she pushed his papers back into the manila envelope. Nothing should remain of him. Nothing at all.

He was pulling up a sock when she returned.

"My socks don't match." He grinned. "I believe if the mystery of the Bermuda Triangle were ever to be solved, it would contain at least five dozen of my socks alone."

"And pens," she answered before thinking. "Boxes of pens that seem to evaporate the moment they're opened."

Why did she answer him?

He laughed, and she shoved the blazer and the envelope at him. "Here."

For a moment he seemed startled. "Thank you. By the way, last night was grand."

She said nothing.

"I was wondering if you would like to have dinner again tonight. There's a place in Donnybrook I've heard of, very posh. I would even drive, so you can wear stilts if you please."

"No, thank you."

"No?"

"That's what I said. I appreciate the offer, but no, thank you."

"Tomorrow night, then?"

"No, thank you. Listen, I really have to be going now."

"Maura, I . . ."

"Good-bye." She hesitated just a moment before closing the door. From the other side he could hear the latch tumble into place. She was locked in, he was locked out.

Slipping on the blazer, he stood staring at the park across the street. A child ran from its mother, and an old man walking a tiny dog stopped to light a cigarette.

It was an odd house, to be sure. And the woman residing within seemed to fit it perfectly.

So why did he feel as if he had just been kicked in the stomach? It was an unfamiliar, uncomfortable reaction, one he did not like. Not one bit.

The meeting was going well.

Donal stood at the podium, looking down at all of his superiors from the pharmaceutical company. He knew them all, had known them and worked with them for a decade.

Yet somehow, here in Dublin they seemed like strangers. They whispered in German and spoke to him in German, even though most of them spoke perfect English. It was as if they felt it necessary to assert their nationality, to make sure they did not become Irish during their three-day stay.

Had he been like that in Munich?

"Ladies and gentlemen," he began, fumbling with his papers. This was to be the final meeting. Once they saw the factory, the possibilities, it was a done deal. "The Irish government is prepared to make a very generous deal in terms of tax benefits."

When he was in Munich, he remained stubbornly Irish. He spoke his German with a broad West Cork accent, even though he could speak the language fluently, idiomatically. Just as the Germans held on to their language, he had done the same.

As did Americans.

What had happened with Maura?

"Furthermore, should any land adjoining the property become available, the government will match, punt per punt, whatever we negotiate. In other words, we will get the land for half price."

They did not seem to understand him. There was a delay, then murmuring, and finally slow applause.

Had he said something to cause offense?

The night before, at dinner with Maura, he had tried to behave correctly, but he had been taken by surprise when he discovered how very much he enjoyed her company. There were moments, long stretches, when he actually forgot why he was with her, who she was and his ultimate goal. She was simply a delightful companion, fun and bright and so beautiful that he found it almost painful to look into her eyes. Could she be angry about his behavior? No. That wasn't it. The evening had been exactly as he had described it—grand.

Someone was asking a question, a stout man in the back. He knew the man's name, could even envision the man's wife—an equally stout woman with a single graying braid wrapped around her head. Yet he was unable to recall his name.

Donal had not been listening.

"Excuse me?"

The man repeated his question in German.

Suddenly Donal couldn't understand the words. They all ran together, spilling into the air like so much muck, meaningless, almost funny.

He had never been nervous in front of an audience, never thought twice about getting up and speaking before large groups. Now he felt silly and self-conscious.

"Um," he said clearly. "Yes. Of course."

He tugged at the button on his jacket cuff as he spoke. "Now, of course . . ."

The entire sleeve tore away.

There was a hush over the room as he very deliberately pulled the sleeve off, watching with a detached fascination as he held up the blue blazer sleeve. He placed it on the podium, and yanked at the other sleeve. That, too, pulled from his body, smooth as silk.

He laid the second sleeve next to the first on the podium.

"Any more questions?"

At that a few of the people began to laugh. Gingerly at first, then, as he smiled back, the laughter exploded. They all thought it was planned, part of his presentation. And they loved it.

He slipped his hand into a pocket as they applauded, and felt a piece of paper there. As some of the Germans rose to their feet, he glanced at the paper.

The memo. He hadn't been able to find it. He'd written it days prior to her arrival. There wasn't even a date on it. It had been his smug plan to remove her, the faceless American.

Not that he would have carried through with such brutal force. The memo had been more of a sabre-rattling exercise for himself than an actual game plan. He had used the words *obstacle* and *force* and, to add to the insults, *persuasion.*

And with certainty, he knew Maura had read it.

"Thank you," he said, stepping down from the podium in his blue blazer vest, threads waving at the armholes.

"Donal, don't you have more to say?" hissed the red-haired fellow from the government. What was his name again?

"Could you take over for me? I have a telephone call to make." He shook the man's hand and headed for the exit, leaving the sleeves dangling.

All he could think of was how she must have felt when she read the memo.

That, and how cruel he had been to a woman whose only crime so far had been that her refusal to sell her company was standing in the way of his dream.

Something was wrong with him. Perhaps he should have heeded the advice of his physician. When Donal had made a simple request for something to help him sleep at night, the doctor had suggested he see a psychiatrist instead, that sleeping pills would only mask the symptom but not address the problem itself.

Then again there were the dreams, always the dreams, of a house and time, of people who seemed vivid in bursts of light, so real at moments they overshadowed his waking hours. He had invented an alternate life for himself, one of love and joy and even fear and confusion, a place he could forever dwell without the risks of reality. He needed to speak to someone about it all, and someday he probably would.

But what could a psychiatrist tell him that he didn't already know? That he was lonely, that the success of his career had not filled the hole that seemed to be at his very core, the emptiness that was now so ingrained it was a part of his identity.

No, it *was* his identity. He was defined by this aloofness, the brittle veneer that kept most people safely at bay. Without another person questioning, wondering, he could avoid peering into his own depths and exploring all that was lacking.

So he had been taking over-the-counter sleeping pills, not that they did any good. Slumber and peace still eluded him.

The way he had treated Maura was part of the problem now, and he had no right to make her miserable simply because his own life was so empty. He had no right at all.

He needed to make a telephone call, and he needed to do it before he lost the courage.

Chapter 8

The idea came to Maura that afternoon. Like most great ideas, it occurred while she was doing anything but trying to come up with a great idea.

It was so obvious, the way to save Maiden Works, that she dropped the paper towel she was using to clean a front window and simply stared back into the parlor. Her eyes did not take in the mess, the dirt and dust it would take weeks to even make a scratch in. Instead she saw the future.

She would turn Maiden Works into a successful business.

The smile spread across her face as her mind elaborated. The building was quaint, in a tumble-down sort of way. All she had to do was add a thatched roof, and presto, Maiden Works could go from a money-losing furniture factory to a folk museum. The employees could stay on, from Kermit MacGee to Jimmy O'Neil and everyone in between, but they would be dressed in authentic period clothing.

Of course, she could decide on a specific period at a later date. That didn't really matter.

What did matter was that the building was on a main road, directly en route to the Wicklow mountains. The workers could go from manufacturing unsold furniture to manufacturing tourist goods. The possibilities were endless—they could make doll furniture. No, better yet, Fairy Furniture. Spelled "Faerie" or in some other archaic fashion. They could also make shillelaghs. And, of course, wooden shamrocks and key rings and perhaps even tiny villages.

But before the busloads of tourists would be taken to the shop, they could watch the men working away, sipping their tea and chatting among themselves.

Perhaps the tourists could even have tea with the workers!

Hopefully, these changes would bring in enough money to save her father's company. But until then, she would probably have to sell the town home to keep everything afloat. The house alone would fetch a good price, as would the contents, the furniture, and carpets.

But what about the ghost?

"Don't think about that," she said to herself. Perhaps this was better, just to sell the house and get on with her life. Perhaps she was becoming too absorbed in the life of a dead man to be considered altogether sane. The house, with all of its secrets and charms, was making her downright wiggy.

Of course she would need to convince Charles MacGuire of the importance of the plan. There wouldn't be much of a problem there. He seemed to . . .

"You!" Maura had very nearly walked right through Fitzwilliam Connolly, who stood leaning against the doorway.

"Indeed."

"Please," she gasped, placing her hand over her racing heart. "Please don't do that again. You scared me to death."

"Well, at least then we'd be on equal footing," he grinned. "I do apologize for not announcing my arrival in a more suitable fashion."

Finally she, too, smiled. "It *is* your home, Fitz. You just startled me."

"I've been meaning to ask you something."

"Really? Go ahead, I'm waiting."

"Why in the name of Jesus do you call me Fitz? In my entire lifetime, and as far as I can tell beyond that, I have not been called Fitz. Only rarely was I called Fitzwilliam, and that was mainly from blood relations who had lived under the same roof for more than a decade."

"What did your younger brother call you?"

He laughed, and Maura was taken aback by how white and strong his teeth were, whiter even than his shirt. A piece of hair had fallen from the leather tie that held it, and he pushed it out of his way with an impatient hand.

"Andrew called me Fitzwilly. I suggest you refrain from addressing me thusly."

"Why is that?"

"Because I was usually forced to halt him by means

of physical force, by tickling or holding him by his ankles over a horse trough." As he spoke, the smile gradually faded.

And Maura, as she watched his expression change, realized the same thing: He could no longer perform even the slightest of physical tasks.

"Oh," she whispered. "I'm sorry."

"Nay. Do not worry yourself." He straightened. "How can a man who is unable to hold a piece of paper be a threat? I am far from even becoming a nuisance."

"Ha. That's what you think, barging in here unannounced."

He remained silent, nodding once in acknowledgment of what she had said.

"I do not know precisely why I am here now," he admitted, glancing around the room.

"Have you ever been here in the daytime? I mean, since . . . well. You know what I mean."

"Not that I can recall. It all seems . . ." He rubbed his eyes, suddenly fatigued. "I feel as if I have been asleep for a long time. And during that slumber I have been dreaming all sorts of peculiar things, of people I've never seen coming and going, of extraordinary clothing—women in monstrous attire, men in strange cloaks, with hair shorn and whiskers long. And I dreamed of children, unfamiliar children who seemed to grow quickly, and then they were gone."

She wanted to ask him questions, yet did not wish to invade any sort of sense of privacy, to strip away the only thing he had left.

"And then I recall a funny old man in a tasseled hat."

"Delbert! I'll bet that's who it was—the man who I inherited this place from."

"Is that who it was?" His gaze rested on her for an uncomfortably long while. "And then I saw you."

She swallowed and began to look away, but his eyes, his very presence was far too compelling.

"I watched you while you slept."

"You did?"

"I should probably apologize for that as well, for watching a woman as she slumbers alone in her bed."

Shifting her weight, Maura crossed her arms and shrugged. "These are rather extraordinary circumstances. I don't suppose there are any set rules of etiquette for this situation. It's a far cry from no white shoes after Labor Day or chewing with your mouth closed."

Again he said nothing for a long while, simply watching her movements. He remained motionless.

A chill seemed to flutter through the room, to fill the corners and cause the drapes to move so lightly, it may have been her imagination.

When she turned around he was gone. She knew, even before she looked, that he had left. The emptiness had already told her.

"I hope you come back," she whispered.

The telephone rang, an intrusive, angry sound in the quiet gentleness of the moment.

"Please come back," she repeated as she went into the kitchen and picked up the phone.

"Hello?"

"Maura, this is Donal Byrne."

Her first instinct was simply to hang up, but she resisted. Instead she remained silent.

"I know you're there," he said. "I can hear you breathing."

"Yes. I'm still here."

"Maura, listen. I have to explain something—this isn't easy for me. Will you hear me out?"

"For a few minutes."

"Thank you. First of all, I have to tell you that I enjoyed last night. I did not know what to expect, but much to my surprise I truly enjoyed your company."

"Much to your surprise? How very kind of you to . . ."

He laughed, but this time she did not feel herself responding. "Poor choice of words. I am not used to wearing my heart on my sleeve. In truth, at the moment I have no sleeves at all."

"Would you, by chance, be wearing your blue blazer?"

"As a matter of fact I am. It is more of a blazer-vest now. Sure to set a fashion trend in Germany."

"Germany? Why in Germany?"

"Because that's where the executives are from."

"You've lost me."

"The executives to whom I was giving a major presentation. They seemed delighted with the pull-away sleeves."

"Well . . ." She would not feel guilty. She refused to allow herself any regret for what she had done. "Why don't you just write them a memo? You seem to have a gift in the realm of brief, concise statements."

"Maura," he began, then he stopped. "I wrote that sometime last week, and I never did send it. It was pure business. You know, it was a bluff—really bluffing no one but myself."

"So you wrote a memo that you had no intention of sending?"

"No, no. I was just trying to psych myself into being able to maneuver this business deal. I am not really the cutthroat type in business or anyplace else for that matter. You know what I mean. I have to do a little posturing to myself. It honestly makes me feel uncomfortable, but I have to do it for the overall good."

"You do well enough."

"Maura, please. May I see you again?"

She closed her eyes and leaned against the kitchen doorway. "There's really no point. I can't imagine you and I having any sort of relationship, not after that memo. And as for the company, well, I've decided to keep it."

There was a long pause on the other end, then what sounded like a pen tapping on a desk. "Fine. You certainly have a right." The tapping stopped. "But once it goes into bankruptcy, which it should in a matter of months, if not sooner, I will be able to pick it up at a much lower price."

"It will not go into bankruptcy."

"It won't, eh?" A new edge came to his voice. "I suppose you'll use the same magical touch you've used on your company in the States. Have you notified your employees yet that the company can only stagger on for a month or so before you're going to have to cut jobs?"

"How . . . Who . . ."

"I made it my business to learn as much as possible about you."

"And of course you are not cutthroat."

Although she'd thought about it, especially with

Donal, she couldn't recall ever hanging up on someone, slamming down the phone in midsentence without at least saying good-bye. But this time she did. The receiver hit the cradle with such force, her hand stung with the vibration.

Hanging up on Donal Byrne did not make her feel any better, did not give her any sense of triumph or satisfaction. Instead, it made her feel worse than before.

Somehow, in the back of her mind, she had thought they might become friends. The mishap with the memo aside, they had shared a fabulous evening. More than just a fabulous evening, they seemed to have shared something else, something special, although she wasn't exactly sure what. Maybe it was nothing more than a mutual interest in the factory. Maybe it was just the normal tension between a man and woman. Yet it had seemed deeper, somehow more potent than those everyday explainations.

It was a nasty memo, but if he had written it the previous week, his explanation made some sense. For a brief moment she thought perhaps they could recapture the warmth of some of the quiet moments they had shared the evening before.

But she knew, with bitter certainty, that she had been wrong. He was just like Roger. Never ever could she be friends with Donal Byrne.

The ghost appeared again just at dusk.

Maura was slumped on the least uncomfortable couch, a half-finished cup of tea and the real estate sections of the *Irish Times* and the *Independent* spread out before her. Her reading glasses were forgotten on top of her head.

"I need your help," he snapped without preamble.

"Sure." She moved the newspapers into a stack, with a legal pad on top to cover the copy. Of course he wouldn't realize the meaning of the sections or of the estate agents she had circled to call. Yet she did not want him to know she was planning to sell the house.

He moved about with large, sure strides, devouring the space with every movement.

"There is much amiss."

"That's an understatement."

"I fear I will not be able to rest until I know what occurred."

Maura glanced up at him. He seemed to glow, almost as if his entire being was incandescent, as if he were pure energy. A breeze rustled the papers as he paced nearby.

"I have a question to ask you." She put down the pen. "You want me to help you, and I will. Of course I will. But do you really want to rest?"

"And I cannot discover what occurred . . . Pardon me?" He stopped midstride.

"I asked you if you really want to rest." She took a swallow of cold tea. "You just don't seem like the resting type."

"That's absurd." He ran a hand through his hair, loosening it from the tie.

"How do you feel? I mean, this restlessness. Is it uncomfortable in any way?"

"It is bothersome, like an aching tooth. It needs attention."

"Yes, but will it make any difference? I mean, what

can you do from your side? The past is the past. I don't understand how finding out the ugly details will help you at this point in your life, eh. Well, whatever this is—at this point in your existence."

"Are you going to quarrel with me at every turn?"

"I hadn't thought about it. Probably."

"Damn." For the first time he seemed to relax. "Is that a chair?" He pointed to one of the more unfortunate examples of postwar furniture, an enormous, battered lounger that had at one time reclined. Now it simply squatted in its brown tweed cloak, as if shabbily confident of its rightful place.

Maura frowned. "Of course it's a chair. Granted, it may not be the most attractive bit of furniture, but it's still a chair."

"Forgive me. I have been unable to distinguish objects from my time to yours. They have blended together, a jumble of sorts."

"Can you still see stuff from your time as well?"

"Not well. They seem to be pale outlines, like shadows in the daylight, not dark enough to discern. Whoa . . ."

"Watch out! That's a recliner."

The chair performed for the first time since perhaps the days of Sputnik, the bottom panel glided out, bumping him into the seat. Simultaneously the back fell away, propelling him into the uncertain middle, cradled with his legs over one side and his arms flaying.

"Good God! Am I being devoured?"

Maura jumped up and pressed the old wooden handle on the chair forward. "Here." She grinned, and just as quickly, she stopped smiling.

"Thank you. This is quite comfortable, indeed. What is . . . Maura? Is there something wrong?"

"You moved the chair, Fitz."

A stillness settled over the room, a calm tension as they simply stared at each other.

"Impossible." His lips formed the word, no sound seemed to escape.

She reached out her hand to touch him.

"No. No, do not!"

Immediately she withdrew her hand.

His voice softened. "I apologize. It is simply that—should my"—his hand clenched into a fist—"should my flesh, such as it be, prove to be unpleasant, I should not wish to offend."

She wanted to reassure him, but he was a man of enormous pride. No words could possibly change his belief.

"Oh, Fitz."

"Oh, Maura." At last the smile returned. "So you will assist me in my efforts?"

"I really don't know what I can do."

"Is there a place where you can procure old newspapers, books? If Marsh's Library is still in existence, they might be of help. Anything that might assist me in reconstructing what happened at the end, anything at all, would be most appreciated."

"I hate to sound like a broken record, but—"

"A broken what?"

"Sorry. I hate to repeat myself, but what good will this do? It's not as if we can go back and punish the guilty party, or parties. It seems already that your friend Patrick did this to you, and that your younger brother came to the rescue and married Kitty."

"Please. Please—I am not good at begging. If you are too engaged in other affairs, I will most certainly understand and try to discover the truth myself. If not, could you assist me?"

This is not normal, she thought, watching his features. Instead of dealing with reality, with the very real issues pressing on her, it was all too easy to become entangled with Fitz and his long-vanished world. Still, he had become a friend and an important one. The truly unusual thing about his request for help was that she knew he was not the sort of man to have ever required much assistance from anyone about anything. That alone made his plea impossible to refuse.

"Of course," she said at last. "I'll be more than glad to help you."

"Thank you. Then I shall leave you." He rose from the chair with only slight difficulty. "Is this meant for comfort?"

"Yep. All you need is a wide-screen television and you'd be set."

His expression was blank. "I do not believe I wish to know what your meaning is. No good can possibly come of it."

"You're right." She looked at her watch. "It's just after six—I'll bet the library is still open. I'll check out whatever I can on you."

"I appreciate that."

Before she could respond, he was gone.

The library at Trinity College was open, filled with students looking tired, intelligent, and panicked. It was too late for her to find another library or Marsh's, and this one was the nearest to her home. She was just curious if there were some books on Fitz, if not, perhaps he would be mentioned in a general history book on ascendancy Ireland.

The atmosphere, with the milling students speaking in hushed voices about upcoming exams and papers due, was enough to give Maura a math anxiety attack, so she headed directly to the biography section.

There were no less than five biographies of Fitzwilliam Connolly, the oldest with a publication date of 1873, the most recent was from only a few years earlier. She wasn't able to check the books out, since she did not yet have a library card, so she took all five back to a desk and began to page through them.

After scanning them, it was obvious that the best of the lot was a book by an author named B. D. Finn. Maura was initially drawn to this particular volume because of a caption next to that loathsome portrait from the National Gallery. It read: "Posthumous portrait of Fitzwilliam Connolly, painted the year after his death. That simple fact may account for his sour expression and perhaps the uncharacteristically foppish choice of attire. From contemporary accounts, Connolly never wore brocade or satin, and, indeed, never sat still long enough for a portrait."

Maura laughed out loud—the author expressed exactly what she herself had known. She turned to the copyright page and discovered the biography had been published in 1976, well over two centuries past the time the writer could have known Fitz.

An odd thought crossed her mind—could Fitz have visited this author the same way he had visited Maura?

"Ridiculous," she muttered into the pages. A student who had just pulled up a chair at the same desk grinned in agreement before returning to her own work.

But the further Maura read, the more certainly she felt that this book was an accurate assessment of his life and, more significant to Fitz himself, of his death. And with each page, her sense of acute embarrassment grew. As an American, and an ignorant one at that, she'd had no notion of his importance not only within his own circle of friends but within the vast scope of the eighteenth century in general.

It wasn't simply his political views that set him apart from his peers. There were many liberal-minded men in the years leading up to the American Revolution. Fitz, however, had been a man of wealth, born to privilege as few were in those days or after. And rather than espouse his opinions, which included a complete repeal of the Catholic Penal Laws, which stripped the vast majority of Irishmen of their rights as both men and human beings, Fitzwilliam Connolly worked quietly from within the buffered, refined circle of the ascendancy. He attended the Rotunda balls, the hunts, the gaming tables on occasion, yet all along he was undermining the very foundation of the society that had given him wealth and position.

It was only after his sensational murder that his true character became generally known.

Before that, Fitzwilliam Connolly was considered one of the most important figures in Dublin society as well as in Dublin business. The two were rarely meshed—success in both arenas. Acceptance in one was usually a grudging result of mastery of the other, and merchant hands were considered base and too soiled to hold in refined society.

Connolly, however, was the eldest son of an established peer. His father had left him a fortune in estate holdings, horse flesh, artwork, a shipping concern, and that rarest of all commodities, cash. He was also given his father's title, which he used only when necessary to avoid a scene.

"He was a marquess?" She hadn't meant to say the words out loud, it was simply that Maura had never met someone with a title.

The lights flashed in the library, a signal that it would close soon. Reluctantly, she flipped to the back of the book, to the end of his life. A heavy, unsettled feeling weighed on her chest, as if simply reading the words would cause him to relive the pain.

"Are you researching the evolution of the wee people or perhaps the origin of the tourist?"

Maura jumped and looked up to see Donal Byrne staring at her with his strange, beautiful eyes.

"I . . . neither, if you absolutely must know." With a theatrical thud she slammed the book closed, causing a cluster of students to jump, pens to be tossed reflexively in the air, and more than one startled cry of "Jaysus!"

"Sorry," she whispered to the assemblage, then she looked back at Donal. "What are you doing here?"

He shrugged. "I like libraries, the people, the smell of the books, the quiet." He craned his neck to read the title. "So you're reading the biographies of your illustrious forebear. This one's the best of the lot." He pointed to the book she had been reading.

"I'm sure the author would be delighted to know that you approve. Now if you don't mind . . ."

"She was my mother," he blurted, then seemed to stiffen.

"Your mother?" She looked again at the book. "It says here the author is B. D. Finn."

"She used her initials and maiden name. See?" He turned the book to the back flap, where there was a black-and-white photograph of a lovely woman with dark windblown hair and the overly large collars of the mid-seventies. The copy said the author lived in the rural west of Ireland with her husband and young son. "I am the young son," he said so softly she could barely hear him.

"Why didn't you tell me?" Maura continued to look at the picture and could indeed see a strong resemblance. Without color, she couldn't be sure if his mother had the same eyes, but even in black and white they were striking, almost haunting.

"I didn't really get a chance to tell you. We're not on speaking terms, remember?"

"Ha ha." She smiled but did not look up at him. Instead she looked at the photograph of his mother, and out of the corner of her eyes she saw his leg, now leaning against the table. She could almost feel the warmth from him, he was so very close. "I'd love to meet her. I mean, she knows so much about Fitz, it would be incredible to actually discuss him with her. Does she ever come to Dublin?"

"She used to." A faint smile traced his lips as he stared at the picture of his mother. "When I was at university, she used to come here often, sometimes just to watch a hurling match of mine, other times she would come to my dorm room unannounced. The funny thing is, none of the other fellows minded. Other mothers used to send us fleeing to the nearest pub just to escape. But with my own mam, well, she would more than likely take *us* to a pub."

"She sounds great. Will she be coming to town anytime soon?"

He blinked at her, as if confused, then shook his head. "She died a while ago."

Instinctively, she reached out and touched his wrist. "I'm so sorry. I really didn't know."

"I know you didn't," he said softly, his gaze slowly shifting to her hand.

"If you ever want to talk . . ." Then she stopped. What was she doing? He clearly wanted no comfort from her.

He stood up before she could say anything else. "Good evening, Maura." He did not look back as he walked away.

It was probably for the best, she mused glancing down again at the photograph of his mother. They had nothing to say to each other, nothing at all. It was probably all for the best.

"Bastard, bastard," he mumbled to himself as he crossed the Trinity College courtyard. A few people turned to stare, but the sight of a young man mumbling to himself during final exams was all too common on the campus.

She had offered to talk to him about his mother. Maura, who had only just then learned that he, too, had lost parents recently, reached out to offer her warmth.

All along he had known that her own father had died a death every bit as slow and painful as his mother's. Yet even in their more extensive conversations, he never once mentioned the fact or offered the most basic of condolences. He should have, he knew that even as he avoided the subject. Any human being with an ounce of integrity would have offered some sort of compassion.

He felt himself becoming more detached than ever from the rest of the world. Lack of sleep, perhaps. Or the unsettled state of his business affairs. Whatever the reason, he was uncomfortably aware that his behavior was not as it should be, that his actions did not reflect his feelings or his intentions. Instead of being kind, he was cruel. Rather than exercising patience he was intolerant and demanding.

What the hell kind of person had he become?

"Bastard, bastard," he repeated. This time no one gave him a second glance.

CHAPTER

9

Maura was relieved, and a bit disappointed, that Fitz didn't come during the night. She had stayed awake, puttering about the bedroom, stifling her yawns behind her hand, waiting for him to appear. The absurdity of the situation struck her just before she gave up and finally decided to go to sleep. After all, she was a grown woman, a businesswoman at that, with the responsibility of two companies in her control.

Yet here she was in her nightgown waiting for a ghost.

By the time she had given up and turned off the lights, she was exhausted and feeling more than a little foolish.

Pulling the covers up under her chin, she closed her eyes and thought about what she would do the next day. There was no use waiting. It was time to contact a real estate agent. The sooner she could secure a buyer for the town house, the sooner she could begin the alterations on the factory and pay off Finnegan's creditors.

Not seeing Fitz made the decision easier.

But, as she began to drift off to sleep, she did not see him appear in the corner of the room. He made no sound, no rustling, no movement at all. Instead he simply watched her, a faltering smile on his face.

"Good night, Maura."

Almost asleep, she murmured something and rolled over to her side, punching a pillow beneath her head.

"Good night," he repeated.

Maura took another sip of tea as she scanned the yellow legal pad filled with the name of real estate agents she had taken down from the newspapers. One name seemed to pop out: Biddy Macguillicuddy. Anyone with a name like Biddy Macguillicuddy was bound to be sympathetic or at least have a sense of humor.

The odd thing was that Maura used to have a doll named Mrs. Macguillicuddy, a ridiculous felt creature with purple hair made from yarn, a purple dress with red plastic cherries and matching purple shoes—felt feet pointing outward.

She called the number listed in the ad. It was an answering machine with a shockingly jolly voice that seemed to speak in exclamation points.

"Hello! This is Biddy Macguillicuddy! Please leave your name and number, and I'll be sure to ring you later! Cheerio!"

Maura left a message and hung up. Almost immediately the telephone rang.

"Hello! This is Biddy Macguillicuddy!"

For a startled moment Maura thought the machine had returned the call, and then she realized that it was Biddy herself, the voice of merriment.

Maura explained her inheritance, and Biddy seemed all too familiar with the entire will, stanza by stanza.

"How very lucky you are!" Then her voice dropped, still booming but somewhat less explosive. "Why would you wish to sell the gem?"

Maura cleared her throat. She needed to sell the place, she didn't need everyone—especially Charles, at this point—to know the precise details.

"Oh, well . . ." she stammered.

"Enough said," Biddy cut her off with friendly efficiency. "Shall I come round today and take a look?"

"That would be . . ."

"Grand! I'll come over at half ten. Cheers!"

The telephone line went dead. Maura felt as if she had just been confronted by an entire platoon of Welcome Wagon ladies, well meaning and relentless.

At precisely ten-thirty, Biddy Macgillicuddy herself stepped through the threshold of number eighty-nine and a half. She was just under five feet tall, with the face of a dried apple—cherubic and care-worn. Her generous frame was cloaked in a turquoise garment festooned with plastic cherry clusters. Her hair was pinned to her head in steel gray twirls—the only color on her body that had not been the product of a natural accident or a cruel prank in the dye vat.

"Hello." Maura extended her hand. "My name is . . ."

"But of course you are!" Biddy Macguillicuddy pumped her hand vigorously.

Maura was momentarily stunned. It was as if her felt doll had come to life as a real estate agent in Dublin.

"Now tell me, Miss Finnegan." Mrs. Macguillicuddy gave Maura a swift yet piercing glance. "Are you any relation to the Dalkey Finnegans?"

"Not that I know of."

"Splendid! They were a wretched lot, every last one of them. There was Sean, the well poisoner, his eldest son Peter, the sheep molester, and Peter's wife, Peggy, who was known to make bangers from the carcasses of stray dogs. Shame. And believe me, they were the best of the lot, the cream of the sorry crop of Finnegans from Dalkey. The rest don't bear mentioning."

Her face settled into an expression of expectant tranquillity.

"I'm sorry the house isn't in better shape at the moment," Maura began, leading the agent into the parlor. "I just arrived a few days ago and haven't had much time to really fix it up."

"Not a worry, my dear. You'll be in quids when this house goes on the market." With that she opened a roomy vinyl bag and produced a rhinestone-studded pen and a worn spiral notebook. "Do you mind if I jot down some notes for the advert?"

"Of course not. Would you like some tea?"

"Oh, there's a darling girl! No, thank you. Not at the moment. After I see the house, perhaps, perhaps. Now, let us take a look."

It was as if a shade had been drawn over the agent's

face. She was all professional appraiser, her voice lost its roller-coaster dips and peaks.

"There is not much molding left, is there?"

"I'm afraid not," Maura apologized.

"Perfectly fine." She touched the tip of her glittering pen to her tongue before writing in the notebook. "Let me see . . . 'Free of cumbersome, dust-catching details.' How does that sound?" She beamed at Maura. "The trick, you see, is to turn everything into an asset. The kitchen is in the back?"

Without waiting for a response, she strode into the kitchen with military precision. "We must use our imagination. Do you have much of an imagination, my dear?"

"No." Maura crossed her arms defensively. "No, I'm afraid not. I've always been rather pragmatic and . . ."

"A bit pokey and outdated, is it not?"

"A little." Maura began to twist a piece of her red hair with her fingers as she stepped aside for Mrs. Macguillicuddy to pass.

"Splendid! 'Cozy kitchen ready to move through the nineties." Her expert hand pulled back a bit of the shabby curtain. "Goodness! The backyard is in even worse shape than the front. 'Nature enjoys her freedom in both gardens.' That sounds rather nice, does it not?"

Finally Maura smiled. "It does. I'd be tempted to buy it myself." Then she took a deep breath. "What do you think the chances are of the house selling quickly? It's just that I would like to resolve everything, and I've heard of houses being on the market for months, even years."

The agent gave a peculiar half smile. "This house will sell. Believe me."

"But it's in such terrible shape."

The perpetual cheer seemed to vacate her face for a moment. "To tell you the truth, the house will sell on the basis of its location, my dear. Whoever buys it will no doubt gut the interior—it would be far simpler than trying to make anything of this mess. But have no doubt, it will fetch a brilliant price. These homes come on the market so rarely. When they do, they are gone in a blink. Now am I to be the exclusive agent?"

The smile had returned to Mrs. Macguillicuddy's face, but Maura failed to notice. "They'll gut the interior?"

What would happen to Fitz?

"Why, of course. Shall we journey upstairs?"

Maura followed in pensive silence as Mrs. Macguillicuddy continued her note taking. "We'll punch up the location in the adverts. This is a prime piece of land. Of course, since it's a landmark, any changes would have to be approved, but that mainly pertains to exterior alterations. And since this was the home of Fitzwilliam Connolly, well, that's as good as gold. There are always people willing to pay a few thousand punts for a patch of history."

Earlier Maura had thought along the same lines. Now she was beginning to feel sick to her stomach, physically ill at the thought of someone ripping out the insides of her house.

"Will the furniture be included in the sale?"

Maura didn't answer, and Mrs. Macguillicuddy did not seem to require one. "Well, we can decide that later. Best to get the advert off and running on the house. Good Lord, look at this jumble!"

They stepped into the room adjoining the yellow parlor. "And the other room is vacant! My, what a splendid example of Georgian wallpaper! I have seen . . ." Her voice trailed off.

"Hum," the agent said pensively. "There is something peculiar. It must be the lack of furniture."

Maura gasped when she saw Fitz standing, arms crossed, in the corner of the room. He stood glaring at her, with such fury that for the first time since she had seen him in her bedroom she was actually frightened.

"Is anything wrong, Miss Finnegan?"

"I'm sorry. I must have pulled a muscle climbing the stairs," she stammered, leaning down to massage her leg and to get Fitz to go away. She jerked her head to the right, toward the door, but that seemed only to add to his anger.

Mrs. Macguillicuddy had grown very quiet. "Oh, dear," she whispered.

Maura stood up and, turning toward her, instinctively reached out an arm to steady the older woman. Her bright face had paled, and suddenly she seemed quite elderly and brittle. "Are you okay?"

The agent was staring at the corner of the room where Fitz lounged. She took a step back in her sturdy shoes, not answering Maura's inquiry. The pen slipped from her hand. Maura bent down to pick it up, and as she leaned forward, Biddy Mcguillicuddy pushed her in an attempt to escape.

"There's something in here! There's something in here and I believe it's evil!"

The rage left Fitz's face as Maura glanced at him with an openmouthed expression of surprise. Before she could say anything, the sound of the estate agent's clattering footsteps in the marble hall downstairs rang throughout the house. Even as Maura followed, she wondered how the woman had moved so quickly. Then she heard the front door thrust open, the sound of footsteps fading.

When Maura reached the first floor, the front door was still swinging on its hinges from Mrs. Macguillicuddy's exit. There was a package leaning against the threshold that appeared to be a book wrapped in brown paper with her name written in black marker. There was no return address, no postage. Whoever the sender was, he or she had placed it there rather than send it through the mail.

Maura scooped up the package and slammed the heavy door shut just as Fitz descended the staircase. The sense of fear she had experienced before was gone.

"She saw you."

"I know." Fitz rubbed his jaw, shaking his head. "I don't think this has ever happened before, other than with you. She must have seen me, but I did not make myself visible to her."

"She must be psychic or something." The book was heavy, and as she spoke she held it against her.

"Pardon me?"

"She must be psychic. You know, able to see ghosts and tell the future and read tea leaves."

"In my day we called such women either mad or drunk with spirits."

"Yeah, well. I should think you would be a little more open-minded now, Fitz."

"She saw me,"

"I know."

As if coming out of a stupor, he suddenly looked directly at her. "You are selling the house."

"I was going to mention that." She held the book more tightly against her chest. "I have to, Fitz. There's no other way. I need the money for the factory and to save my father's company."

"Then you will sell me as well." He spoke from between clenched teeth.

"No, no. It's not like that at all."

"Is it not?"

"Wait a minute. I almost forgot—I found some information on you at the library. I wrote down some facts and dates. I couldn't take out any of the books since I don't have a library card yet. I think I have to establish some sort of residency."

"In that case, you need not bother. It seems you will not be a resident long enough to require library privileges."

He spun around and began to ascend the staircase.

"Don't you want to hear what I learned about you?"

There was no response as he continued his climb. Just as the steps rounded toward the first floor, he paused, hand gripping the banister.

"I believe I want nothing more of you."

"Fitz, you have to understand—I really have no other option. I was hoping I could take you with me, maybe. Do you think you could leave here?"

He stared at her for a long time before answering.

"This whole time I felt 'twas I the unnatural, cold thing. You I envisioned as warm and alive. I longed so to be like you, I, the unnatural, cold thing."

Just before he vanished, he hit the banister with such force that it rattled the entire snaking length of the staircase, vibrating the spokes, causing chunks of paint and plaster to explode through the air.

"It seems I was very much mistaken. You, my dear, are the cold, unnatural thing."

"No, wait! Please . . ." But he was already gone.

The house suddenly seemed empty as it never had before, a sense of nothingness that seemed to permeate through to her bones.

"He doesn't understand," she said in a voice uncertain, unsteady. "He has no idea of what modern business requires."

It was painful to swallow, and she squeezed her eyes shut and gripped the package.

The package. She had almost forgotten all about it.

Taking a deep breath she walked over to the staircase and sat on the second step. With her thumb she unfastened the tape holding the brown wrapping paper together.

When she flipped it over, the wrapping open, she simply stared for a while.

The book was familiar. *Fitzwilliam Connolly: The Soul and Conscience of Ascendancy Ireland,* by B. D. Finn, the book Donal's mother had written.

Unlike the library copy, this one was in pristine condition, free of the scars and coffee circles and dog-eared pages that a book earned after two decades in a university library.

She opened up to the title page. There was writing

there, a neatly penned cluster of words. The script was rounded and precise, a style she had noticed that seemed to be the product of Irish elementary schools.

To my son, who, while still young, is no longer as little as I would wish . . . All my love, Mam.

It was his own copy, signed by his mother. For what seemed to be forever she was unable to breathe, simply staring at the inscription.

Donal had given her his own copy.

A small slip of paper was poking out from the pages of the book.

Maura, I do hope this book is a help. I can personally vouch for the character of the author, if not the subject. Please enjoy, Donal Byrne.

His handwriting was similar to his mother's perhaps less slanted. She stared at the two samples side by side, wondering why she was so reluctant to stop studying them. There was no point, except that the more she concentrated on something as benign as handwriting samples, the less time she would have to contemplate why she suddenly felt like laughing and weeping at once. Or why she felt a lump in her throat which wasn't completely unpleasant, yet not entirely comfortable.

No matter how long she sat on the steps with the book and brown paper wrapping on her lap, one stark fact remained. He had given her his own copy of the book.

Not for the first time, surely not for the last, Maura wondered if she would ever in a million years understand the workings of a man's mind.

Chapter 10

She felt as if the house itself were closing in on her. As large as it was, the rooms suddenly seemed oppressively small, the walls too close together, and the ceilings too near to the floors. It was like being at a gathering of too many relatives, no place to escape, no corner to collect one's thoughts. To preserve her sanity Maura had to leave, to escape if only for a few hours.

Instead of calling Charles MacGuire or Biddy Macguillacuddy or any other deed that might require some sort of intelligent conversation, Maura decided to visit the furniture factory. Should Jimmy O'Neil be there, she knew she would not have to hold up her end of a dialogue, since understanding him was out of the question in any case. And if Kermit MacGee was no longer ill she could see firsthand what others found so appealing.

Maura dressed carefully, in a linen suit and skirt

that seemed to proclaim business acumen with every no-nonsense inch of sensible beige fabric. Her only concession to a remote fashion sense was a well-hidden blue blouse with removable shoulder pads. She left them in, hoping that the more she resembled a linebacker, the more respect she might gain from the employees.

Arriving just before three in the afternoon, she entered the front door just as the workers were about to embark on a tea break. Her arrival did nothing to deter them from their respite.

The first person she saw was Jimmy O'Neil. As usual he wore a black jacket and black trousers with a crumpled white shirt printed with a tiny geometric design. Whether it was the same outfit or if he had a closet filled with identical frayed trousers and thread-bare jackets, she couldn't be sure. But through the transparent shirt she saw his sleeveless undershirt in some sort of thermal weave. The front seemed to have been pulled out of shape, for the neck scooped almost to the bottom of his chest, and when he removed his jacket in the afternoon warmth, she couldn't help but notice that one of the sleeves draped over his arm like a woman's errant bra strap. His hair, as usual, stood proud and erect in almost military white splendor.

"Thath a geekoma hey." He waved boldly and pointed to a gentleman with alarmingly wide side-burns. Swinging the jacket over his shoulder, he nodded toward his companion. "Kersther Math-eraga."

The whiskered man stood and bowed at the waist. His trousers seemed to have been sewn at home by someone who had not yet mastered the art, yet had a great deal of multicolored yarn at their disposal. His tie, knotted into a small bulb at the base of his throat, dangled well past his belt and was knit of the same yarn. It was unraveling at the bottom, and she had a sudden image of him cutting the tie off as it stretched.

"It is indeed a pleasure to meet you," he pronounced. "Jimmy here has told me so much about you, Miss Finnegan."

Maura blinked. "I'm sorry, I didn't catch your name."

The man seemed surprised. "Well, it's just as Jimmy said—Kermit MacGee."

"Oh, of course!" She leaned forward and shook his hand, which seemed to please him immensely.

Jimmy stepped forward and said something, while Kermit listened with a barely restrained grin. Then Jimmy stopped, nudged Kermit, and nodded.

"Nah, Jimmy! I can't tell herself the punch line, not to this joke. It's not fit for mixed company."

"Please," Maura urged. "I'd love to hear the punch line." She almost added that it didn't matter, since she had no clue as to what the rest of the joke was but was afraid that Jimmy would merely repeat it.

"Are you sure, miss?"

"Absolutely," she said with confidence.

"Well, so then he says . . ." A hush fell over the workroom. A few workers scrambled closer, hunched forward in eager expectation. "So then he says . . ." Kermit repeated, slowly savoring their reaction.

He was milking the room like a real pro, she marveled.

At last he seemed to rise upon his toes, and in a high-pitched voice he shouted "Knickers!"

The place went to pieces. Maura alone was not doubled over with laughter, clutching her sides, gasping for breath and repeating the hilarious word to herself over and over.

When he finally caught his breath, Jimmy looked at Maura and frowned, wiping a tear from his reddened cheek.

Kermit also stopped and seemed to stiffen. "I'm sorry, miss, if that joke was in any way offensive."

"Not at all." She tried to smile but was so confused by their reaction that she was reluctant to admit she had no idea what had been so funny.

Slowly a somber cloud seemed to descend over the factory, and they whispered to each other and shook their heads as they relit pipes and returned to work or tea.

"No, honestly. That was a very funny joke." But they didn't really believe her.

Jimmy O'Neil gave her a disappointed shrug, then suddenly he glanced just over her shoulder and his face brightened.

"Dotha misser blothdea!"

She knew better than to hesitate for an instant. "I know! Isn't that a riot!"

Without missing a beat, she clapped her hands and began laughing, bending forward and hoping that she looked convincing.

It took a while for her to realize she was laughing alone—the deafening sounds she was making by herself drowned out any other noise. She stopped and cleared her throat, a few giggles still coming out.

Someone was behind her.

"Well, I'm certainly glad the announcement of my arrival has put you into such a good mood."

She spun around and was face-to-face with Donal Byrne.

He continued. "After our last conversation, I wasn't quite sure how you would react to seeing me."

Jimmy said something and Donal gave Maura a look of surprise. "You must be joking," he said at last.

Jimmy shook his head, shrugged at Maura, and left to finish his tea.

"What did he say?"

A slow smile spread over Donal's face, a face she couldn't help but notice was absolutely wonderful in the natural afternoon light.

"You haven't the slightest clue as to what old Jimmy is saying, do you?"

"Not the foggiest. What did he say?"

"The less you know about that unfortunate joke, the better." He was wearing a pinstripe suit, a look she always thought was rather stuffy, but it seemed to work on him. He shifted, his own eyes perusing her, and she fervently wished she hadn't worn such a classically mannish outfit.

"Oh," she said uncomfortably.

"Did you get the book?"

"I meant to tell you, yes, thank you. That was incredibly generous of you." She lowered her voice. "I really can't accept. It's far too precious a gift."

"No. She would have wanted someone with an interest in Connolly to have it." He glanced up and waved at an employee who called his name.

"But, Donal, it's inscribed to you. I can't accept

your only copy, not one that your mother meant for you alone."

"Nah, it's fine." He looked directly into her eyes. "I have boxes of books at home."

"Why?"

"She kept them for when she had book signings. Unfortunately, there never seemed to be the great demand we had all hoped for, although in scholarly circles she was quite the celebrity for a few months, at least until someone else came out with an interesting biography. I have my very own copy. Not to worry."

She simply watched him, the light reflecting off his hair and causing his eyes to turn into an extraordinary shade of deep blue. There was just something so fresh and real about him, so very vibrant.

And then a thought occurred to her.

"Hey, what are you doing here?"

He pointed to himself. "Me?"

"Yes, you."

"You seem to be quizzing me a great deal lately concerning my right to be in Dublin locations. If you will please remember, you are the visitor, and I am the native son."

She ignored his answer. "Does this have something to do with your takeover attempt? It won't work, you know. I was going to discuss some of my plans with Jimmy O'Neil, just to see how he felt about the changes."

His eyebrows raised just slightly. "But you don't understand a word that he says. How on earth do you intend to work with a man you can't understand?"

"Well," she began. He grinned, and she was unable

to stop from returning the smile. "The language barrier between Jimmy O'Neil and myself is the very least of my concerns."

It felt good to hear Donal laugh, to see the way his entire face seemed to light up from within.

"So tell me," she prodded. "What *are* you doing here?"

"Well." He began to reach for her hand but stopped short and shoved his hands into his pockets. "I just thought I would come by and see if you would care for some lunch."

"It's past three-thirty."

"Well, then. How about a very early dinner?"

"How did you know I would be here?"

"I telephoned your house, and when there was no answer, I took a wild guess. My office isn't far from here. Shall we go, then?"

He crooked his arm in her direction, hands still in the jacket pockets. With only slight hesitation, she accepted the arm.

"You know, I don't believe you," she muttered as they left. "And after lunch I have to come back to see about the changes."

"Best do that tomorrow. They'll close up early today."

"Why is that? Kermit is keeping everyone entertained, so there's no reason to leave."

"Because it's such fine weather." He paused, his tone more serious. "The bottom line is that there isn't enough for them to do. There just aren't the orders they would need to work through the day."

There was no use arguing.

"I still want to know why you are here, Donal."

"For a meal. I owe you something posh after Nino's."

"I loved Nino's!" She hadn't meant to exclaim, but he just smiled.

"I was afraid of that." He looped her purse more firmly about her shoulder, and they left.

"I believe there is romance in the air," someone said from a back room.

"How right you are, Jimmy. How right you are indeed!"

Then another man added. "It's a good job she left before the Germans got here. What time are they to arrive?"

"About half four, I believe. Donal has a government man to show them about, so it won't matter if he's not here."

The only word Maura could come up with to describe the restaurant was the same one Donal had used: posh. From the moment they entered the small stone building, when she battled an instinctive urge to genuflect, she spoke in a hushed whisper.

The place looked as if it had been stripped from the pages of *Architectural Digest,* with majestic windows and gleaming crystal vases on each table blinding her, every noise muffled by the rich carpets. The ceiling was beamed with what seemed to be ancient wood. The overall effect was one of modern lines blending in perfect harmony with classic details.

She also knew this would be a very expensive meal. Not knowing who would pay the bill—after all, his track record indicated a distinct ability to allow the guest to pay—Maura decided that no matter what luxuries were available or what out-of-season delicacy awaited her command, a simple bowl of soup sounded just perfect.

Donal, however, felt more than comfortable.

"Is Kevin here today?" he asked as the host greeted them.

"I'm afraid not, Mr. Byrne." The host was an elderly gentleman who seemed to treat his position with great solemnity. Every word was spoken with the precision of an accomplished curate. "He has gone to cheer on his cousin at the Wicklow Sheep Shearing Festival."

"Is it that time already?"

"It is indeed, Mr. Byrne. And I hear the Kennedys from Galway have brought their cousins from Australia to compete. It should be brilliant."

"Not the same Kennedys with the sister who . . ."

The host's voice overlapped. "The very ones, sir."

"That should liven things up a bit." Donal then turned to Maura. "Excuse me. Maura Finnegan, this is Dermot Hayes, the best restaurant host in Dublin. In all of Ireland, for that matter."

The man flushed with pleasure, the tips of his ears reddening, before modestly denying the claim. Then his thoughts turned to business.

"I'm afraid we are between seatings, Mr. Bryne. But I daresay Hans will scare up something for you."

"That would be grand, Dermot."

They were ushered to a large table by a window, and much to her delight, she discovered the view was of an old wooden mill with a rocky stream propelling the paddles.

She was so entranced with the scene that she was only vaguely aware he had ordered wine.

"No. I can't," she hissed the moment Dermot left.

"And why ever not?" His face held all the innocence of a choirboy. That illusion, more than the wine itself, alarmed Maura.

"Because I have work to do. Stuff that needs to get done. Telephone calls to make."

"And the weight of the world is on your shoulders. Let it rest a while, Maura. It's late afternoon, it's Friday, and anyone you'll call will not be in. Now, what are you in the mood for? More prawns, perhaps?"

"No. just some soup."

"Soup? Is that all?"

"A bowl of soup," she said. Dermot had returned with a bottle of white wine, so chilled the glass was dotted with beads of condensation after the ceremonial pouring. Donal took a sip and smiled.

"Tell me all you want is a bowl of soup when you taste this," he urged. Reluctantly, she took a small sip.

It was the best wine she had ever tasted. In fact, it was the best liquid of any sort she had ever tasted.

"Oh."

"I believe she likes it, Dermot."

"I believe your assessment is correct, Mr. Byrne."

When Dermot left, Maura felt an uncomfortable quiet settle over the table.

"So I guess this is an old mill," she said after taking another sip of wine.

"It is. It was owned by a family with a singularly odd name for their chosen profession. Here, have some more."

"This is wonderful. What was their name?"

"Miller."

It took her a moment to respond, and then she began to laugh. "I wonder what came first, the profession or the name."

"A chicken or egg proposition, if you ask me." He tilted his head. "Do you ever wonder about names? My own, for example. Now I've often wondered if someone in my family had their ambitions thwarted because of the name."

"I don't understand."

"For example, I have a little-known talent."

"I'm not sure if I want to hear this."

"I bake bread."

The swallow of wine almost choked her. "Excuse me?"

"I'm serious. My mother made sure that I knew how to make soda bread. It was a point with her—she always wanted to make sure that if I had a pound of flour and a cup of buttermilk, I would not go hungry."

"Did it help?"

"It did. There were times when I first moved to Munich that I could barely afford the flour and milk, but I did have bread. And then, later on, the bread became a thing of comfort for me. No matter how cold or lonely I felt, the smell of the soda bread brought me right back home."

As he continued he refilled her glass. "So I've always wanted to be a baker. Now that's a secret, and I would appreciate it if you would treat it as such. But who would hire a baker with a last name of Byrne?"

"I once knew a veterinarian named Dr. Yelp."

"A banker friend of mine is named Swindler," he

laughed. "And a fellow I know from university is a psychiatrist. How would you feel about telling your most private thoughts to a Dr. Frankie Strange?"

Dermot magically appeared at the table. "Hans has some lovely dishes, if you're ready to hear them."

"No, thank you. Just a bowl of soup, please." All she would have is soup. Nothing else.

"Could you give us a few minutes, Dermot?"

The host bowed and left, leaving a basket of bread on the table.

"Hey," she said before he could speak. "Do you know anything about how Fitz died?"

"Who on earth is Fitz?"

"You know, Fitzwilliam Connolly."

"You call him Fitz? I suppose as a distant relation you are granted intimacy." He smiled. "I . . . well, let me see. It's been a while since I've read about him, but as I recall, he was murdered by his good friend Patrick Kildare, who was in turn lynched by a mob of Whiteboys."

"Whiteboys?"

"They were a gang of young men. At first they caused mischief in the name of the Catholic cause. Nothing terribly serious, tearing down fences to allow their livestock to graze, minor vandalism of tithe collectors' property. They disappeared for a while, then reemerged with a more vicious bent."

"Why were they called the Whiteboys?"

"Because although they blackened their faces to escape recognition, they wore white smocks and feathers in their hats. The feathers were supposed to be a tribute to the Wild Geese."

"Who were they?"

"They were the Irishmen who fled their native land because of the Protestant oppression. The penal laws prohibited the Catholics from military service in the British Army, so the Wild Geese went to Europe, mostly France, where they became brilliant officers, absolutely brilliant. Even back then it was difficult for an Irishman to make a living in his own country."

At that he grasped the bottle of wine and poured a bit more into her glass, then dumped the rest into his. "Dermot, may we have another bottle?"

"Wait, Donal. I don't think this is a good idea."

"I think it's a brilliant idea."

There was no use arguing with him, she realized. When the wine came, he held the bottle over her glass until she moved her hand.

"The Whiteboys murdered Patrick Kildare because Kildare murdered Fitzwilliam Connolly." Donal wasn't looking her directly in the eyes. Instead he looked at his hands, the rim of the wineglass, the prongs on a fork.

"How did they know that it was Patrick Kildare?"

"Because Andrew Connolly saw the murder."

She gasped, and that sound brought his eyes to hers. "How old was he?"

"I believe he had not yet turned twenty."

"My God. Can you imagine what that must have done to his mind?" She thought of herself at nineteen, how sheltered she had been at that age, so sheltered she hadn't even realized it. What a different person she would be today had she witnessed a murder. It was the sort of thing that would change a person forever. Poor Andrew.

"Was he sure it was Patrick Kildare?"

Donal nodded. "Absolutely. And even if there had been any doubt, there were papers to prove his intent. Andrew himself found them, evidence so damning that it removed every question. They've been lost, of course, but they were seen by Andrew, and he told others of their content."

"How depressing. So then he married Kitty?"

Finally Donal smiled. "You are on intimate terms, are you not? Kitty. Her name was Katherine Burbridge, the only daughter of Sir Garrett Burbridge. She was known as a beauty and a wit and an accomplished artist, as well. And, of course, she had been the intended bride of Fitzwilliam."

"That's one bit I knew about. They had been planning a big wedding. But that's about all I know about her. Do you know anything else? I mean, what her personality was like. I don't even think I've seen a picture of her."

"There's one in my mother's book."

"Really? There must be a section I missed. I thought I saw all of the illustrations." The moment she got home she was going to look for the picture of Kitty. She must have been beautiful, one of those delicate Gainsborough types draped in lavish folds of rich blues and greens and reds, her bare white shoulder rouged, perhaps a single gold or amber or sable tendril curled against her long neck. She must have been beautiful. "And I suppose Andrew and Kitty had children."

"No. Actually, Katherine died the following year."

"I didn't know that. My God, I didn't know that she died so soon." Why wasn't she with Fitz now?

Had she truly fallen in love with young Andrew? Another thought crossed her mind. "She died the same year she painted the portrait of Fitz."

"I suppose so."

"Do you remember any details of what she was like? Or how she died?"

"Who? Katherine?"

"Of course I mean Katherine. How old was she when she died?"

"I believe she was of an age with Andrew, perhaps a few years older."

"That's what he said."

"That's what who said?"

She was still wondering about Fitz and his Kitty, how he loved her. "That's what Fitz told me. He couldn't believe she would marry Andrew after they used to tease him so much . . ."

Her words trailed off as she realized what she had just said. Donal was watching her, his expression unreadable.

"Go on."

"No. Nothing." She took a large gulp of wine. "What I meant is that in the books I've read about him, that's probably what he would have thought. After all, Patrick was supposed to watch after Kitty should anything happen to him."

"I've never heard that. Where did you read that about Patrick Kildare?"

"I don't remember."

"It certainly wasn't in my mother's book."

"No, I don't think it was. Maybe I made it up or got it mixed up with another story."

Dermot was again at the table. "May I suggest some supper?" His expert gaze rested on the nearly empty second bottle of wine.

"Whatever you suggest." Whether he was speaking to Dermot or Maura, she could not be sure. Yet his eyes were decidedly fixed on Maura, on her face, steady and unwavering.

A warmth seemed to rush through her, and she had a vague sense of her face flushing from the wine or the length of the day or, more likely, Donal. It was Donal who caused the flush and the pleasant discomfort and the breathlessness.

"Let's go," she said.

Donal did not respond at first.

"I want to go," she repeated, heedless of the sharp intake of breath from the host.

"Dermot," Donal said, not looking up. "May we please have the check?"

"There is no charge, Mr. Byrne. You've given us so much business, with your friends in town and . . ."

"Thank you, Dermot. Thank you very much."

The drive back to Merrion Square took both a moment and an eternity. In what seemed a few seconds they were back at her home, a blur, a hazy moment. She fumbled with the keys, and they did not speak. There was no need for words.

A warmth radiated from him in the cold marble of her front hallway. For long seconds they simply stood, bodies not touching yet somehow feeling every inch of each other. He reached up and traced her cheek, tenderly, with such gentleness she closed her eyes, unable to watch the emotions shift and deepen on his exquisite face.

Did he whisper her name?

Her hands touched the fabric of his jacket, hesitantly at first, then more boldly she caressed his upper arms and slid to his shoulders. With one move he shrugged free of his jacket, and carefully slid her jacket from her arms, resting it on top of his on the floor.

Her throat had suddenly gone dry, and she savored the feel of him, the hardness of his muscles, the sharp angles of his collarbone. Beneath her palm she felt his heart pounding strong and hard, and he pressed a kiss on her temple.

The next moments seemed a dream, at the same time inevitable.

"Maura." This time she knew he had said it, her name softly on his lips, his tongue trailing along her ear, then to her throat.

They sank to the floor as one. He held her closely, cushioning her with his body. The marble floor seemed warm now, warm and welcoming and perfect.

She kissed his chest and heard him gasp so wantonly she did it again, thrilling in the power she held to give him such sublime pleasure.

Everything was new, every inch of skin and flesh untried and untested, and they explored sensations together, ethereal emotions raw and poignant. They shared joy and desire and a sense of awe, an overwhelming awareness of each other.

Never had she experienced anything as powerful, as if every nerve and feeling was sharpened to extraordinary sensitivity. Even as he moved without touching her, she knew his every motion instinctively.

At last, on the cold marble floor, now infused with

their shared warmth, they fell asleep, clothes pushed heedlessly aside. In slumber she did not fear intimacy, and he awoke for a moment and smiled, stroking her cheek, reliving in his mind the memories they had just created together.

The smile faltered for a moment.

He was washed with a feeling of unease, almost as if his thoughts had been able to step away and view him objectively.

This had not been his intention. At least, he did not believe this had been his intention.

Good God, he thought to himself. *I am falling in love with her.*

There had to be a way to salvage the situation. Perhaps if he could have a little more time with her before she learned what he had done, she would understand. They could work together.

A sudden chill ran down his bare arms, and he held her more closely, tightly against his own body as if that would absorb the cold of the room and the cold of what he had done.

How could he ever explain that he had found a loophole in the will? Indeed, he was rather surprised that Charles MacGuire had not spotted it earlier and warned his client that if she took steps to sell the primary piece of real estate—the house—within less than twelve months of inheriting, the factory would automatically be put up for sale.

Could it be that Charles didn't know of her plan to sell the town house? In any case, within a matter of days the factory would be his, with or without her consent. In truth, he had intended to tell her over dinner, but before he could make sense of the evening, they were on this marble floor.

"I'm so sorry, my love," he murmured against her hair.

This could very well be the last time he would ever hold her. In all probability it was. The realization made him hold his breath, and his heart did a painful flip, as if accusing him.

He closed his eyes, willing the sun to remain hidden so he could cherish each second.

A few minutes later they were both asleep. His face had relaxed in drowsy contentment.

And from the top of the staircase another man glared at the two in unbound fury. All along he had been there, watching them, seeing their movements.

He would finally exact his vengeance.

CHAPTER 11

Maura awoke with a start, her head resting on something warm. That something spoke.

"Good morning."

She jumped, and he chuckled, a noise rumbling from deep in his chest.

"Oh my God," she moaned. "I can't believe we . . ."

"Shush."

"But don't you think we should have . . ."

"Shush," he repeated.

"I'm really not the type to . . ."

Before she could continue, his mouth was on hers, soft and silencing and feeling every bit as right as it had the night before. It was almost a challenge, a dare to pull away. And it was a challenge that seemed very right to decline.

"Mmmm," she sighed.

"That's better." Although she couldn't see his face, his cheek resting against hers, she felt him smile.

"I can't believe we camped out in the hallway," she said after long moments of comfortable silence.

"I can't believe we made it this far. I've never . . ." He didn't finish the sentence.

"You've never what?"

He cleared his throat. "Nothing."

"No, please tell me."

"I've never done anything like this," he finally admitted.

She turned to face him, a hint of whiskers on his jaw that seemed to make him even more handsome. His dark hair was tousled, more curly and unruly, lending him a rakish look.

"Neither have I." She touched his mouth, and he kissed her fingers softly, then his eyes closed, and he pulled her closer to him.

And a vase came crashing down on the floor right where she had been.

"What the hell?" Donal sat up, his entire body taut. "Where did that come from?"

Maura raised up on her elbow.

"Stay down," he hissed. "Could someone have broken in?"

The shattered vase was in shards on the floor, a blotch on the wall where it had hit, water dripping downward in fingers. The day before she had placed flowers in it, and the stems and broken blooms were heaped next to the smashed china. She recognized it as the blue-and-white antique from the front parlor and knew exactly who must have thrown it.

It must have been Fitz.

The force of his anger both surprised and frightened her. As she touched Donal's arm, for the first time she had a sickening feeling of being in over her head, involved in something she had not been prepared to face. She had thought of Fitz as a friend.

Yet he was dead, a ghost. There was nothing natural about their friendship, nor could there ever be.

"Donal—you'd better go now." Her voice was strained, and he placed his hand on her shoulder.

"No." He quickly slipped on his trousers and shirt, buttoning it as he glanced around. "Maura, love, you'd best get dressed. I don't believe we're alone."

"I know for a fact we're not."

"Who is it then?"

"Please, just go. I'll explain later." She could think of something by then, some rational explanation. If she told him the truth, he's think her a raving lunatic, an irrational American.

Maybe that's exactly what she had become.

When he spoke again, his voice was full of soothing warmth. "I will not leave you alone without knowing what the hell is happening." She could almost believe him, let him take care of everything. Rising to her feet, she paused.

"Please, Donal. Let go of my wrist."

Before he had a chance, a mantel clock flew from the parlor. Maura saw it from the corner of her eye and pushed Donal's head down. It crashed into the wall and splintered into pieces, springs and glass and twisted shreds of brass piled with fragments of mahogany.

"What—" he began.

"Stop it!" she shouted.

"Excuse me?" Donal replied, one eyebrow raised as he glanced about the room.

"I wasn't speaking to you," she snapped. "Please, we'll both be better off if you just leave now. I think you're getting him angry."

"Well," Donal kept his voice low. "Whoever he is, he's not doing wonders for my mood either." Then he began to stand, his eyes narrowed as he searched for the perpetrator. "All right. Your prank has been duly noted, and we are both terribly impressed. Now show yourself before I call the garda."

Maura handed him his shoes and socks, the crumpled jacket they had used as a pillow, and his tie, the knot somehow still in place. "Please, just go now and I'll call you later."

"You're afraid," he said, brushing a bit of hair from her eyes. "Who is it?" Then his expression changed. "Have you had a man here with you this whole time?"

"Not exactly." Just as she was about to gently lead him through the front door, an ashtray from the parlor winged into the hallway like a drunken flying saucer.

"Coward!" Donal shouted to the parlor. "Show yourself—"

And with that a footstool joined the ashtray, mantel clock, and vase, slamming into the wall.

"Good-bye, Donal." Now she was getting worried. Fitz was out of control and seemed bent on hurting someone. That someone was apparently Donal.

"So this is how it is to be." There was a strange, labored quality in his voice, as if forcing himself to remain calm. "After last night, did it mean nothing?"

"It was great, just fine." She turned toward the

parlor and saw the reclining chair inching toward the hall.

Fitz was trying to kill Donal.

"Bye!" With a shove she slammed the door. Outside she heard him curse, then pound on the door with such force she though it would shatter.

"Maura! Let me back in . . ."

For a response she slid the dead bolt into place.

There was silence from the other side, and she leaned her forehead against the thick cold wood of the door. "I'm so sorry," she whispered. She touched the door, wishing she was touching him instead.

At least he was safe.

At least he hadn't been hurt.

And that thought alone would give her the strength to face the culprit.

"Fitz!"

There was no response.

"You'll not get away with this, you bully!"

Again there was no response. She finished buttoning up her shirt and, with resignation, looked about at the mess in the hall.

"I thought you were my friend," she said softly as she walked to the kitchen for a dustpan and brush.

Once again she had been betrayed by a man. As if it weren't enough to have had horrible luck with simple mortal men, now Maura Finnegan had found a way to be duped by a dead one.

Two hours later, when the telephone finally rang, Maura all but tackled it in her rush to answer.

"Hello?" She hoped she didn't sound too eager. Just to speak to him would be such a relief. It helped that Fitz hadn't appeared since Donal left, so she could focus all of her attention on Donal.

"Hello, my dear!" It was the unmistakable voice of Biddy Macguillicuddy.

"Oh." She couldn't help but be disappointed.

"I rang to see if I have earned a permanent spot in the doghouse. I do hope you don't think me a fool for running away yesterday. My eyes must have been playing tricks on me, my dear. I assure you, I will represent your property with utter competence."

"Of course." Maura pulled up one of the wobbly ladder-back chairs and sat down. "Do you need to come back and take more notes?"

"Ah, there's a kind girl! No, not at all. In fact, I believe I may already have a buyer for your house."

"You're kidding." This was so soon. She had expected the process to take weeks, perhaps months.

"An estate agent never kids about potential buyers. I have a bit more work to do on this lead, but I do believe it's as sure a prospect as I've ever seen."

"Great."

"And he's willing to pay an enormous sum of money."

"How much?"

There was uneasy giggling on the other end. "I almost hate to say for fear of jinxing the deal. Let me say this—there will be a lot of zeroes on your check."

"Great," she said with even less enthusiasm. This just didn't seem right. It was too fast, too easy.

And there was another problem. Where would she go now? Of course she could return to the Mont Clare or perhaps stay at the Shelbourne. Hotels were expensive, though. She couldn't possibly bear the mere notion of spending close to a hundred dollars a day for a hotel.

If only Donal, if only they were . . .

"Does that sound good?" It was Biddy, but Maura hadn't been listening.

"I'm sorry. I didn't catch that last bit."

"I was just wondering if your solicitor knew. We will, of course, go through him when it comes to changing the deed and all of the other particular legalities."

Charles. She hadn't thought of how she'd be letting him down. He'd recognize the necessity for the sale, of course, but he was just so pleased with her arrival on Merrion Square, she couldn't help but think her selling the place would seem a sneaky, underhanded move.

Biddy's voice continued nonstop. "So I will indeed let you know if our buyer comes through. Cheerio, my dear!"

The line went dead, and Maura hung up.

Rubbing her upper arms, she walked into the parlor and sat down. She felt odd, as if something was terribly out of place, yet she couldn't identify what it was. There was an overall sense of unease, like the ghastly still before a storm.

"Maura."

He had come so quietly, she jumped.

"You," she snapped, then raised her chin. "I'm not speaking to you."

Fitz stood in the wide doorway, the smile leaving his face.

"Pardon me?"

"You know very well what I mean. You could have

killed him, me, too, for that matter—your aim was not exactly major league. That vase was worth something, by the way."

He stepped forward, running his hand over his mouth. "Please, tell me what you're talking about."

"Oh, Fitz. Don't make me go through this again."

"Maura, you must. Tell me exactly what happened."

"Well, I guess you'd had enough of armchair quarterback. It was an audience participation thing. You threw a vase, an ashtray, a mantel clock, that little footstool. You were working up to the lounger when I finally pushed Donal out of the house. I haven't heard from him, by the way."

Fitzwilliam had remained silent, his arms crossed as she spoke.

"Maura, it wasn't me."

"Of course it was you."

"I was not the one who threw those objects. It was not me."

Now it was her turn to be quiet. The moment he had told her, she knew with absolute certainty he was telling the truth. He seemed every bit as baffled as she was, and something else.

He stared out of the window, and she realized with a jolt that he was worried.

"There is another here," he said softly.

"Who?"

"I cannot be sure. I've sensed it for some time now, that I did not walk these halls alone. When you arrived, I assumed that was what I had felt, your presence. Now I feel something else."

She simply glanced up at him, and his eyes looked

directly into hers. A strange communication passed between the two, and she took a deep breath, unable to look away.

"I fear for you," he whispered. A cold breeze ruffled her hair as he spoke. "I feel malice. Unmistakable and spreading, as if it's evolving and becoming stronger."

"From this other person?"

The nod he gave was so brief, she would have missed it had she not been so attuned to his movements.

"I believe it is the one who murdered me."

"Patrick Kildare?"

"I do not know. It is an encroaching darkness. You sense as well. I know you do."

She did. Although the feeling of unease seemed to grow, she had assumed it was her own guilt taking shape, her guilt at selling the house and abandoning Fitz. Part of her longed to ignore it, hoping the entire dismal cloud would just evaporate.

"I believe you must leave, Maura. Do not wait until the property is sold. You must leave to protect yourself."

Her own mind had been veering along the same lines, yet the moment he uttered the words, she realized she needed to stay. There was no question in her own mind. She belonged there.

"No. I can't leave, Fitz."

"There is no choice." Very slowly he closed his eyes, as if seeing her as he spoke would be too difficult. "I do not believe I can protect you."

Glancing down, she tried to stop the tears, tried to ignore the overwhelming loneliness that gripped her so tightly she could barely breathe.

What a stupid time to feel sorry for myself, she thought. *Stupid, stupid.*

"Maura," he said. One single word, and the tears were released fully, unrepentantly. It was as if she had waited her entire life to cry, to weep for everything she had become and everything she was not. For all of the dreams and aspirations of childhood that had been dropped one by one, forgotten in the sand.

She was so very alone.

And then he was beside her. Still she turned her face away, an absurd attempt at hiding her shameful tears.

"Maura," he repeated.

There were so many things she wanted to say, that she was nothing, that she had failed miserably in every venture upon which she had ever embarked, that unlike him, she would never leave a single mark on the world. And above all, she was alone.

"No you are not."

Had he spoken or had she merely imagined the words?

"Ah, Maura, you are so wrong, so very wrong."

Tilting her head toward his voice, she realized they were nearly touching, so close she could see every solid detail of his face, each strand of hair. But it wasn't Fitz she was seeing—it was Donal. Emotions welled within her, churning from a depth she had never even imagined.

What was happening?

She opened her mouth to speak, and he shook his head, and she understood. There was no need to speak. Words were redundant, useless, trite.

Her eyes fluttered shut as he seemed to fill her with

his very being, Donal's arms floating toward the heavens as his presence mingled with hers. It was like being on a cloud filled with love. It was nothing of this world, nothing lingering of a mortal touch—every fiber of her was saturated with a bounteous sense of being treasured by Donal, of being cherished as no one else had ever been cherished.

Slowly she opened her eyes, but she saw Fitz again smiling down at her.

What has happened, she wondered. Had she just imagined seeing Donal—loving Donal?

And then Fitz looked deeply, boundlessly into her. Without uttering a word, he told her.

"Our souls have touched."

She knew that was it, the only possible explanation.

She was still in a daze when Biddy Macguillicuddy rang the doorbell.

"Hello! I do hope—oh, my dear! Are you quite well?"

It was like being assaulted by a vociferous cherub. Her small, plump hands waved in the air as if she would take flight, the plastic cherries clinking together in accompaniment.

"I must be a bit tired," Maura understated.

"Oh, you poor, poor thing! But I do have some grand news. I do believe our buyer will make a firm bid in the next few days, perhaps as early as tomorrow."

"Tomorrow?"

"Yes! Splendid, simply splendid—far better than I had ever hoped. Now, have you had a chance to chat with Charlie MacGuire?"

"No, I'm afraid not."

"Well, not to put too fine a point on it, but we really had best let him know all of these exciting goings-on. Can't have the solicitor left out in the cold, can we? Or is it out in the blue? I can never remember. Shall I give him a jingle?"

"Well . . ." She couldn't leave here. Not with everything so up in the air.

Not without Fitz.

"Please, dear. Do us both a favor and call Charles first thing in the morning."

"Do you suppose you could stall the buyer?"

Biddy looked stunned. "Why ever for? In hopes of getting a higher price? My dear, I can't imagine a higher price."

The telephone rang. "I'll be right back."

"Not to worry, my dear. I had nothing else to say, just popped by. Cheerio!"

And she vanished before Maura had a chance to ask her in. The phone rang again, but not before she realized why Biddy had left in such a rush.

The poor woman had sensed Fitz and probably the evil presence as well. She simply could not tolerate the place, and only the anticipation of a fast, lucrative sale could induce her to enter the doorway ever again.

"Hello." Straightening the cord, which had become entangled with a corner of the curtain, the phone slipped from her hand, clanking on the floor before she could return to the call.

"I'm sorry," she laughed. "I just dropped you. I'll begin again. Hello."

"Perhaps we should begin again." His voice was low, without any warmth or humor.

"Donal! Oh, I'm so glad you called. I can explain this morning."

"You already have. There was another man there, and he was justifiably angered by my presence."

"No, no that's not the whole story. It's more complicated than that."

"There is nothing complicated about the situation. It's the oldest story in the world, Maura."

"Believe me, this one's got quite a twist."

"I'm sure it does."

With an exasperated sigh, she realized the only thing to do was to tell him the whole story. She had tried and utterly failed to come up with some logical explanation, but the further the tale would develop, the more questions arose than were answered. Perhaps he would think her insane.

On the other hand, Biddy Macguillicuddy might back her up on this one. She was most certainly aware of Fitzwilliam.

"Donal, I will explain, but I have to do this in person, face-to-face."

"I'm not sure that's a good idea. We seem to get into trouble when we see each other."

"Please. I really have to tell someone, and you're the only one with whom I feel comfortable sharing the whole story." That wasn't quite true. She'd rather not be forced to tell anyone, especially not Donal, but the fact was he had been witness to something that had to be explained.

"Fine. Where would you like to meet? There are a few things I need to tell you, as well."

"Could you come over here tonight?"

"Will your friend mind?"

"Don't make this any more difficult than it already is."

"I'm not the one making the situation difficult. Remember, I was the target, not the vase assassin. So I repeat, will your friend be there?"

"I'm not sure. He more or less comes and goes as he pleases. You'll understand better once I explain."

"That's unlikely," he muttered. "All right, fine. Should I come round at half six?"

She flipped up her wrist and checked her watch. That was a little more than two hours away. "Great. I'll see you then."

"Good-bye, Maura." There was a slight hesitation in his voice, as if he would say more.

"Bye."

Then she heard a gentle click and the peculiarly tinny dial tone.

At least she would see him tonight, she thought.

When the doorbell rang just a half hour later, Maura wrapped in a bathrobe, her hair scattered in wet tendrils about her shoulders, assumed it was Donal.

"An hour and a half early?" There wasn't time to do much more than shake her head like a retriever and answer the door.

It was Charles Macguire.

"Oh, dear me!" His face turned a mortified shade of red, and he turned his back. "I am sorry. I tried to ring you a few moments ago, but there was no answer, so I just thought I'd pop these papers over. Oh, dear."

"Don't worry, Charles. Please come in. Could I get you something?"

He nodded. "Perhaps a better sense of timing." When she laughed in response, he finally relaxed.

"Now what are these papers about?" She gestured to the envelope under his arm.

"Oh, yes. They are about the sale."

Maura was momentarily stunned. "You know about it?"

"Yes. I was informed today."

"I . . . I'm so sorry, Charles. I should have told you myself." Hadn't she told Biddy she would tell Charles the next morning?

"Not to worry. All we have to do is sign a few documents to release the property for sale."

"Charles, I really don't want to do this. I just have no other options."

His craggy face softened. "I understand, my dear. You have been placed in a most difficult position. The best thing is to sell it off, get a good price, and be done with it."

"So you're not angry?"

"Me?" He seemed genuinely surprised. "Why on earth should I be angry that you wish to sell what is yours? Here, sign this one first."

"Oh, I'm so glad, so relieved." With just a slight hesitation, she signed.

What would happen to Fitz? She pushed the thought away. Somehow she would manage to resolve the situation. No buyer could push her out of the place right away. Most certainly she could arrange to stay for a while.

"Fine, excellent. The buyer is ready, as I understand it."

"That's what I hear as well." She tightened the belt on her robe.

"I'm surprised you know so much."

"What do you mean?"

"Nothing, really. But from what I was told the buyer wanted this thing done swiftly and quietly. You understand, so as not to upset anyone."

"Oh." She really didn't understand, and was just relieved that Charles wasn't angry. "Well, I suppose I should finish getting dressed."

"Right! I'll get these going on their way." He paused. "By the way, are you free this evening?"

"No. Well, I'm not sure, maybe later."

"Grand! Come round Nesbitt's if you wish, the later the better."

"Thanks. I'll try." She smiled, and Charles blinked once before returning the smile.

Once he was back on the street, he kept thinking of her smile, the way she looked in that bathrobe with her hair all wet and smelling like a pine forest. If only he could be ten years younger. Make that fifteen.

Folding the papers up, he also wondered about how easily she had signed them. Perhaps he had misunderstood her in the beginning.

In any case, within a few short days Maiden Works Furniture would be in new hands, financed by a German pharmaceutical company, and run by Donal Byrne.

And he whistled as he walked to the Shelbourne for his first Jameson of the day.

Chapter 12

Donal, usually pathologically prompt, was almost twenty minutes late.

"I apologize," he said the moment she opened the door. "I lost track of the time at work."

He stepped into the hallway, a tweed jacket slung over his shoulder in spite of the chill in the air. Maura simply took in the sight of him, the strength and sheer vitality of his presence. Even standing still, he exuded energy, as if simply standing was something of a trial.

Polished though he was, with expensive clothes and impeccable grooming, beneath the veneer there seemed to be a wildness just waiting to spring forth. He was about to speak again, when he seemed to have lost his train of thought.

They stood in silence, as his gaze remained fixed on her face, drifting only long enough to take in her body, lingering at her waist, where a belt cinched a pair of jeans. Instead of making her feel self-conscious and underdressed, his languid perusal made her cheeks burn with a tingling warmth, as if she were suddenly cloaked in the most sumptuous of garments, the most beautiful of gowns.

Even after a full day of work, he was crisp and fresh. His eyes settled again on her face, and a softness was there, one she had never noticed before. As if he'd been caught, his thoughts transparent in turbulent blue, he looked quickly down, shifting slightly as he stood.

For a moment he stared at the floor, the exact spot they had been the night before. Her gaze followed his downward, and she cleared her throat for lack of anything better to say or do.

"Would you like to come in?" She was halfway to the parlor by the time the words were out. Instead of answering, he simply stared at the floor.

"Yes." He moved quickly into the parlor, leaving his briefcase and jacket in the hallway.

There was an uncomfortable tension between them, and Maura wasn't sure how to clear the air, to ease the tension.

"Please sit down." She motioned toward an overstuffed couch. He nodded once and sat, one of his legs nervously moving up and down, heel tapping against the floor.

"So, shall I go first or should you?"

"I . . . maybe I should." She settled on the same couch, close enough that they could touch if either seemed so inclined. For the moment they remained stiffly apart, in separate corners, as if awaiting the ding of a bell.

"All right." She tucked her legs beneath her. "I really don't quite know how to begin."

"How about by telling me who tossed all of those objects? That seems a good place to begin."

She swallowed, realizing when asked point-blank that what she was about to say sounded absurd. For the past couple of days she had grown so used to Fitz, the strangeness of the situation seemed to have faded on her. He wasn't a ghost, a man who had been dead for well over two centuries. He was just Fitz, her friend.

"He's a friend of mine," she said at last.

"I see. I had already assumed that." Donal rubbed his jaw, producing a slight scratchy sound from a new growth of barely visible whiskers. "Is he an American staying here with you?"

"He's not American, he's Irish."

"Irish, is he?" Donal seemed surprised. "From Dublin?"

"Originally, I believe so." This was getting uncomfortable.

"Did he attend university? Perhaps I know him."

"Well, yes he did, but I doubt you would know him. He went to Trinity."

"He did? I know many folks from Trinity. When did he graduate?"

"Oh, he was way ahead of you. Way, way ahead."

"I see." Donal frowned, casting her a sideways glance. "Is he a relation of yours?"

"Yes, but a distant one." How much longer could she keep this up?

"Distant. Does he have any claim on your inheritance?"

"Well, not exactly. Although he should, by all rights. He just doesn't have much need of the factory or the deed to the house at the moment. He's a wonderful man."

"Interesting. May I meet him?"

"I'm not sure. There's a little problem."

"What sort of little problem?"

"Well . . ." Now she began to tap her foot nervously, and she crossed her arms, as if giving comfort to herself.

"Come on, Maura. There is something wrong here—you've behaved strangely since this morning. I've managed to control my temper. I'm all ease and serenity. Tell me. I believe I have a right to know."

"Would you like some tea?"

"No, I would not." He was unable to hide his irritation. "Can you just tell me the man's full name? Surely that would not put too much of a strain on you."

"His name." She began to pull a thread from her cuff. "Well, his name is Fitzwilliam Connolly."

The thread unraveled further, and a button dropped to the floor.

"His name is Fitzwilliam Connolly," Donal repeated. "So he must be a descendant. But wouldn't he have been more likely to inherit than you? I know they searched all over for you, and I can't imagine how they managed to miss a Trinity graduate named Fitzwilliam Connolly." Then he paused before reaching down for her button and handing it back to her.

"And my mother," he said. "She was brilliant at digging up unlikely sources, not to mention the more obvious ones. She spent months at Trinity, looking through their archives for information on the original Connolly. I can't believe she would have missed him."

"Well." She tucked the button into her jeans pocket. "He may not have been available for comment when your mother was working."

"Quite possibly. Still, she was very thorough."

"Donal." She took a deep breath. "I don't know how else to say this but to just come out with it—Fitzwilliam Connolly is a ghost."

Very slowly, he turned his entire body to face her. "What kind of a bloody joke are you playing?"

"It's not a bloody joke. Just listen to me and remain calm. Please hear me out."

He made no attempt to move, nor did he encourage her in any way. He simply stared in blank disbelief.

"Okay, this is what happened. On the first night I was here—right before I met you, in fact—he came into my bedroom. I thought he was a burglar or at least some sort of intruder. Then he walked through my luggage, and I realized he was a ghost."

"Maura, I . . ."

"Please listen! He didn't know he was dead. He thought I was the intruder, and I had to convince him what had happened. He thinks there's more to the story, by the way, much more than Patrick Kildare killing him. So I told him I would do anything he needed. That's why I was researching him, trying to find out the basic facts."

Donal remained silent, and then he reached out and touched her face. "Maura. Come closer."

She slid across the sofa, perplexed but relieved that he didn't get angry or accuse her of some sort of trickery. His arm went about her, and he kissed her forehead. Before he could pull her closer, she leaned back.

"What are you thinking?" She needed to know.

"It really doesn't matter."

"Yes, it does! I've just told you that there's a ghost in this house, and you don't seem to react at all."

"Now let me get this straight." His voice was soft and rational. "Fitzwilliam Connolly has been living here with you, and it is he who asked you to research his own life, and it is he who threw all of those items at me this morning. Is that right?"

"Well, not exactly. He says that someone else threw the stuff at your head."

"Ah. I see. Would this other person also be of a deceased nature?"

"As a matter of fact, yes. You don't believe me, do you?"

"Maura. How shall I say this?" His hand dropped over hers. "I believe I have underestimated the strain you've been under."

"You mean you . . ."

"Please." His hand tightened. "Now it's my turn. Listen to me."

"You don't believe me," she said, her voice hollow.

"Maura, hear my side of this tale. Your father died last year, and I must apologize for not being more sympathetic. It had more to do with my own self-centeredness than with you. I believe I was afraid to let our relationship go from business rivals to something more intimate, and I wrongly thought mentioning personal events would muddy that line."

"What are you saying?"

"Maura, I was wrong. I was blinded by my generic dislike of Americans. I've been stubborn and narrow-minded, blaming you for my own problems."

She simply stared at him, her mouth slightly open.

"I know. I'm more surprised than you are." He smiled. "But it's true."

"What about the ghost? Do you believe in Fitz?"

"Oh, Maura, I'll help you through this. Perhaps together we can find the help you need. You've been trying to do this all alone, first the company in Wisconsin, now over here the demands on all sides. I felt that way in Munich, as if the weight of the world rested on my . . ."

"You don't believe me, do you?" She withdrew her hand from the warmth of his, and he looked down at his open palm.

"I believe you believe it," he hedged.

"In other words, you think I'm crazy."

"No. Not crazy, not at all." When he reached for her again, she ducked and pressed herself into the far corner of the couch. He continued speaking in a soft tone, as if coaxing a cat from the limb of a tree. "Listen to me. When my mother died, I thought I heard her when it rained."

Maura didn't answer. She just watched him.

"My mother used to love the rain. She's the only person I ever knew, especially in Ireland—where fine days are prized and few—who actually preferred rain to the sun. She would sing along to the patter of the drops on the window, make up silly little songs, nonsense lyrics, just because storms used to frighten me. And the month after she died, there was a great downpour, and I was going through her papers and suddenly heard her voice again, singing some song I had never heard but knew she had made up."

"You heard your mother, so why won't you believe me?"

"But I didn't hear my mother. Don't you see? I missed her so much, longed for her so very much, that I imagined hearing her voice. And strangely, I felt much better after that. It was my mind's way of coping, I suppose. My mind's way of fooling my heart and of easing my loss."

"But this is different," she pleaded. "Why would I imagine Fitzwilliam Connolly? It's not as if he was someone I knew."

"Oh, Maura, don't you see? You could use him right now, someone to help with the burden. Who better than the man who began all of this? And there is the added attraction as well."

"What added attraction?"

"He is safely dead. Unlike someone like me, your ghost can make no demands. Since you don't have to risk a real emotional tie, where by necessity you put yourself in a vulnerable position, you cannot be hurt."

She blinked. "God help us, you minored in psychology at college, didn't you?"

"Well, yes, as a matter of fact I did. But that doesn't invalidate what I just said. Now tell me, did you invent him before or after you did your research?"

"Ugh! Can't you be more open-minded about this? I mean, don't you believe in ghosts just a little?"

"I do not, Maura. In fact, I am fundamentally

opposed to the very notion. Such superstition has held the Irish back for generations now. No. I do not believe in ghosts or witches or fairies or little people."

"Donal . . ." She thought of Fitz, of the way he had reached her. "Donal, do you believe souls can touch?"

"Souls can touch?" He shook his head. "No. No, I do not simply because I do not believe in the idea of a soul. We are human beings, we forge our own paths with our minds and ambitions. Souls fall into the same realm as other superstitions, Maura."

"I think you're wrong. I mean, why would people be attracted to each other? All of us are basically the same, flesh and blood and bone. Then what quality separates us, makes us different from every other human being? What attracts or repels others? Well, it's clear to me it must be our souls."

"Maura." He smiled. "I was attracted to you because I find you beautiful, and then I realized I enjoyed your personality as well. It has nothing to do with souls, everything to do with the mortal body and character and intellect—which has nothing to do with a spirit."

"You're wrong."

"So be it. You have every right in the world to disagree with what I'm saying. I simply do not believe in anything I cannot see or touch or feel. But does it really matter?"

"Yes, it does. To me it does, because our souls have touched."

"That is ridiculous. This is the product of stress and imagination."

"No, it's not! This is important to me, Donal. You

don't believe there's a ghost here, and that's understandable. But the belief in a soul is so fundamental, I can't fathom not believing in its existence."

"Enough, Maura. Let's change the subject. Now, I really want to discuss a way to help you with everything that's suddenly been placed on your lap. You've gone through so much, been asked to carry the weight of your father's company as well as everything here, that you must find a way to distribute the responsibility. I was unsure before tonight, but now I realize how vital this is to your emotional and psychological well-being."

Suddenly she stood up. "Fitz! Fitz, could you please come down here and talk to Donal? He doesn't believe in you. Please, Fitz?"

Donal stood up next to Maura. "Maura, just sit down. I'll get you something to calm you . . ."

"I am calm!"

"No, you aren't. You are angry at me, and all because I believe in a scientific approach to life and do not believe in goblins and souls and little men in pointed shoes."

"Fitz! Please come down here and meet Donal!"

"You are getting yourself all worked up over nothing." His hand rested on her shoulder. "I'm here to help you in any way I possibly can."

"You are not. You just want to butter me up to get hold of the factory. Well, it won't work. I will never give it up. Never. Fitz! I need you . . ."

And then a chill encompassed the room. Maura halted mid-sentence. "Uh-oh," she breathed.

"Is there a window open?" Donal glanced behind

him to see where the breeze came from, but the windows and the door were all firmly latched against the outside.

"Let's go," she said. "We can argue about this over at Nesbitt's. I just want you to leave."

"I will not. Let me check in back and upstairs, Maura. We can't have the place open."

"Donal, please. It doesn't like you. I think whatever it is thinks you're Fitz, and it's trying to kill you again."

He grinned. "Not to worry, Maura. Remember—I have no soul. No one, in this world or another, could ever mistake my soul for another. Stay here while I check in the back."

"No." A sense of fear seemed to close in on her, and Donal paused, as if listening for something.

"Maura, there's an intruder upstairs." All traces of humor vanished.

"It's the other, evil thing. It's not Fitz. Please, Donal, let's just leave."

"Whoever it is, I need to stop him. He must not be allowed to frighten you like this." Donal took both her hands. "Go outside, Maura. There's a phone box on the corner—I don't want you in the house a moment longer. Call the garda."

Upstairs there was an enormous crash, as if a large piece of furniture had been hurled into a wall.

"It's in the yellow parlor just above," she whispered. He nodded once. The sense of approaching doom was almost choking her, and she looked up at Donal to see if he felt it, as well.

He did. She knew it by the slight frown that creased his forehead and a very light sheen of perspiration that dotted his temples. She reached up and touched his face, but he did not react, his eyes focused on the staircase.

He felt it, too.

In one swift movement he took her hand. "Forget catching anyone, Maura. Let's just go," he mumbled as he pulled her toward the door.

She nodded, and in an instant they were at the front entrance. He moved the bolt, but the doorknob would not turn.

"Hurry," she urged. There was another crash from upstairs, and then something much worse. The sound of heavy footsteps treading across the floor above, and then the door from the yellow parlor creaked open.

"The damn thing's stuck," he rasped, and hit the brass knob once before trying it again. "The back door?"

"The yard's enclosed. There's no way out except through the front. Donal, please hurry."

It was coming, she could feel it. By the frantic way Donal was working on the door, she knew he was aware of the thing approaching. She slipped her arm about his waist, as if his body could infuse her with strength, and she turned back to face the staircase.

There was something there. Unlike Fitz, this was not the clear form of a man, it was not a clear form of anything at all. It was a churning darkness, like malevolent spilled ink, changing and shifting as it moved.

She was unable to speak, unable to breathe, as if her entire being was suspended.

Donal continued to fumble, cursing and slamming his hand against the lock and the bolt and the doorknob. Still it came closer, liquid movements soundlessly winding across the marble floor.

Maura glanced at his hands, blood dotting them where he had hit the sharp metal, yet still he struggled.

And then he stopped.

"Donal?"

She could hear him breathing, and turned toward him. The thing was on them.

She backed away and realized it was only on him, on Donal. And it seemed to have him by the throat.

"No!" she screamed, and she tried to bat away the blackness. All she hit was Donal.

His chest was heaving, struggling for air, and she could tell that he was unable to get any, none at all.

Donal began to slump forward, and Maura pulled and pushed at the lock, beating it with both hands and even her foot at the base of the door.

"Open," she prayed. "Please, open."

There was a roar in her ears, and miraculously, the door flew open. She grabbed Donal, who fell forward, his forehead on her shoulder.

"Run with me," she begged. "I can't carry you."

Somehow he stumbled forward, still gasping. He began to stop at the base of the steps outside, but Maura knew it wasn't safe. They had to get across the street.

A green bus veered to avoid hitting them as she pulled them across to the park. Behind her she heard the front door slam shut.

The moment they reached the grass, he fell to his knees, his breath ragged and painful.

"Donal, are you all right?"

She knelt beside him, her hand resting gently on his back as he leaned forward. He nodded once, his hair tumbling over his face as his arm propped him up. Finally he took several deep, shuddering breaths.

Suddenly he looked up at her. "Are you harmed?" His voice sounded like sandpaper, and he took more breaths.

She shook her head. "I'm fine."

Even in the darkness of night she could see red marks on his throat, large and right over his Adam's apple. And when she looked closer, into his eyes, she saw they were glistening unnatural brightness.

It hit her with a startling force: He had very nearly died. A few more moments, and the life would have been squeezed out of him.

"Maura?"

She tried to smile. He pulled her toward him, and she closed her eyes against his shoulder.

"What just happened?"

It took her a moment to think. "I don't know. It was all so fast. Nothing like this has happened before, nothing at all."

Straightening, she leaned back to look into his face. He wasn't smiling.

"I don't know about you." His voice was heavy, weary. "I could certainly use a pint."

And shakily, they both stood up and, without even looking at number eighty nine and a half, walked over to Nesbitt's.

Chapter 13

Nesbitt's was packed as usual. Elbow to elbow, patrons were laughing and toasting and talking, their images reflected in mirrors clouded with age, smiles distorted, faces blurry and indistinct.

"Here." It was the first word Donal had spoken to her since they left Merrion Square. He took Maura's arm and led her to the rear, where there was a bit more space. Voices raised in merriment greeted them, and they nodded as they tried to inch by the clusters of people.

"Good God, Byrne! Have you been in a row?"

"Look at his eyes, Seamus! Who was it, Donal? And does he look worse than you do?"

"My sage guess is that it was a 'she,' not a 'he,' that did this to our man."

Maura glanced up at him, and realized he did, indeed, look as if he had just gone several rounds in a brawl. But considering what had just actually occurred, he seemed remarkably composed.

"Would you like a glass of wine?"

She nodded, and he ordered wine for her, a pint of Guinness for himself.

After the initial comments, everyone left them alone, with only intermittent nods and acknowledging, speculative winks. He took a long pull on the stout before speaking.

"What the hell happened back there?" His voice was still raspy.

"I think something wanted you to leave."

"That I gathered." He patted his shirt and seemed surprised for a moment. "Damn, I left my jacket back there. Do you happen to have a cigarette?"

"You shouldn't smoke," she said automatically.

"I am aware of that, my dear," he said between clenched teeth. "But I believe being very nearly choked to death is less healthy in the long run than a thousand cigarettes."

"I'm sorry."

He acknowledged her apology with a very slight nod.

"How does your throat feel?"

For a long while he stared at the Guinness, the thick beige foam leaving waves on the glass like an outgoing tide. He took another drink before answering.

"I didn't think we would make it out of there," he said at last. "I honestly didn't think we would live."

Someone in the front of the pub called his name, and he automatically smiled and raised his chin in response, but Maura could tell he was thinking only of the hallway and what had happened.

"I know," she whispered.

"Has anything like this happened before?"

"No. That wasn't Fitz, by the way. I don't know who it was, but it wasn't Fitz."

"How can you be so sure," he began, then stopped. A small chuckle escaped his lips.

"What's so funny?"

"I was about to discuss this with you in all seriousness."

"How else can you discuss it?" She was completely baffled.

"There must be some other explanation."

"Just a moment ago you seemed to believe it was a . . . well, a . . ."

"Let me complete the sentence for you. I seemed all too eager to suddenly believe it was a ghost. Is that what you were going to say?"

"What else could it have been? You were there, Donal."

He remained silent for a few moments, not looking at her, not looking at anything.

"I've just been thinking." With one swallow he drained the contents of his glass and motioned to the publican for another. He wiped his mouth with the back of his hand, too intent on his thoughts to realize what he had just done. "Is it possible someone doesn't want you there?"

"Well that's just the point." She frowned. "Fitz is fine, but it's the other person who doesn't want any interference."

"No, no. That's not what I mean at all." The second pint was handed to him. He tilted his head toward her own glass, but she shook her head. He continued. "Who would have the most to gain from you leaving?"

"A person, you mean?"

"Yes. A person or an organization or business. Who would gain the most if you left?"

"That's immaterial. Whatever is in there, it can't be reasoned away."

"Maura, listen to me. There are no such things as ghosts."

"How can you say that? It almost killed you!"

"Someone did. Someone very clever, someone who wants you to leave, to give up. Think, Maura, who would want you to go back to America and in a hurry without looking back. Whoever it is wants you to just drop your entire inheritance without a second thought down the road."

Maura cleared her throat and shook her head.

"What is it?"

"You're not making sense. Even if someone wanted me to leave, how could they have managed the trick we just experienced? Think, Donal. There is no way someone could have become invisible."

"I've been thinking about that. Of course, you're right, but we may have been drugged."

"Drugged? How is that possible?"

"There may have been some sort of hallucinogenic gas passed through the pipes or sprayed from the top of the steps."

"Right. And we both imagined the same thing."

"It could be the power of suggestion, Maura. You're right—what happened was fast and confusing. We need to figure out who would want you to go away, and then we can work backward on exactly how they managed this production."

She watched his features as he spoke, convincing himself with every word that what he was saying was the only possible explaination for what had just occurred.

"The truth is, Donal," she said at last, "you are the one who would have the most to gain if I left. You're the only one I can think of."

After a stunned pause, his expression shifting to anger, he balled his hand into a fist. "Yes, that must be it, Maura." He slammed the still-full pint onto the bar, causing a brief pause in the pub's buzz of conversation. He waited until the noise level again rose before continuing. "I wanted your goddamned town house so much I tried to kill myself. How clever you are to have discovered my trick."

"You're being impossible." She tried to keep her voice low and even. "I can't believe you refuse to admit what happened. I'm just saying that no one could have staged what happened back there. Don't you get it yet? This is real. We were just attacked by something that is not of this world. My God, I've never in my life met anyone as stubborn and . . ."

"Maura! Donal! How grand to see you, and together yet!" Charles MacGuire seemed to embrace them both with his exuberance.

"Hello, Charles." Donal did not take his eyes off Maura as he spoke.

"Charlie! I can't tell you how happy I am to see you." Deliberately she turned away from Donal, relieved their argument had been halted.

"So, is it a toast to the deal you're having?" Charles held up a finger, made a circular motion to the publican, then returned his attention to Donal and Maura.

She flushed, not wanting Charles to continue. What would Donal think, knowing that she was selling the town house anyway in order to save the factory? When she tried to gauge his reaction, he glanced away.

"Ah, here we go now!" Charles handed her another glass of wine, Donal and himself pints. "Let's have a drink to the prosperity of the Maiden Works Furniture Factory. Here's to a flourishing future to equal and exceed its illustrious past."

"Thank you," Maura murmured.

"Ta, Charles," Donal said at the same time. Their eyes met over the rims of their glasses, both slightly perplexed as they raised a toast and took sips.

"How refreshing, how absolutely refreshing entirely that the two of you have buried your differences, and you with all the reason in the world to have . . ."

"Charles!" Donal's voice seemed to surprise himself every bit as much as it surprised the other two. "I, well, I just wanted to know how have you been?"

"Grand, Donal." He shrugged. "Just as I was this very afternoon." He paused, leaning closer to Donal's face. "Good Lord, what the devil happened to your eyes? You look as if you've been pub-crawling for the past twelve months altogether."

"That's how I feel." Donal smiled. "That's exactly how I feel."

"But what happened?"

"Nothing, Charles. I suppose I'm just tired."

The three remained in uncomfortable silence,

glancing about the room, smiling uncertainly at each other, struggling for something to say. This had never happened before, a strained inability to make conversation. Finally Charles spoke, his face brightening.

"So tell us the plans for the factory!"

"Oh, well . . ." she began.

"I really don't think . . ." Donal's words overlapped hers.

"Can we talk about something else?" She used her perkiest tone. Donal eagerly joined her.

"Charles, what do you think of Jack Charlton and the boys on the football team?"

"They're brilliant!"

For the next hour Maura heard more details of Irish World Cup soccer than anyone, including the team itself, would ever want to know.

Exhaustion set in, and she searched for a break in the conversation to announce her leaving. Finally, between the finer points of heading a ball and the outrageous injustice rendered by a specific referee, she was able to speak.

"I'll be off now." She put down the empty wineglass.

"No," Donal said, then smiled, softening the bite of his objection. "I mean, I will walk you home, Maura."

"How gallant! Donal, you do all men proud. It's proud I am to be a member of the same sex as yourself." With that Charles was engulfed by a motley trio of men, one wearing sunglasses although it was close to midnight, another sporting half a mustache.

"We are at present searching for the rest of Willy's facial hair," announced the man in the sunglasses.

"When last seen it was drifting down Lower Baggot Street with a fancy lady from Kilkenny."

Donal gently led her to the door.

"Thanks, Donal. I can find my own way home."

"You can't go back there."

"Why?"

"For God's sake, Maura. You know very well why."

"I thought you didn't believe in ghosts."

"I don't, but I do believe in someone wanting to frighten you into selling the house."

"Oh, Donal." They were now on the street, the cool night air a relief after the swirling cigarette smoke in Nesbitt's. "Didn't you hear what Charles said?"

He seemed genuinely mystified.

"I signed papers today to sell the town house. There is no reason anyone would want to frighten me out of the place. I'm leaving it willingly."

"I don't understand."

"Come on." She felt like crying. How much more explicit was she going to have to be? "I'm selling the Merrion Square place to save my company back home and to help finance the changes at the factory."

For a moment Donal simply stared just beyond her. What was she talking about? Didn't she realize that the papers she signed were for the factory, not the town house? "Oh, Maura," he sighed, shaking his head. "Did you read the papers you signed carefully?"

"Of course, I did." Then she remembered how hurried she had been, how many demands seemed to have been pressing on her when she was presented with the papers. All she had wanted to do was get the signing out of the way before she could change her mind. "Well, no," she revised. "Not really. I mean, Biddy Macguillicuddy told me all the details. She seems very competent, and I'm sure she must be familiar with this sort of thing."

He did not respond, and she peered into his face in the darkness, the handsome face, all planes and angles. "She's my real estate agent."

"I know who she is."

"Oh, all right." She crossed her arms, suddenly cold.

"Are you this way about all business matters?"

"What do you mean by 'this way'?"

"Lax."

"I am not lax."

"Why didn't you thoroughly examine the papers you signed? You should have taken your time, held on to them overnight, called Charles or another solicitor in to assist you with any details that you may have had questions about. Did you do that, Maura?"

"Not exactly. But I knew what they were about, just a standard form about the rights of the real estate agent to handle the property."

"Bloody hell. You may have donated your body to science or agreed to be used as practice skin for a tattoo school."

"Why are you so angry? It's my property. I know you and Charles see it as some sort of betrayal that I could ever part with the place. But don't you see? I have no choice—and it's all for a greater good, to save my father's company and to turn the factory around. I figured that would be more help to everyone than fixing up a town house. And maybe if the factory does well enough, I could buy the town house back."

His hands clenched, and she reached out and closed one of her own hands over his fist. He jerked away, as if she had touched him with a burning match.

"What have I done wrong?"

"Nothing, damn it, nothing at all." He seemed to be struggling with himself, biting back words he was aching to say.

"What? Please tell me what's the matter."

"Has it ever crossed your mind that you're no businesswoman?"

She did not reply for long moments and merely stared at him.

"Other than as an insult, is there a point to this?" she asked quietly.

"Yes! Damn it, why don't you do something you're good at?"

"Thank you so very much." Stiffening, she walked ahead, her eyes painful and prickling with tears.

He sighed, and followed after her, placing his hand on her shoulder.

"Please let go of me." Her voice was unsteady.

"That came out all wrong. It's just that there are so very many things you could do. You have so many talents and gifts yet to be explored, but circumstance has put you where you are. You remind me so much of someone."

"And who would that be?"

"It's simply that you have other abilities and interests, but you've been stuck as head of your father's company, now all of this. You've never really had the chance to explore what you want. And that's a shame."

"I suppose that's why you were so kind before in

offering to take my latest burden from me. It's not that you were interested in the factory. It was altruism, pure altruism."

"Maura . . ."

"Good night, Donal."

"You can't go back there."

She looked him full in the face, her own hurt and disillusionment reflected in her eyes.

"I believe I'll be better off inside than out here with you."

The house was just across the street, and without even waiting to hear what else he had to say, she began to walk, and then, when walking wasn't fast enough, she ran.

"Maura!" He called her name once, only once, before she disappeared into the house, the door neither slamming shut nor closing softly. It simply opened, and then she was gone.

"Maura," he said softly. "It's my own mother you remind me of. You remind me of her." And after he stared at the closed door and the flickering lights of Merrion Square and heard the sounds of the late night traffic, of laughter far away and a cat in an alley round the corner, he went home, too.

Perhaps the problem with being an American in Ireland had nothing to do with reality and everything to do with expectations—not just Maura's own expectations or those of the Dubliners she had met but the expectations and assumptions of the generations before her.

No matter how clear-cut a situation seemed, such as the simple fact of inheriting property, there were layers upon layers of misunderstandings and confusion.

The main problem seemed to be communication. The very words the Irish used were colored with shades of mythology, of Gaelic expressions that didn't quite translate into English, while Americans used their words plainly with curt sentences and direct statements. She was accustomed to the American plainspokenness, the no-frills business talk of her economics professors.

The Irish instead lulled and wooed, instilling nuance and meaning into every word, even in business. Donal was almost an exception. Almost. Still he charmed and courted with his manner, an eloquence every bit as powerful as the words employed. Yet she had the distinct impression he was holding something back.

That seemed to be the only explanation for the way Maura was feeling, of the rioting emotions she was unable to shake off, emotions of such intensity that she didn't hear the tea kettle whistle as she sat in the kitchen. And when the sound finally did pierce her consciousness, she didn't jump as she usually did. Instead she moved slowly, with a languor she didn't really feel.

She hadn't seen Fitz all day and was beginning to wonder if Donal was right, that she *had* just imagined him. It was entirely possible, even probable, that he did not exist. The whole country seemed locked in a conspiracy to drive her if not insane, then just slightly off balance.

When the telephone rang, she wondered who on earth would call at such an early hour. Then she realized it was well past noon, and only she herself had been in a world of ponderous thoughts and drowsy movements.

"Maura." It was Donal. "I'm calling to see how you are. Did anything unusual happen last night?"

"No." She really didn't want to speak to him. There was nothing to say, nothing at all.

"You don't sound well."

She did not reply.

"Maura, there is something else. Two things really. I was going over my mother's papers, the ones from when she wrote the book on Fitzwilliam Connolly."

"Hum." She was more tired than she had realized, and suddenly all she wanted to do was sleep.

"She had doubts about Patrick Kildare being the killer. It seems her editor advised her against publishing her thoughts, simply because her notion of Kildare's innocence would raise more questions than it would answer. Would you like me to bring these over?"

Her eyes, which had been growing heavy, now closed. Never in her life had she been so exhausted, so utterly drained. She was also aware of a vague feeling of nausea, but that would go away once she slept. She knew it absolutely. All she needed was sleep.

"Maura, are you there?"

It was rude not to answer, but she was so tired.

"Maura? Answer me, or I'm coming right over. . . ."

That was the last she heard, and then she was embraced by a dark, consuming slumber.

CHAPTER 14

The fragrance of some sweet confection awoke her.

"Um," she sighed, both in sleepy confusion and at the delicious aroma. Even before she opened her eyes she realized two things. One, she had not eaten since the night before. No wonder she was so exhausted.

And two, she had tied her bathrobe too tightly about her waist. Maura could barely draw in a full breath.

"Ah, there we go now." It was the voice of a woman, kind and consoling. "Have a dish of tea. He will be here presently, and we wish him not to see you so."

Slowly Maura opened her eyes. Almost immediately she recognized the front parlor, the way the sun streamed through the windows.

But instead of the shabby room with worn furniture and dust, she was in a beautifully restored Georgian sitting room. It was straight out of a museum, magnificent wood gleaming, elegant shutters on the windows. Blinking, she glanced into the hallway. The familiar black-and-white marble was there, but above was a tinkling chandelier with thick candles set into the crystal. Ornate molding, painted in a pale blue to contrast with the white walls and marble, was lavished on the ceiling and along the staircase.

Her feet hurt, and glancing down she saw they were encased in tiny satin slippers, embroidered with delicate shimmering threads. The heels were triangular, the toes pointed.

"I . . ." she began, and then saw the woman who had spoken.

Before she could even ask who she was, the woman patted her hand.

"There there, Kitty dear. Your Fitzwilliam promises to return from his journey by this evening. He never speaks but the truth, and I have known him since he was a babe."

Maura barely heard the words. The woman was in full Georgian costume, from a lace cap upon her gray curls to the wildly exaggerated, lavish folds of her skirt, two humps on either side of her hips like an upturned camel.

"Oh," was all she could say. The woman handed Maura a cup, and with trembling hands she accepted.

It was, indeed, tea, but more pungent than she was used to. A gleaming service was placed on a nearby table, with covered dishes and pots and a small stack of cups. And there she saw a silver basket filled with what appeared to be scones.

The older woman laughed. "Yes, my dear, we had them made for you just this morning! Let me fetch you one." Her accent was most peculiar, not quite English, not quite Irish.

The scone was delicious, although the flour used to make it felt grainy on her teeth. So far she had said nothing, only stared at the surroundings.

From outside she heard the heavy roll and crunch of carriage wheels, the nickering of horses, the jingling of reins and gentle whispers of coachmen and riders.

This was the most fabulous dream she had ever had, and she was determined to make the most of it.

"Thank you," she finally said when the last crumb was gone. She was also clothed in costume, her own dress seemed to be a cream muslin, but light and airy, less structured than the stiff brocade of the older woman. She did, however, have the odd hoops at the sides, and beneath her skirt she could feel layers of petticoats and lace.

"Now, my dear," the older woman said. "We must discuss the wedding."

Maura smiled. "Of course!" Why not? This was her dream, she could do with it what she wanted. Might as well plan a wedding.

"Now, Connolly will have none of this, as you know."

"Connolly?" That was a relief. At least her dream involved a groom she knew. "I know. He cares nothing for fripperies."

What the hell was a frippery?

The older woman seemed to know, and she laughed a friendly chuckle. "Men! What do they know of weddings?"

"It is very nearly a shame we require them to round out the ceremony," Maura added.

The older woman again laughed. "Oh, my dear! But with such a groom—can you imagine how he will appear? Gracious! 'Tis a good thing an autumn ceremony is planned, for there will be enough swooning at the sight of him without the heat of summer. Now, you did say you wished him in pale blue satin . . ."

"Ugh!" Maura's gasp startled the woman. "Excuse me, Aunt Sarah." Aunt Sarah? Well, it was as good a name as any, she supposed, and the woman didn't seem startled. "Aunt Sarah," she tested the name again, and the older woman merely peered at Maura more closely.

"Yes, my dear?"

"Well, I do hope no preparations have been made. I just feel Fitz," she paused and repeated his name. "I just feel Fitzwilliam would look ghastly in pale blue."

"But it is such a fashionable shade, dear Kitty. And pray, what other color should he wear? The world will wish to see him in colors other than the blacks and browns and grays he always wears. I declare, one would never take him for a peer from the plainness of his clothing. He appears more the clerk than the lord."

"I like that about him," she said more to herself than to the character in her dream. "He wears his hair unwigged and unpowdered, his waistcoat unadorned with flowers, his blouse free of lace. It suits him, for he is most certainly no fop."

"Of course! I would never accuse Connolly of being a fop or a dandy. Yet, well, my dear, he is just a bit coarse at times."

"Coarse?"

"Not in his speech or manner, mind you! No fault

could be laid at his boots for that. Still, a bit of polish would be splendid on his wedding day, think you not?"

"I think not. I have chosen Fitzwilliam, not Andrew." Her mind whirled for a moment. Andrew? Who on earth was . . .

Then it came to her: Andrew was Fitz's younger brother. She congratulated herself for remembering, even in the deep recesses of a dream, some of the secondary characters.

The older woman seemed shocked. "Of course! Why, never would I compare Andrew to his brother. Indeed, I wonder that they are of any relation at all, most especially brothers. There are times when his odd fancies cannot but make me laugh. There is such a vast difference twixt the two gentlemen . . ."

"Is there now?" The voice came from the doorway, and both women turned.

Maura almost laughed aloud when she saw the young man lounging against the arched threshold. He seemed to have stepped straight from a stage production, listed in the playbill as Languid, Useless Buck.

He wore green satin and lace and brocade, from the top of his outrageously wigged head to the silver decorative spurs in his glimmering boots. His slender frame betrayed youth, but there was a softness to him that spoke of little activity and much leisure. She looked at his face, pale with white powder, and wondered if the beauty mark just to the side of his chin was fake or real.

"Excuse us, Andrew," Aunt Sarah said crisply. "We were discussing your brother's upcoming nuptials. Pray leave us to our chatter."

"Of course you were! And may I again add my heartfelt felicitations, Sister Kitty? How I do look forward to having your presence in this house even more constant. And I can think of naught that will give me pleasure as the very imaginings of a little Fitzwilly or Kitty to run about, chubby hands clutching all of value."

"How kind of you, Andrew." Maura smiled and nodded. "And indeed, what a charming image you conjure. I'm sure you will be much gratified to at last have playmates of your own intelligence and aptitude. I trust they will set you a good example."

Aunt Sarah gasped, but Maura barely noticed. Andrew's face twisted, a look of such malice and pure hatred, she held her breath. Instead of the languid youth, he was suddenly an image of ruthless fury.

Before she could speak further, the front door opened.

"Kitty?"

Immediately Andrew's face resumed the bland expression.

"Dear brother! How pleased I am that you have returned safely! And here is your dear Kitty!"

And then Fitz stepped into the room.

Maura simply stared, her heart pounding so hard she placed her hand over her breast, startled for a moment at how closely he reminded her of Donal.

Fitz cuffed his brother lightly on the chin, causing the beauty patch to flutter to the floor and powder from his wig to puff to his shoulders.

"Aunt Sarah, you seem in high joy and spirits." Fitz smiled. The older woman gave some sort of response Maura didn't hear.

Never once had he taken his eyes off her, and never once had she been able to even blink.

He was a wild vision in a battered three-corner hat, his hair bleached by the sun, his skin bronzed. With one sweeping gesture he threw off the hat and was at her side in two long strides.

Somehow she had managed to rise to her unsteady feet.

"Kitty." He spoke the name as an embrace.

"I . . ." she began, and then his lips touched hers.

"Now really, Lord Connolly, I cannot tolerate this behavior from anyone, even you. I am here as chaperon."

He pulled away for just an instant. "Go away." He grinned, and then tightened his hold on her.

And through her delirium she realized that Aunt Sarah, clucking to herself, had indeed gone away, as had Andrew.

"My love," he whispered.

Still unable to catch her breath, she merely looked up at him, touching his face lightly.

"How is it possible?" As he spoke she wondered at the warmth of him, the solid strength.

"How is what possible?" Her own voice was a rasp, but she didn't care.

"How is it possible that you have grown yet more beautiful these past four months?"

"Four months?" Her hands clutched his arms, his shoulders. "It seems forever."

"It does." Then he reached into the pocket of his jacket. "Here."

It was a sprig of purple flowers, pressed and dried.

She smiled, touching the petals. "Whose estate did you plunder these from?"

He laughed, a joyous sound that seemed to fill the corners of the room. "Alas, my bride knows me all too well! I merely relieved a garden outside of Paris of these weeds."

"Weeds." Maura couldn't believe she was seeing him in the flesh. "These are most likely the rarest of flowers, grown with years of care and love."

"No." The smile left his face. "That is you, Kitty. The rarest of flowers."

"Oh," she sighed. He plucked the flowers from her hand and tucked them gently into the waist of her gown.

Suddenly there was the sound of someone clearing his throat from the doorway.

"Andrew," Fitz acknowledged.

"Fitzwilliam. I do hate to interrupt you . . ."

"No you don't," she muttered. Fitz frowned and tilted her chin up.

"Now Kitty." He smiled and kissed her temple. "Come in, Andrew. Why, just look at you! Is that yet another new suit of clothes?"

There was no censure in his tone, not a single hint of sarcasm or reproach. Fitz was genuinely pleased his younger brother had purchased the clothes.

"Yes, it is." There was an unmistakable note of pride in Andrew's voice.

"Now what would one call that particular shade?" Maura could tell Fitz was making every attempt to withhold a chuckle.

"Pomona," he replied, standing straighter as if to admire his own suit more fully.

"Bilious green," she whispered, and Fitz very nearly chortled out loud.

"It's splendid, Andrew, absolutely splendid."

"I need to speak with you, brother," Andrew said. Maura noticed in the brief time he had been out of the room he had managed to replace his beauty mark and restore his carefully rolled curls.

"Well, go on."

"Alone." Andrew smiled at Maura, but the smile did not reach his eyes. It crossed her mind that his more pleasant expressions seemed to pain him.

"Come, come Andrew." Fitz wrapped an arm around her. "Kitty will be my wife in a matter of weeks. You may speak freely before her."

"She's to be your wife, not mine." His mouth made an ever-so-brief petulant turn downward, so swift was the change in his countenance that it would have been easy to miss. "Fitzwilliam, please. I am desirous of speaking to you on business matters, and surely Kitty would find the topic dull as dishwater."

"Not at all! Honestly, I long to hear more of business. If I find anything dull, it's French fashions and new bonnet designs. I saw a woman last week with such a feather whim in her hair she looked quite mad!"

"That you find all matters of fashion dull is quite apparent," Andrew said between clenched teeth.

Fitz merely took a deep breath and coaxed her onto the sofa. "Very well, Kitty. Please, sit down lest you faint from the tedium."

"She already fainted today. I wonder Aunt Sarah did not tell you." Andrew made a great show of examining his fingernails.

At once Fitz was beside her on the couch. "Kitty, are you unwell?"

She placed her hand along the side of his face. "I am well, indeed. I was simply hungry. I had not eaten since yesterday—I suppose I was just too excited about your arrival to think of food. I am fine."

His eyes searched hers, and she felt a strange tightness in her throat.

"Oh, Fitz," she breathed.

"Fitz," he repeated. "I like it, Kitty. But only from you. Only you."

He leaned forward, and she felt his warm breath on her cheek as he kissed her.

"I wish to discuss some business matters," Andrew stated. Fitz halted, a faint smile on his lips.

"Go on then, Andrew." He ran his hand through his hair once before turning his full attention on his brother.

"I wish to know if you have fully considered the matter I presented to you before your voyage." Now Andrew seemed to inflate with his own words.

"Please refresh my memory. What matter was that?"

"It was about trading in a certain item."

Suddenly he stood up. "I do hope you are not referring to what I am thinking of."

Maura looked up at him, his body tight with what seemed to be anger.

Andrew smiled. "Indeed I am. Why will you not hear me out on this? You have no idea of the riches that are to be gained from this venture. Vast, vast wealth awaits us, and we are perfectly poised to accept our due."

"No. No, I will not even speak of this." Fitz clenched his fist, then slowly released it when he saw her eyes.

"What is this about?" she asked softly.

"Matters that need not concern you," he said, reaching out and touching her shoulder.

"Nay, brother. Do not play the role of hypocrite. It does not suit you. The fair Kitty requested to hear this conversation. Think you her too dim to comprehend?"

Fitz was silent for a moment. "I merely believe she will look upon your suggestion with the same abhorrence as do I."

"Why do we not ask her then? Since she will soon be your wife, you are denying her the right to make her own life more luxurious. Pity."

"Very well." Fitz turned toward her. "My young brother wishes to embark on a new business venture. The item he mentioned earlier refers to human beings."

Maura shook her head, uncomprehending.

"Kitty, he wants to use the shipping concern for the transport and sale of African slaves."

The notion took her by surprise, and she gasped.

"Oh, Kitty, don't be such a simpleton," snapped Andrew. "There are far less savory things than the slave trade. And with all the money you would make, you could give freely to charity, to all of those filthy little urchins you are always knitting caps for. The Africans are little more than animals, less than the value of a good horse or dog, certainly . . ."

"Stop!"

Fitz's voice boomed, and both Maura and Andrew jumped.

"I am ashamed of you, Andrew." Although he spoke softly, there was a quiver of danger in his tone that made him far more frightening than when he shouted. "Never before have I been so basely insulted. You wish to bring us all down in the greedy quest for more money. How much would you require, Andrew? Do you not have a suit of satin in mulberry, in peacock blue, in jardin yellow, and now, what be this vile color?"

"Pomona," Andrew whispered.

Andrew knew he had gone too far, Maura realized. He had always known when to pull back from his brother, but the lust for more of everything had made him incautious.

"Pomona," Fitz snapped. "Pomona."

"I must go now." Andrew backed away. "I am expected at Lord and Lady Downe's ball. And you are invited as well, Fitzwilliam. Good day, and welcome back."

It was astonishing how quickly, and with what agility, Andrew left the house.

"Pomona," Fitz murmured as the echoes of the slamming door faded.

"Kitty, what are we to do with him?"

"Fitz, does Andrew have any percentage of your business ventures?"

He slumped into the sofa, bumping the back of his head.

"Sorry." She winced, sitting next to him and gently rubbing the back of his head, the thick ponytail coming loose.

With a swallow he looked at her, a brief smile before he spoke. "No, my love. Not yet. I am waiting for Andrew to pass this unsupportedly troublesome age. Patrick does hold some shares, although Andrew doesn't know it yet."

"Patrick Kildare?" She almost shrieked the name.

"Of course. He owns shares of the shipping concern, a brilliant businessman and an even better friend. What ails you, Kitty?"

Part of her wanted to tell him she was not Kitty, she was Maura, and this was a dream, and Patrick Kildare was very likely plotting to kill him. She wanted to take him by the shoulders, warn him to stay away from the front steps. Perhaps he could go to America and get away from the politics and danger of Ireland.

Instead she simply leaned over and lightly kissed his cheek.

"Ah, Kitty." He sighed heavily. "What do you call this power you have over me?"

"Pomona," she breathed in his ear.

And after a stunned silence, Fitzwilliam Connolly literally roared with laughter.

"Maura!"

Someone was speaking to her from the end of a long tunnel, the voice was male and urgent. She tried to utter his name.

"Donal?" But it came out as a groan, and for a brief moment she was embarrassed.

"Maura, please."

In her half slumber she reached out and felt a powerful arm. He seemed to be holding her upright. Slowly, reluctantly, she opened her eyes.

"Donal," she murmured.

"For pity's sake, don't you know how to operate the bloody gas?"

It was hard to focus. He seemed to fade in and out of her vision like a withering dream.

Still he spoke. "You turned on two burners, but only lit one."

"One what?"

"For your tea. On top of the cooker, you switched on two burners but only lit one. Damn it, Maura, I shudder to think what would have happened had I not called."

Now she could see him fully, his strangely modern clothes, hair slightly ruffled where he had pushed a hand through. There were beads of perspiration at his temples, even though the day was chilly.

It struck her then Donal and Fitz were so alike—it was no wonder she had been confused in her dream. It was not so much a physical resemblance, although they were quite similar in build and coloring, and they both even had the strange bent finger on the left hand. It was Donal's expression more than anything that reminded her of Fitz, perhaps the way both men looked at her with complete, unwavering concentration. Perhaps that was it.

"I had the strangest dream." She sat up fully. Somehow she had ended up on the kitchen floor. Donal, too, was on the floor, and beside him was a jacket he had either been wearing or carrying, now in a crumpled heap. All of the windows were wide open, a breeze passing through the house.

"Here." He pulled the jacket over and placed it

around her shoulders. "I had to break a front windowpane to get in. Sorry. I'll have it repaired as soon as possible. And the other windows are open to air the place out."

Then, for no apparent reason, a feeling settled over her, a sense of sadness, as if she could cry at any moment.

"How do you feel?" His tone was unexpectedly gentle, so soft she looked at his face. So handsome, features of pure masculine beauty.

"I had the strangest dream," she repeated.

"Did you now?" Adjusting the jacket over her shoulders, he gave her a slight smile.

"Would you care to tell me about it?"

"About what?" A vague panic rose. Did he want to hear about how she imagined him two hundred years earlier? How she made them a couple in love?

"About your dream. Would you care to tell me about it?"

"Oh, yes. The dream." Taking a deep breath, she tried to recall the details. "I was in ascendancy Ireland, right here in this house. It was absolutely gorgeous, really lovely, with crystal and candles and silver. It must have been about 1767, because we were planning the wedding."

"We?"

"At first it was just me and Aunt Sarah, but then Andrew came in, spoiled and petulant."

"I see. And you were engaged to Andrew?"

"No! Of course not. I was engaged to . . . Fitz."

"The ghost?"

She shook her head. "In my dream he was real and

vital and alive. He had just come back from a voyage, and he gave me sprigs of dried flowers from a lawn outside of Paris."

"That was very thoughtful of him."

"Yes. It was. Aunt Sarah wants him to wear pale blue at the wedding, but I can't imagine it."

"So you were Katherine Burbridge?"

"I'm not sure. I seemed to be me, although everyone called me Kitty." She bit her lip. "Funny. I just realized they called me Kitty, but in my mind I heard Maura. I was the same person, though. My hands and arms were the same. A piece of hair was on my shoulder, and it was my hair."

"Interesting. Anything else?"

She thought for a few moments, oblivious to the expression on Donal's face, of the way his gaze traced her form, every detail.

"Yes! This is amazing, Donal—I don't think Patrick Kildare killed Fitz. I can't explain it, just a feeling that I have, but it's too strong to ignore. Did you know Kildare was a business partner of his? Fitz seemed to trust him completely, as both a friend and an associate, and gave him shares in the shipping concern."

"Shares of the shipping concern? I don't believe so. I've read all about Kildare, and never have I heard it mentioned that he was a partner of Connolly's. But Maura, do you remember our phone conversation right before you fainted?"

"No," she replied uncomfortably.

"I called you because I was going over some of my mother's notes. She didn't think Kildare was guilty, either. Her editor didn't want her to delve into that angle—too complicated, and she could not find the solid proof she needed. If it wasn't Kildare, then who was it? If Kildare was truly innocent, that meant he had to have been framed, and there was no logical winner in that situation, no reason for anyone to have killed Kildare."

"Ah ha." She brightened. "But what if Kildare was indeed Fitz's secret partner, then who would gain the most if they were both dead?"

Donal thought a moment. "That's easy enough—it would have been Andrew."

"Andrew. Honestly, Fitz has a blind spot when it comes to his brother. He's so astute in other ways but is unable to see Andrew for the rotten, spoiled twerp that he is. You should see the way he looks at me with those beady eyes, and that stupid beauty mark . . ."

"Maura, it was a dream."

She crossed her arms, about to speak, and then remained silent.

"You had this dream because you and I were discussing this very situation when you passed out. Remember?"

"But Donal, this dream was so real, far more vivid than most of my real life seems. Even the scones, the tea. And my God, my corset was so uncomfortable."

"Maura," he warned. "Don't get too carried away."

He was right. Of course, he was right.

"But what about what happened to you last night?" His shirt was open at the collar, and the red marks over his throat had dulled to purplish blue.

"I still believe someone wants us to stay away, but that had to do with very human, earthly greed. That's why I was so worried when you dropped the telephone today. I thought whoever it was had harmed you."

"Oh." Then she looked directly at him. "Have I thanked you?"

"No. As a matter of fact you have not."

She leaned forward and kissed his lips.

Donal was right. She had imagined most of it, the rest had nothing to do with the supernatural and everything to do with property values.

He pressed his mouth lightly against her forehead. "Before I forget, the National Gallery has just put up the portrait of Katherine Burbridge Connolly. It's been down for over six months, a cleaning they said, although how long can it take to clean one canvas? Would you like to see your rival for Fitz's attention?"

It did seem absurd, especially in the light of a brilliant afternoon, in the sure safety of Donal's presence.

"Very funny." She grinned. "Just let me get dressed." Then she stopped. "I really should get over to the factory today. I want to talk to some of the old-timers about the changes coming up."

He rose to his feet, lifting her with him. "Plenty of time for that. No need to rush. You're in Ireland, not the U.S."

"Well . . ." She did want to see the portrait. "Fine. Just give me a few moments to get dressed."

He smiled as she left, although there was something strained about the expression. She couldn't quite put her finger on it, a sense of discomfort, perhaps. Or maybe he just thought she had an overactive imagination.

In any case, she was looking forward to seeing what Kitty looked like.

"She's not at all what I expected."

Maura and Donal stood before the large portrait. He had seen it before and was more interested in Maura's reaction than in the painting itself.

The woman was attractive, but in a pale, limp sort of fashion. Everything about her seemed tired, from her flat brown hair to her nondescript eyes. It looked like a hundred other portraits of some long-ago woman wearing quaint fashions and no makeup.

"A bit of mascara would have done wonders," she mumbled.

Donal shrugged. "The poor thing was not well, Maura. And she'd had a rough few months, from the murders of her fiancé and then his friend, the sudden marriage to Andrew. To top it off, she was ill with some fatal disease. Can't remember what it was, undoubtedly the symptoms were elegant and ladylike. I don't believe mascara could have helped a jot with her life."

"Hm. She looks tired."

"She does. And I'll bet she knew it, too."

"Why do you say that?"

"Look at what she's holding in her right hand."

"Wait, there's a glare." Maura shifted position to get a better view. "I still can't see what it is."

"Dead flowers. She'd holding a bunch of dead flowers. Rather macabre, even for the eighteenth century, don't you think?"

They were small purple flowers. And Maura had

seen them before. They were the flowers Fitz had brought back from Paris.

"Is anything wrong?"

"Donal, those are the flowers."

"What flowers?"

"The ones from my dream. The ones he gave her."

"No, Maura, really."

"I'm serious. He put them into the waistband of her dress."

"I'm sure you've seen this portrait, and then dreamed about the flowers."

"How could I have seen the portrait? It's been gone for months and months! Donal, this means my dream was true! It wasn't a dream at all . . ."

"No," he said firmly. "Maura, you have seen this portrait. It's in just about every biography of Fitzwilliam Connolly, including my mother's. You may have just glanced at it, but surely you remembered the details of the flowers."

She suddenly felt ridiculous. "You must think I'm insane."

He grinned. "I do. But that's another matter altogether. Now let's see, where is your Fitz? I believe someone with a very high moral tone has moved him to another wing. Wouldn't do to have them together." Then he whispered. "She married his brother, you know."

"Very funny." She couldn't help but giggle as they crossed into the next room.

"Ah, here we go. Would the two of you like to be alone?"

Maura didn't answer. Instead she simply stared at the portrait of Fitzwilliam Connolly. Everything was the same from the last time she had seen the painting, including the too-large nose and the too-sinister eyes. Everything except for one vital aspect.

The man in the portrait was not wearing blue satin. Instead, he was clad in a simple black jacket, his hair free of wigs and powder. His breeches were a buff color, the boots gleaming but just slightly worn. It was very nearly her Fitz.

And it was exactly what she had tried to tell Aunt Sarah he would wear to the wedding. In short, the man in the portrait was dressed as the groom of her dreams.

Chapter 15

Donal followed Maura as she ran from the National Gallery.

"Can you slow down and tell me what's wrong?"

No response followed his question. She simply kept walking, her face drained of color, her expression both resolute and flustered.

"If you won't tell me, tell George over there on the lawn." He gestured toward a bronze statue of George Bernard Shaw, but it took her a few moments to realize who he was talking about.

"George? Oh, I see." Finally she paused. "Donal, may I ask you a question?"

"Certainly."

"Has Fitzwilliam Connolly always worn black in that portrait?"

Donal blinked. "Do you mean has he ever changed outfits?"

"Well." She stepped aside to allow a group tour to

pass. "I mean, is there a portrait just like that one, only he's wearing different clothes? Perhaps pale blue satin with a brocade waistcoat and powdered wig?"

"Maura, you must be joking. Of course not. That painting is the only known likeness of the man. And frankly, from what I've read of him, you couldn't pay him to pose as Little Boy Blue."

"But that's just it!" She grasped one of his wrists. "Before I had that dream, he was to be married to Kitty in pale blue satin. Aunt Sarah had determined it, but I talked her into letting him wear plain black."

"It was just a dream." He reached forward and brushed a piece of hair from her eyes. "What you probably imagined was the blue portrait. The one you just saw is in every biography of him and in every illustrated history of Ireland I can think of."

She was about to argue, and stopped. "Oh my God, you're right," she said softly. "I must be losing my mind."

"No. Of course you're not. You've just had some very vivid dreams. You're in a new country with unfamiliar surroundings."

He glanced at her with a wary smile. Clearly she did not believe him.

"I have to go," she said abruptly.

"Where?"

"Anywhere. I just have to think for a while. Maybe I should call home and find out what's going on with the company. Or perhaps visit the factory. Maybe both or neither. I just have to focus, to think."

"I see." Shoving his hands into his pockets, he shrugged. "Well then, would you like to have dinner tonight?"

"I, well. I'm not sure." She just needed some time alone to gather her thoughts and try to figure out if she was headed for a nervous breakdown or simply addled. "When I decide, should I just give you a call later?"

"That would be grand. And if I don't hear from you by half seven, I'll ring."

"Fine. And, Donal?"

He turned, and she was struck by how incredibly handsome he was.

"Thank you for everything."

With a hesitant nod, he smiled. "Good-bye, then."

"Bye."

And he watched her as she passed through the gates on her way home.

Jimmy O'Neil was about to fetch another cup of tea when a suspicious movement up front caught his eye. When he saw who it was he smiled. "Mr. Byrne, good day to you!"

"And to you as well," Donal greeted as he walked through the factory door.

"And now are there to be any Germans with you this afternoon?"

"No, no Germans today, Jimmy. May I speak to you?"

"Certainly, Mr. Byrne." Jimmy's face became serious, an expression that struck Donal as particularly incongruous.

"The truth is, Miss Finnegan may be coming here this afternoon."

"Herself?"

"Herself," he confirmed.

"How kind of herself to be showing an interest in the factory, and she no longer owning stick nor stool of the place."

"Well, that's the problem, Jimmy. She doesn't know I'm in charge."

A reddened hand pushed one of his ears forward. "What was that you were saying?"

"You heard me." Donal sighed. "Lord help us, she thinks she is still the sole proprietor of the Maiden Works Furniture Factory."

"If I may ask, how did you manage that triumph of surgical wordplay? A genius you must be, a rare bard of the nuance, if you don't mind my saying so."

"No, Jimmy. I'm afraid it's worse than that. Well, she didn't ask, and—I just haven't told her."

"You haven't . . ." The sputter of his sentence dwindled to nothingness.

"Excuse me?"

"It just seems to me, sir, that you have not been fair with the lady, not fair at all at all." The last four words were pronounced as one rolling word.

"Well, the situation became rather complicated."

"And are you thinking that I didn't see that, and me with two perfectly good eyes and ears?"

"I know. What I'm saying is that I would like you to listen to her as if she still owned the place. Just for today, you see. Just until I can find the proper way to tell her."

Jimmy O'Neil's eyes narrowed to a pair of pale blue slits, more eloquent than any words could possibly be.

"Oh." Donal straightened. "And have you had a chance to look over my proposed improvements?"

"I have indeed, sir."

"And what do you think of them?"

"Not much."

Donal was about to continue, and stopped. "Pardon?"

"I said, I don't think much of the proposed changes, nor do the other men."

"Come, Jimmy. Your job is secure."

"Mine and mine alone. What would you be needing an air vacuum for, built into the walls to suck away the wood shavings? And who's to operate the computers?"

"We will try to retrain the men. Those who would rather not, well, we will give them a very handsome severance package."

"Fine. Just enough for a wake."

"Jimmy, let's discuss this calmly."

"I am perfectly calm," he stated, although with every other word he rose on the balls of his feet in an effort to meet Donal eye to eye. "We are artists, Mr. Byrne. We make furniture by hand, as did out fathers and, in some cases, grandfathers. And are you saying that running a computer will give the same results?"

"No, no, of course not. But this company is doomed to fail unless it can turn a profit. The overhead is too high, the materials too costly, and the work too slow for us to do so at present. By using less expensive materials, pressed woods with fine wood overlay, for example, we can reduce the production costs. And by programming automatic cutting and sanding machines, we will also reduce the manual labor involved, thus reducing the price we will have to charge to clear a profit."

"And thus reducing the men in the company's employ."

"Jimmy, listen. Many of the men are past retirement age anyway. With the pension they can relax and enjoy their days . . ."

"Most of the men are the sole support of their entire families! Don't you see? In many a case their sons and daughters are still unemployed or underemployed, at best. It's not just the man and his white-haired wife anymore, sitting about and enjoying their golden years by stitching tea cozies and watching the grandchildren. Perhaps they should have taught you that in Germany, with all those fancy school courses."

"Jimmy, please." Donal realized they had attracted a crowd, and he waved uneasily at the rest of the staff. "Gentlemen. Hello."

A few murmured "hellos" were returned.

"I'll do as you say, Mr. Byrne," Jimmy O'Neil said at last. "For today I'll do as you say because I would rather not cause the American lady any distress. It seems to me that meeting you may have already done that, and I'll not add to it."

With that, Jimmy O'Neil left to fetch his tea, and the other men scattered, shooting Donal pointed glares over their shoulders.

"I'm only trying to help." They didn't seem to listen. "Fergus? Mike? Did you hear what I said?"

But they all left. For the first time since he began this project, Donal Byrne had a terrible thought: What if he was wrong?

* * *

It took Maura several tries to get through to her secretary back home in Wisconsin. When at last she did, a flustered Rachel Wells answered the telephone on the fifth ring.

"Maura Finnegan's office," she said weakly, as if expecting someone to disagree. There was either commotion or static from the telephone lines in the background.

"Rachel? Hi, it's me."

"Maura! Thank God you called! Things have been insane here." She seemed to be on the verge of tears.

"What's happening? Why didn't you call me if things were so terrible?"

"The phone company wouldn't let us." She sniffed.

"That bad?"

"That bad. I have dozens of messages for you—so many, we've used up all those pink pads. Some from the bank, some from vendors wanting to be paid, the packaging plant, the caterers from that launch party last month. Oh, Maura, it's really hit the fan here."

"Rachel, I'm so sorry. All I can say is that I'm trying to sort it out on this end."

"You should really speak to Peter Jones. He's been shouldering all the mess, if you know what I mean."

"Thank you, Rachel. Yes, can you transfer me to him?"

"Oh, wait a minute—before I forget. Roger Parker called a few days ago."

Her throat went dry. Roger. The cause of her troubles, most of them anyway. She attempted to sound casual, and hoped that transatlantic static would assist.

"Roger? Hum. How is he?"

"He wanted to see you. When I told him where you were, he seemed to know that already. Anyway, I gave him your Dublin number and address. I hope that's okay."

"Of course!" She hadn't meant to shriek. Thank God, he hadn't called. That would be the last thing in the world she needed. "Thank you, Rachel. Hang in there, all right?"

"Sure, Maura. I'm transferring you now."

There were some clicks and a buzz, and then Peter Jones.

"Well, Maura. I'm afraid Finnegan's Freeze-Dried is in a fine kettle of fish."

"Oh?" Maura bit her lip. "A new recipe?"

"Very funny. No, Maura. I don't know exactly what's happening, since you have not given me much authority here. I'm just putting out the smaller fires as they occur, and doing so blindly, I might add."

"I'm so sorry." She swallowed. "All right. I'll call up bookkeeping and grant you permission to see the books. You won't like it, Peter."

"I'm aware of that already." She thought she had lost him, and then he spoke again. "Maura, just what were you thinking?"

Instead of hedging, she answered plainly. She was simply too tired of the whole thing to come up with anything except the truth. "I don't know. I thought that I could save everyone, everything. That just maybe something wonderful would happen in Dublin, and I could bail us all out."

"Well. I'll take a look at the books."

"Peter?"

"Yes."

"You're upset."

On the other end she heard him sigh. "Maura, you're like a daughter to me. I love you dearly."

"Thank you."

"It's just that, well, my dear . . ."

"Yes?"

"I've never thought you had much of a head for business. I told your father this, and he wouldn't listen. He always said you were a financial whiz."

"And you knew better?"

"Not necessarily. I just saw a very sweet redheaded kid in a step dancing costume, trying her damnedest to please everyone. You were always doing as you were told, always smiling and making everyone happy. Everyone, that is, except yourself."

"Oh." Her voice had become very small. "I'll straighten things out in bookkeeping."

"Accounting," he said. "I need to talk with the accounting department."

"Oh, sure. Right."

After she hung up the telephone, she felt miserable. Everything she touched seemed to turn to coal.

The kitchen was strangely comforting in its stark plainness, and her gaze went to the stove. Here she had experienced such a wonderful dream in a magical world. Perhaps it was not a real place, only a corner of her mind where tranquillity and happiness dwelled. Still, it was her place, her happiness.

Was it better to live in a miserable real world or a wonderful imaginary world? Did it really matter, as long as she was content?

Her fingers ran over the knob, lingering, touching it with a gentle caress. All she had to do was turn the knob, and she could see Aunt Sarah, sullen Andrew, and, of course, Fitz.

Then she stopped, withdrawing her hand.

What am I doing? she thought.

She was both appalled and frightened, confused by the way her mind had nearly betrayed her.

The factory. She would go to the factory and start rectifying the situation. That would straighten out her mind, perhaps help her regain her sense of self.

She had to do something, anything, or else she would surely go mad.

The men at the factory did not seem surprised to see her.

In fact, it almost seemed as though they had been expecting her. Jimmy O'Neil met her at the door, his white hair stiff and splendid, his ubiquitous black jacket and trousers, frayed at the cuffs, a slight moss color in places.

"Athugh gothether motergergle," he waved.

"Good to see you, too, Jimmy." Maura smiled. "I have some ideas to discuss with you. Do you have a few moments?"

He nodded, and gestured to the table where the workers had their tea, the oilcloth table covering swept free of crumbs.

"Thank you." She sat where he indicated, and he settled across the table. "I have an idea of how to turn this factory around."

"Grand," he said clearly, although with a distinct lack of enthusiasm.

"Now, I'm sure you've noticed that Dublin attracts a great number of tourists."

Jimmy grunted, neither a yes nor no, just a simple grunt.

"Well, I'm sure you've also noticed that the Maiden Works Furniture Factory isn't exactly beating off customers with a stick."

To that Jimmy did not respond at all. He simply stared at her with his pale blue eyes, bloodshot and shrewd.

"Instead of furniture, we will make items appealing to tourists. Small things, key chains, ashtrays, blackthorn walking sticks, cottages—you know, the sort of stuff tourists pay way too much for."

"Why do we need to make them at all?"

"Excuse me?"

"It just seems to me that places in Dublin sell those things at every corner and shop front. Why would they come halfway down the Wicklow Road for more of the same?"

"Well, you see, that would be the real draw. They could actually watch you make the items. The employees would be dressed in costumes, and the tourists would get a big kick out of seeing you make their key chains, then maybe having tea with you."

"So it's a sideshow we're to become, is that it?"

"No, no. Not at all . . ."

"Miss Finnegan," he began, standing. "Ather motherbillight keptheings."

"I'm sorry, I didn't quite understand . . ."

"Gother dallagh." And with that he left.

Maura sat for a few moments longer, waiting to see if Jimmy would return. When it was clear he would not, that she would just sit until the factory closed, she left, wondering how she would ever have the nerve to return.

There was solace, peace to be had at the town house.

How could she have sold it? Of course, nothing had been finalized—perhaps she could still get it back.

From Jimmy O'Neil's reaction, she knew that her idea of changing the factory would not work as easily as she had hoped. Indeed, she questioned whether she would even repeat her suggestions. Spoken out loud, with Jimmy's face a mask of censure, it seemed crass and insulting.

But the town house welcomed her, a non-judgmental friend, an oasis of peacefulness. She slumped into a sofa in the front parlor, not terribly comfortable, but hers, all hers.

Closing her eyes, she imagined a scent of scones, of sharing a dish of tea with old, very old, friends.

The doorbell rang. Perhaps she could just ignore it, the intrusive blare, and they would just go away. The bell rang again and again. And then she heard the sounds of a key in the lock, the slow turning of the front door.

"Here we go!" It was Biddy Macguillicuddy, her voice drifting across the marble hallway like a merry cloud. "Lucky I have a set of keys . . . Why, Maura, my dear! I had no idea you were in! We rang and rang, and since there was no answer, in we came."

At last Maura opened her eyes. There stood the real estate agent, and she could only see the shadow of another person.

"Ah, and with me is a fellow Yank, here to look over the house."

Reluctantly, Maura stood up, prepared to meet the stranger.

And from the doorway, out stepped Roger Parker.

CHAPTER 16

"Hello, Maura." His voice was still smooth as polyester silk.

She walked slowly toward them, her surprise giving way to anger as she approached. It was really Roger, her tormentor, the man who had made her entire life wall-to-wall misery. Roger.

"You know each other?" Biddy Macguillicuddy was delighted, her face becoming alarmingly red, the plastic cherries pinned to her lapel quivering with the wearer's glee.

"Know each other?" He winked. "We were engaged to be married."

Roger smiled, his too-perfect teeth out of place on his mouth. To Maura his smile suddenly looked like a packet of white Chiclets gum, lined up in symmetrical rows. Once she had kissed that mouth, she thought with perplexed distaste.

"Roger, what are you doing here?" The question was almost comically understated.

Biddy clapped her hands. "Now isn't this something?"

Roger continued to smile, his sweater tied with calculated ease around his shoulders, one thumb looped around his belt.

He just didn't fit in Dublin. He was utterly out of place, all slick charm and pale facade. Everything she had so admired about him in Wisconsin looked glaringly absurd, from his Montgomery Ward catalog pose to his perfectly combed hair.

And, of course, there was the little matter of his lying about every aspect of his life, making an utter fool of her, then dumping her when he discovered she wasn't quite the wealthy heiress he had believed.

"May we have a few moments alone?" She actually managed to smile at the real estate agent.

"Of course! I'll step away and leave you lovebirds together." With great squishing of her rubber-soled shoes, she crept into the kitchen.

"I can't believe you're here," she said between clenched teeth.

"Happy?" A lazy smile flit across his mouth. "Your secretary said . . ."

"My secretary has no idea you give pond scum a bad name."

An expression of smug satisfaction was on his face as he reached for her. She ducked, but he was undeterred, his features remaining unruffled. "You're more beautiful than I remembered."

"I can't tell you how pleased I am to hear that." She refused to meet his eyes.

"No, Maura. Truly. There's a look about you now that wasn't there before, a softness, a sparkle. This place suits you."

"The way Harvard suited you?"

For a moment he seemed stunned, just a brief flash of confusion crossed his blandly handsome features. "What do you mean?"

"Don't play dumb, Roger. I called the Harvard alumni office when you disappeared. They had never heard of you. You are not in any of their records."

"So, you were worried about me?"

"No. I just wondered who the hell you really were. Who are you, Roger?" She at last looked up at him. He placed his thumb on her chin.

"Don't you dare," she warned.

"Dare what?" His voice had that quality that used to make her knees wobble.

"Don't you dare chuck me on the chin. I've always hated that. You were forever chucking me on the chin."

"Why, Maura. I don't recall any complaints."

"Ugh!" She turned toward the kitchen. "Mrs. Macguillicuddy! I believe your client wishes to leave now."

"What, dear?"

Roger stepped closer. "Maura, I am interested in this house."

"Do come again after I have an alarm system installed," she hissed.

"I've come all this way to personally tell you some good news, and this is how you treat me?"

"Good news? Is Interpol onto you?"

"Why, Maura"—he chuckled—"you've grown a sense of humor!"

She refused to give him the satisfaction of knowing how much she hated him. He wasn't worth the energy.

"Good-bye, Roger."

"You're a wealthy woman now, Maura."

"I know. That's why you're here, isn't it? You dropped me when I was broke, and now you're here hoping to claim the inheritance. Right?"

"No. You misunderstand. I've always been in love with you but felt unworthy. And do not forget, I'm a man of action, Maura. I crave adventure and danger and feared that getting too involved with you would curtail my life."

She simply stared at him. A man of action? Craved danger? The most risky thing she had ever seen him do so far had been a brief jaywalking spree in downtown Milwaukee and a tussle with a baby goat at the petting zoo.

"But now, Maura, I'm the man you need." His bearing became almost military. "I'm not afraid of commitments. I'm finally ready for us."

"You're ready for us?" The urge to laugh was so powerful, she bit the inside of her cheek to keep quiet. "Roger, please. It's over. Let's at least keep some dignity."

Suddenly she felt sorry for him, as if seeing him for the first time. It was sad, really, sad and funny and certainly not worth any more angst. He had managed to fool both of them once, and now he was only fooling himself. For that she was almost grateful—how could she ever have thought herself in love with him? He belonged in the same category as her brief crush on Billy Kennedy in fifth grade, a romance that ended when he wrote her a note reading "You are a pig." She still had the note somewhere, a torn page from a loose leaf folder, and all of her memories of Roger would soon join her Billy Kennedy collection.

"Oh, Roger," she said. It was more of a sigh to herself, a realization of how very foolish people can be.

Biddy returned, flush with the notion of romance. "What a charming couple you two make! Now, Mr. Parker, would you rather Miss Finnegan alone shows you about the place?"

"Roger has a previous appointment. Don't you, Roger?" Her smile defied argument.

"Alas, that is true," he said.

"What a shame! But, Mr. Parker, I thought you had cleared this entire afternoon to see this house?"

"I've seen all I need to see."

"Good-bye, Roger." She reached behind him to pull the door wide open.

"Well, I suppose we will return." The agent shrugged with less enthusiasm than Maura thought her capable of.

Roger waited for her to leave, then looked directly at Maura.

"I'll be back, sweetheart," he murmured. Just before he passed through the entrance, he chucked her on the chin.

"Roger." she shook her head as she watched him walk away. Had he always walked like that, with his hips swinging and his arms dangling so awkwardly at his side? His head seemed tilted, as if he was straining to hear some silent message, a dog whistle only Roger could hear. Again she smiled.

Poor Roger.

She had a choice later that night. Either she could spend the evening alone with a pot of tea and a stack of books or at Nesbitt's, with dozens of her closest friends, many of whom she was not yet acquainted with. Donal had mentioned something about having dinner, but the plans seemed casual at best. The choice had not yet been determined when the telephone rang.

"Maura."

The voice was so clipped, she didn't realize who it was for a moment.

"Donal?"

There was a sound of voices in the background, bursts of laughter, and a woman's high-pitched giggle from somewhere in the distance. A man began to sing a song she couldn't identify, but other men joined in, off key and joyous.

"Yes. It's me." There was an edge in his tone she had never heard before.

"Is there anything wrong?"

"We need to talk."

"Sure. What do you want to talk about?"

"Not over the telephone. We need to speak in person. Shall I come by?"

Although she was quite certain now that she had dreamed the entire Fitz episode, she still wasn't sure what, or rather who, had attacked Donal. That had been real.

"No, no. I'll meet you someplace. Where are you now?"

"Nesbitt's."

She laughed, but he did not return the laughter.

"Will you come soon?"

"Yes, of course. Just give me a few minutes to . . ."

"Fine. Good-bye then." And he hung up.

"And I'm so looking forward to seeing you, too," she said sweetly into the dead receiver.

An almost irresistible urge overcame her to call back Nesbitt's and have whoever answered the telephone pass a message on to Donal that she would not be able to make it after all. But then the thought of wondering why he sounded so upset, of not knowing if she had done yet another thing to inspire wrath, was simply too annoying. She had to know, no matter how upset it made her.

"A perfect end to a perfect day," she said to herself as she finished dressing.

Nesbitt's was friendly and welcoming as ever. If only she was not scheduled to have some undoubtedly trying conversation with Donal, she could actually enjoy herself.

Perhaps she was mistaken. Perhaps the tension in his voice was due to overwork or not sleeping or maybe even something he ate at dinner. It was possible, she mused, that she herself had nothing to do with his seemingly foul temper.

She was being rather egotistical, in fact, to assume that she had the power to ruin his day, to unwittingly taint his evening with unpleasantness.

And then she saw him, glaring at her from the end

of the dark wood bar, the solitary grim face in a sea of affability.

"Hi, Donal," she managed to greet him breezily. "I hear you had a very special visitor today."

"Excuse me?"

"Why didn't you tell me you were engaged?"

"Roger? You mean Roger?"

"Yes, I mean Roger. Biddy Macguillicuddy has told all of Dublin about the romance of it all. How could you have kept this from me?"

"But we're not engaged! He said we were, but we never even discussed marriage."

"You planned last night together, didn't you? So he could get the best price on your town house. The whole ghost charade was to throw us all off the track, wasn't it?"

"No! I can't believe you think that! Listen, Roger is a joke—he's a fraud and a nothing."

"When I think of what a fool you have taken me for . . ."

"Donal, no. Please."

There was an empty pint jar next to his elbow, and he made no effort to either signal for more or offer her a drink. "Then I might as well tell you now, Maura, I bought the factory. The papers that Charles had you sign were not about your house, although by signing on an estate agent, you've made your plans clear on that flank as well. Don't look so surprised. You must have known . . . Maura?"

She felt as if the wind had been knocked out of her. All she could do was shake her head.

"No." It came out as a whisper.

The anger seemed to leave him. "Maura, listen to

me. There was nothing personal in this. I was doing my job. It was a business move."

"Yes. Yes, it was personal." She tried to keep her voice even. "I trusted you. I told you things, shared . . . oh God."

Trembling, her hand covered her mouth, as if stopping her words would undo all that had happened.

"Maura." He glanced around, aware that eyes were focusing on them. "Let's discuss this further, someplace more private."

"No." A wave of nausea rose, and she wondered if she would become ill right there. She had to leave. She had to get away from the smoke and the faces and the smell of whiskey and stout and the laughter. Above all, she had to get away from Donal.

Without another word she left, blindly dashing through the crowds that parted as she passed.

He was about to follow her, but someone held him back. "Best let her go, Byrne. Give her a few minutes head start."

"Good God," he mumbled. "What if she was telling the truth about Roger? That they weren't engaged? That she didn't love him?"

"Have another pint, man," another person offered.

Donal stared at the foamy head on the new pint.

He had been so sure. When he heard that a handsome American was claiming to be her fiancé, he had immediately assumed it to be true. Of course she would go with her own kind, good-looking, a Yankee. Of course, how could she be interested in someone like Donal.

But the expression on her face. Would he ever be

able to strike it from his mind? It was raw hurt, visceral pain.

Indeed, if she was telling the truth, he had just offered her the final betrayal. He had been so busy feeling sorry for his own wounded pride, he did not think about anything else.

Maura had seemed so miraculous, he didn't stop to even question the first unfavorable bit of gossip about her. She had been an impossible fantasy. And he had been all too eager to destroy that fantasy, simply because he couldn't trust his own luck.

So he did not trust her.

And what if this Roger was behind the events in the Merrion Square house. That made more sense than any other possibility. And if so, perhaps she was in trouble and did not even realize it. Maybe even real danger.

"I must go," he said to his companions.

"Ah, you can't be going just now. Give her time to cool off."

Another agreed. "Go after her now, and you'll be seeing the flat side of an iron pan before long. She was in a fine state when she left. If I were you, I'd give her a good head start."

"A year, at least," added a third person before they all chuckled.

They were right. He needed to figure out what to say, how to phrase his feelings.

In truth, he'd never done anything like this before. He had always been pragmatic, focused. Until Maura.

With a shock he realized that he couldn't imagine his own future without her. Even next week was inconceivable, let alone a month, a year, a decade.

He didn't need the factory. He needed Maura.

Perhaps the factory had been a red herring all along, some scheme of fate to bring them together. He had fought so furiously for the factory simply because he couldn't face the truth. What he had really been fighting for had been Maura.

"Why, Donal Byrne, you've gone quite pale."

"Aye. He looks as if he's seen a ghost, he does."

All he could manage was a weak smile.

Yes, he would wait a few moments to follow her. He couldn't possibly run now, not with his heart already pounding and his legs threatening to collapse.

"Another drink, Donal?"

He took a deep breath and nodded. This evening he had intended to tell her all of the nasty business about the factory, to watch her squirm and writhe under his astute observations.

Instead, he was about to do something far more dangerous. Donal Byrne was going to declare himself to the American Maura Finnegan.

"A toast, gentlemen," he began. "To wonders, and may they never cease."

Maura hadn't thought it possible. A day that had been turning progressively more horrendous by the hour had managed to become an absolute nightmare within a final span of twenty minutes.

That's how long it had taken. Twenty minutes, start to finish, and whatever she thought she had was gone.

No factory. No house. No way to save the company back home, which meant no job, no future, all of those workers suddenly unemployed.

Above all, no Donal.

Her legs felt so heavy that even crossing the front hallway seemed like trudging through quicksand. Slumping into the nearest chair, she didn't mind that it wasn't comfortable. She didn't deserve comfort.

Taking a deep breath, she closed her eyes.

"Fitz," she mumbled. "What am I going to do."

Drowsy, she did not hear the footsteps on the staircase.

"Hello, Kitty my love?"

His voice was clear, liltingly beautiful, and heart-breakingly close.

His rich chuckle caused her eyes to open, and there he was. Fitzwilliam Connolly.

As she straightened in the chair, she realized she was wearing yet another costume. It must be a different day from the last dream, although he seemed to be in the same loose linen shirt and breeches and boots he always wore, his thick hair tied back.

"Are you feeling better now, Kitty?"

"Yes." There were tea things out, another set this time, with half-eaten scones and bits of white bread. He approached and smiled down at her, resting his knuckles along the side of her face.

"We'll have to get you stronger by the wedding," he said softly. "It would never do to have the bride swoon during the ceremony."

"Why not? The other ladies will when they catch a glimpse of my handsome groom."

Fitz rubbed his thumb gently on her temple, then sat down in the chair next to hers. It seemed impossible that such a delicate chair could hold his solid weight, but it did.

"I will be blunt, my heart," he said, taking one of her hands into his. They were large, rough hands, full of strength. Even the bent finger on his left hand was strong and sure. "I am worried about you."

"Oh, Fitz." She glanced at the tea tray filled with crumbs. "I must have eaten the cakes too quickly."

"You did not take a single morsel. Andrew ate several, I had one. You could not seem to bear the sight of them, and do not deny this. I saw the change in your countenance."

"I must just be nervous about the wedding." A thought came to her. "Are you wearing pale blue?"

The smile left his face. "We just had that discussion. Andrew and Aunt Sarah want me in the blue satin, you wish me in simple black, and I gave you the final vote. Kitty . . ." His fingers tightened around hers. "I am to be your husband. In truth, I feel so now. Tell me what ails you."

"I, well," she stammered. "I guess I'm worried about Patrick Kildare."

"What say you?"

"Do you really trust him? It just seems to me that giving him a share in your company may not be such a good idea."

For a few moments he did not respond; he simply stared at their linked hands. "Do you object because he has not his own fortune? Because, in truth, his own fortune could be covered with the crown of a hat."

She was confused. "Whose hat?"

"Come, come, Kitty. He is not a wealthy man, but he is just and honest, and he is the best friend I have ever had. Besides you."

"Fitz." She leaned forward and kissed his hand.

"Would you rather not see him? He should be here presently with some new shipping orders."

"I'd love to meet him." He had to be better than Andrew, she thought. At least he couldn't possibly be as bad.

"Meet him? Kitty, you've known him almost as long as I have."

"I mean, meet him at the door."

Before the conversation could go further, there was a loud knock, then the sound of a doorbell. She jumped. The house as she knew it had an electric bell, hollow and mechanical sounding. The pleasant gong surprised her.

Fitz made no move to answer, and she was about to rise when a pleasant-looking woman in a mop cap bustled to the door.

"Good day, Mrs. Finnegan. Is the great lord within?"

Finnegan! The housekeeper's name was Finnegan, and Maura craned to see the woman but was unable to see her face. The older woman laughed, a merry, plump sound. "Of course he is, Mr. Kildare. He's just having tea with Miss Burbridge."

"Kitty!" The man's voice was effusive, and it made her smile. He bounded into the parlor, a broad grin on his face, arms opened wide. "How grand to see you!"

She automatically stood up, her own arms open. "Patrick, what a sight you are, you rascal."

It was as if she saw her favorite friend from high school, the guy who never had dates but deserved the best. He was handsome in a bright, clever sort of way—his personality rather than his features made him attractive. Although he wasn't nearly as tall as

Fitz, he was stocky, the sort of build that tended to become stout with the years.

"And there he is," Fitz said. "The prodigal partner. How goes it out west?"

"Things are well, Fitzwilliam. Give me a moment to seduce your betrothed." With that he kissed her forehead, then paused. "Are you feeling well, Kitty?" There was genuine concern in his brown eyes.

"What flattery, Patrick! No wonder you remain a bachelor still. I suppose you approached the girls in Kilkenny with the same accusation of illness. Nothing makes a woman feel more wretched than wearing her best gown, working magic with her hair, and then being asked if she is not too unwell to be out in a public place."

"We are all aware of Patrick's peculiar charms," Fitz approached the two, his hands clasped behind him. "What was that insulting phrase you spoke to the girl last year at the Castle ball? Kitty, you must recall, for you helped the poor thing dry her tears on the verandah."

Patrick himself answered. "Please. If we are to banter about my failings as a suitor, we shall be here through next Easter."

"Now what was it again, Fitz?" She frowned, ignoring Patrick's plea. "I may have removed it from my memory, such nightmares it brought."

"Very well." Patrick tugged at a lock of her hair that was on her shoulder before turning to Fitz. "We may as well have an accurate rendition of the event. It was not my fault."

"Ah, well, there we go, Kitty. 'Twas not his fault."

"It never is," she giggled.

"The girl had a distinct limp. After the first dance, the limp grew more pronounced. It was out of concern that I inquired after her health."

"That's not quite how I recall it," she said, watching Fitz in his failed attempts at keeping a straight face. "The girl in question said you asked her first about her leg, most improper, Patrick. One never discusses vulgarities such as limbs to a gently bred lady. And when she blushed and stammered, which must have been a very pretty sight, you accused her of having a wooden leg."

Fitz burst out with an explosive laugh, and Patrick crossed his arms. "Again I must plead the innocent. With all the skirts and sails and sheer acreage of cloth you women wear, your ability to perambulate, much less dance, is an utter mystery to most men."

"And it is likely to remain so, my friend. At least to you." Fitz gave him a light punch on the shoulder, and they all laughed. Finally Fitz gestured for them to sit down.

Maura was surprised that returning to the chair was a relief. Perhaps she was ill. She took a few deep breaths, glancing up to see Fitz's piercing eyes fixed on her. With a lightness she did not entirely feel, she smiled at him.

He returned the smile, but it was slightly forced. Yet he made no comment. When Patrick began to speak, he turned his attention to his friend, wiping his hand over his mouth as if to remove his concern.

"Fitzwilliam, I must be blunt. There is disturbing news which you, by necessity, must hear." All traces of the previous humor had vanished. Both men and Maura were suddenly serious.

"Continue, Patrick."

"Is your brother near?"

"Nay. I believe he is at present visiting a tailor's shop on Sackett Street. Does this ill news concern Andrew?"

"I fear it does. Andrew, and you, Kitty."

"Me?"

"Kitty?" Fitz burst out simultaneously.

"I'll be brief. There is a general knowledge in the west that Andrew seeks to take over the shipping concern."

"But how could he? My brother has not the means."

"He has offered a large reward to any squireens who will assist him in abducting Katherine Burbridge."

Her hand reached over to Fitz, who quickly enveloped it in his own. Patrick continued.

"He has also sought the services of several priests, couple-beggers who marry for fee. In short, he means to use Kitty's rightful fortune to finance his desire to take over the company or start a rival firm."

It made complete sense, absolute sense to her. As a second son, he was forced to depend on his older brother for everything. Generous as Fitz was, it was never enough for Andrew.

She felt sick at the mere thought of being tied in wedlock to Andrew.

"I will not believe that of my brother," Fitz rasped.

"That I feared." Patrick leaned forward. "Please, there is enough evidence to prove his intentions. He has not been subtle with his inquiries, Fitzwilliam."

"He is my brother, my closest relation. He would not do such a dastardly thing, especially not to me."

"You do not see him. You never have, not as others have seen Andrew." Patrick kept his voice gentle. "He is as unlike you as two could possibly be, filled with jealousy and rage and ruthless greed. For your sake, please consider the evidence I have collected."

He reached into his waistcoat and withdrew some parchments tied with a red ribbon. As he began to hand them over, Fitz dropped her hand and rose to his feet.

"I will not view contrived evidence."

"For God's sake, Fitzwilliam, listen to me! He intends to take her before the fortnight is out. Do you hear me? We are not merely discussing the future of your company, we are discussing Kitty."

"I will not hear these lies! Kitty, he should not have spoken before you. Your ears should not be insulted by malicious falsehoods."

She stood and placed her hand on his forearm. "Fitz, I do not believe they are falsehoods."

Turning toward her, his features reflected such anger she longed to step away from his wrath, but she couldn't. Instead, she spoke.

"I, too, have heard whisperings of Andrew and his covert meetings. Did you know he has been frequenting cockfights and bear-baitings? Did you know the ruffians with whom he habitually shares company? Just last week he reputedly . . ."

"Silence!"

A gasp escaped from her, stunned at the ferocity of his voice. Never had he addressed her thusly. Never.

Raising her chin, she faced him without blinking. "Andrew has always been your one blind spot. I beg of you, please take Patrick's warnings seriously. For our sake, for my sake. Oh, Fitz, I can only plead with you."

"I cannot believe what I am hearing. Kitty, Patrick—you have both turned against me."

"Nay! Fitzwilliam, it is our very fondness, indeed our love of you that causes us to speak," Patrick began.

"Leave! The two of you, be gone from my sight!"

She felt her heart lurch, then begin a dreadful pounding in her chest, so painful she was unable to speak, although she tried. The only noise she was able to make was a strange sort of breathing, but she was unable to hear over the uneven throbbing of her heart. Each beat seemed to twist and burn, and she longed for it to cease, to stop tormenting her.

"Kitty?" The voice was a man, either Patrick or Fitz, she couldn't distinguish. "Place the pillow beneath her head."

Was she standing still? No, now she was on the floor, and it was hard and cold.

Perhaps she should have told him before about the strange flutterings she would feel. But they always passed after a short time. He had other things to worry about, far more important things than a high-strung bride. That's what the physicians would have declared, and what a fool she would be to have summoned one.

With great effort she opened her eyes, and there he was, Fitz. Someone had loosened her corset, and she hoped it had been either Mrs. Finnegan or Fitz, for Patrick would tease her later, had he been the one to unbind her. She knew he would tease.

Better. Now she was feeling much better. Fitz held

the rim of a glass to her lips, and she sipped, thinking it was water or tea. But he had given her spirits, and she was unaccustomed to spirits and began to cough.

"There, there," he said, as if she were a child, and he smoothed her hair.

She could smell him, that fragrance that was Fitzwilliam. Again she closed her eyes, her cheek resting against his shoulder.

Finally she was safe.

CHAPTER 17

He was kissing her.

Maura relaxed for the moment, enjoying the sensation. But the more he kissed her, the more aware she became that something was very wrong. He was being rough, not kind and gentle. There was an overwhelming sense that he didn't really care for her, his fingernails digging into her flesh. Even his mouth was hurting, a grinding pressure rather than a tender kiss, and it was becoming unpleasant.

Too many teeth. There was an sensation of being devoured. And that's when she realized it wasn't Donal, nor was it even Fitz weighing so heavily on her.

"Roger!" Pulling away, she saw his face, partially obscured by a shadow.

"Come on, Maura," he urged. "You left the front window wide open. You knew I would come by."

"It was broken. Get off me," she warned, trying to push at his shoulders.

Instead of rolling away, he began his assault on her mouth again, this time grinning as he pressed down.

"Remember this?" He moaned. She did indeed remember—his appalling habit of tickling her as they embraced.

But it wasn't amusing now or even annoying. He outweighed her by at least sixty pounds, and there was an unsettling intensity to him. Maura was rapidly becoming frightened.

"Please stop."

There was no indication he had heard her.

The way she was pinned under his weight, she was unable to move.

How had she ended up on the parlor floor?

With one hand he began to yank at her blouse, but before alarm could give way to sheer terror, he suddenly rose. Another voice filled the room.

"You bastard! Get the hell off her!"

Donal. He had somehow pulled a stunned Roger to his feet.

"Who are you?" Roger stammered.

Donal merely turned to Maura, reaching down to help her up. His gaze rested on the ripped blouse, and his jaw clenched before he spoke. "Are you hurt?"

"No, I'm fine." She was unable to even look at Roger, the man she had once imagined she loved. With trembling hands she tried to pull her shirt back into place.

"I suggest you leave and not return," Donal said in a low voice.

"What right do you have to—"

"Go away, Roger," she interrupted.

"Maura, I will not be treated this way."

"Oh?" Donal slowly turned toward him. "I believe I could show you far more interesting treatment. And the gardai would be fascinated at what I stumbled upon—it certainly appeared to be the beginning of a felony, at best."

Roger straightened and walked stiffly through the open door. Donal fastened the lock before turning toward her. Very gently, he placed his hands on her shoulders.

"Now tell me, are you truly unharmed?" His voice was so soft, so full of concern, she began to feel the full significance of what had almost happened.

"I didn't want him here," she began. "I must have fallen asleep, and the next thing I knew, he was on me, his hands everywhere . . ."

"It's over now, my love." He tenderly pulled her closer, and she closed her eyes, resting her head against his chest.

"I don't know how it happened." The tears began in earnest now. "It was so dark, and you were not there."

"I was going to follow you, but you were so furious at me, justifiably so. I don't know what happens when I'm with you, I just seem to lose all sense and reason."

Never had she felt so safe, so secure. He began to rub her back as he held her, and he rested his cheek against her head, kissing her lightly on the temple.

"He was just there in the night. I wasn't feeling well, I had retired early."

"It wasn't that early, Maura . . ."

She kept talking, settling further in his embrace, her eyes closed in lethargic peacefulness.

"And as you refused to listen to Patrick, I despaired of how to persuade you. But thank God you arrived. I fear what Andrew may have done."

"Andrew? I thought his name was Roger."

"Have you seen the papers yet?"

"What papers?"

"You must see the papers. I know not what they contain, but Patrick would never mislead you."

"Maura, what papers? The only ones I know of are the papers Charles has, the ones about transferring the factory to, well, you know, me."

As he spoke he led her to the sofa, and together, almost as one, they settled. In her drowsy contentment she snuggled closer.

"I have not been completely honest with you," he began, smiling as she sighed. "All this time I have been battling you, but it's myself I truly battled with. The factory, all the business nonsense was just a distraction. One I maintained because the feelings I have for you, well, to tell you the truth, they spooked me. Are you listening?"

She seemed to either nod or nestle closer.

"I'll take that as a yes."

When she didn't respond, he continued. "Part of my problem, part of my self-imposed solitude, was brought on by my mother's death. We were terribly close, especially after my father died, and the rage and betrayal I felt when she died frightened me. Here I had been operating under the delusion of self-control, a sense of never losing a grip. Then I lost it completely. Life became meaningless. I remember walking down a street in Munich just after I returned from her funeral, and I was angry that everyone else was going about their business, as if nothing was wrong. I had an urge to scream at a woman who was laughing in front of a market, to trip the merrily romantic couple.

"It was a sense of outrage, I suppose. 'How can they go about their business when my world has just collapsed?' So I regained my self-control, vowing never to let myself into such a vulnerable position again. And then I met you."

Pausing to take a deep breath, he closed his eyes. "I love you, Maura. I love you so much that when I heard today some American was in town to see you, I lost my self-control. I love you so much I would rather argue with you than be away from you. I love you so very much that I can't imagine a future without you. It would be blank, desolate—a vast, endless nothing."

She seemed to move, and he waited for her answer. And waited.

"Maura? Have you nothing to say?"

Still she remained silent. And then he heard it, quietly at first, so softly he held his breath to prevent missing a word.

She was snoring.

Only after a jolt of frustration did he begin to chuckle. Of course, she would sleep through the most passionate declaration he had ever made. Of course, she would snore in response to his revealing his heart.

Of course, he would have to repeat the entire scene at a later date, preferably when she was conscious.

Before he fell asleep he had one final thought: At least he'd had a dress rehearsal.

He awoke in a panic.

She was ill, and something else. What was the other thing that had him so confoundedly upset?

"Kitty." He kept his voice so low, he thought only he could hear.

"Yes?" And then he saw her face, beaming in what he could only realize was love, her extraordinary eyes on him.

How had he gotten on the other side of the room, leaning against a fireplace mantel?

Glancing down, he was startled to see fawn-colored breeches and leather boots that came to his knees. He reached back to scratch his head in confusion and was met with hair, lots of hair, pulled back into a ponytail with . . . what was it? . . . a leather tie.

A leather tie?

"I do hope they find him soon," she said.

"As do I," he replied without thinking. "I am ashamed of the way I behaved, ashamed and utterly anguished."

"Do not blame yourself, Fitz." She looked so fragile in the gossamer gown, her delicate face more pale than usual. That was to be expected, of course. After what had happened the night before, it was a wonder she was able to sit so calmly.

"How long have you known about Andrew?" He hadn't meant to ask that question. Part of him hoped she somehow had not heard. Yet he had to know. It was a compulsion to discover how truly blind he had been to his own brother's nature.

"Oh, my love." She sighed as she spoke, a gauzy, ephemeral sound that caused his heart to race just slightly. At once he was at her side, kneeling by her chair, clasping one of her fragile hands in his.

"Can you ever forgive me? That I doubted both you and Patrick . . . I cannot think of it without loathing."

"I would have been sorely disappointed had you not doubted us. Andrew is your brother, and our suspicions would drive a wedge between the two of you."

"But when did you know?"

"About Andrew? Fitz, he has always been thus. You alone saw him through a haze of love. Even your father feared for his character. Do you recall the night his favorite hound was found dead on the lawn?"

"Of course I do. Boru was my favorite as well."

"Andrew killed him."

He tightened his hold on her hand but said nothing, allowing her to continue. "Your father overheard Andrew boasting to the stable boy about how he slit the hound's throat with a dinner knife."

"Why didn't he tell me? Father. He should have told me."

"Your father also protected Andrew, hoping that the black sheep would change color in time. He also knew that you would likely never again trust your brother, and that rift would take years to mend."

"A dinner knife," he mumbled. "I do recall that some silver was replaced around the same time that Boru was found. I myself fetched it from Thomas Read's shop on Crane Lane."

"Your father told me he could not glance upon

those knives without thinking of Andrew or poor Boru."

"Why did he tell you this? You and not me?"

"It was when his health was failing, Fitz. He knew of our feelings toward each other. I suppose he had known for a long time. Your father wanted me to know about Andrew's dual nature, should he grow up in such a way. He feared for you, your father. He knew you only saw the good in Andrew."

"What a complete fool you must think me."

"No." She leaned forward, and he rested his head on her breast. "Had you been any different, had you been suspicious or mistrustful, you would not be my Fitzwilliam."

He closed his eyes as she stroked his hair.

How would he ever be able to protect her?

Marry her. Marry her now before the big planned ceremony. That was the only way to prevent his brother's plan, the one he thwarted—only just—the night before.

By God, he would protect her. And forever she would remain his.

In her sleep she could feel him holding her, and it was wonderful.

As she began to waken, she could even feel him breathing deeply and evenly, and when she moved, he tightened his hold, as if she would escape.

A lovely dream. She resisted the urge to wake as long as possible, delaying the moment when she would open her eyes and find herself alone. If she could only fall asleep again, just for a while, and continue the dream of being in love, of being loved.

"Maura," he whispered, and she jumped.

"Donal!"

They were on the couch in the parlor, a piece of furniture so narrow and uncomfortable that it was difficult to sit without looking around the room for a less jarring place to rest. From the way they were lying, they must have slept there all night.

Maura sat up slowly, disentangling herself from his grasp.

"How did you get here? I thought you hated me." She hadn't meant to say that, but the last thing she remembered he was furious at her.

"I do not hate you." His voice was rough, untried in the morning. He cleared his throat and smiled. "In fact, last night I believe I declared my love for you."

Was he joking?

"What . . . what did I say?"

"You snored."

"I . . . wait a minute. I don't snore."

"That's good to know." The smile left his face, and he, too, sat up fully. "Are you all right?"

"Why?"

"Do you remember last night, with Roger—"

Her voice overlapped his. "Roger. He was here and, and he . . ."

"I know. I saw what happened."

The unwelcome memories flooded back to her, of his hands everywhere, the terrible feel of his body on hers. Then Donal had arrived. She remembered that he came into the house and rescued her and muttered comforting words.

"Thank you." It was pitifully inadequate, but he reached out and brushed a piece of hair from her eyes.

"You're welcome."

A new growth of whiskers lined his jaw, lending him a rakish air, and his eyes held a sleepy look that held her completely. In spite of his rumpled appearance, she had never seen him look so appealing. She had never seen anyone so handsome.

"Did you really declare you love me?"

"I did indeed."

"Would you care to repeat it?"

A slow grin curved his lips. "Not at the moment. Suffice it to say I made a complete fool of myself."

Something about those words made him pause. "You must think me an utter fool."

"Of course I don't. I only wish I had been awake. Is anything wrong?"

"I don't know." He glanced around the room. It had been different before, with crystal and candles and molding along the ceiling. Other things had remained the same, the mantel, the way the sun came through the windows. Another thought occurred to him.

"Who are Patrick and Andrew?"

Immediately she crossed her arms. "Why do you want to know? Did I talk in my sleep?"

"I'm not sure. I had a peculiar dream, all about a brother named Andrew."

"Go on," she said.

"It seems I had a friend named Patrick, and a fiancée . . . Kitty." Then he leveled his gaze at hers. "I must have imagined it, but it was so clear, so absolutely vivid I can even recall what I was wearing. The odd thing was that I wasn't surprised to find myself dressed in eighteenth century clothes. There was barely a sense of wonder, just acceptance."

"Was I there?"

He laughed. "No, Auntie Em." Then he stopped. "But you were. You were there the whole time, and your name was Kitty. And I was . . . my God, this is impossible."

"You were Fitz."

For a long while they simply stared at each other, wondering if what they were thinking was remotely possible. She broke the silence first.

"Do you remember anything about a dog?"

He nodded. "Boru. Andrew killed him and left him on the lawn. My father—" He stopped. "Fitzwilliam's father told her about it."

"Do you remember what happened next?"

"The father ordered new silver. I even remember the shop—Thomas Read on Crane Lane. But Maura, I know the store. It's famous, Joyce even wrote of it in *Ulysses,* on Parliament Street, right next to City Hall. It's been there for centuries, the whole shop sags and leans, it's so old."

"Was Parliament Street ever called Crane Lane?"

"I don't know."

"Do you remember anything else?"

"Andrew. He attacked you and tried to abduct you, and you and Patrick had warned me. Now I don't know how I know this, but he wanted to elope with you for your dowry. And I was completely blind . . ."

"It's okay, Donal."

"And you. It was you. I called you Kitty, yet in my mind and heart it was you. You were ill, something was wrong with you, but we all seemed to be pretending you were perfectly well. In a way this thing with Andrew was a distraction, a relief. It prevented us from dwelling on how sick you really were. Why didn't you consult a physician?"

"Because it wasn't so bad, at least not until just recently. The physicians would just bleed me and pronounce me hysterical or worse."

"You are so pale. I have this notion in my mind that I fear nothing, not a sudden storm at sea or being swept overboard. Yet I have real fear when I look at Kitty, terrible fear that I would never admit to, for admitting to the fear might give it more power."

"Andrew tried to take me."

"I know. It happened the evening before. And I somehow stumbled upon it just in time. Then Andrew vanished, but so did Patrick. He took the papers with the proof with him."

"And you don't know what they say, what evidence they hold."

"Because I was a fool, and refused to even look at them."

Again they lapsed into silence. Outside, across the street in Merrion Square Park, they could hear the shouts of children playing. A motor scooter rumbled by, the engine slowing as it turned the corner. A horn honked from someplace far away. But they did not hear the sounds. They were both stunned beyond comprehension.

"This can't be happening." She turned toward him, and he reached out and brushed his knuckles against her cheek.

"I know," he said.

"Wait a minute." She seemed to be shaking herself back to sensibility. "Okay, do you have a telephone directory?"

"Not on me. Why?"

"I just thought I'd call the shop you mentioned and see if they have ever changed locations."

"Brilliant! The place is a virtual museum, so whoever is there is bound to know the answer. Just call directory assistance."

She was already on her feet and headed toward the telephone in the kitchen. Donal followed closely.

"What do I dial for directory assistance? Four one one?"

"Eleven nine zero."

She dialed, then turned to him.

"Thomas Read on Parliament Street."

When she had the number she rang the store. A man answered, and she suddenly felt absolutely ridiculous.

"Just a minute, please," she said, then shoved the receiver over to Donal. He raised his eyebrows, then got on the phone.

"Hello. I have a question to ask you about your store . . . Yes. Yes, I know that, thank you. But what I was wondering, was the shop ever located on Crane Lane? Yes . . . Of course. . . . Sword making? Indeed, it is a dying art . . . Yes. Yes, I see . . . I remember that as a boy . . . No, I was from the west, but we came here every summer. . . . Cork, in fact. . . . No. I'm afraid not, but the name is familiar. There are a lot of O'Conners in that part. . . . Thank you for your time. I will, and look forward to it. Thank you again. Good-bye."

"Well?" She asked the moment the receiver was on the hook.

"We're invited to a sword-sharpening demonstration this afternoon."

"That's great, but what about the location?"

"The shop was established in 1670."

"So it would have been in existence by 1767."

"The original story was on Blind Quay, which as the man just said was slightly disturbing for a knife company, visions of putting out eyes with single thrusts and all that."

"When did they move to Parliament Street?"

"In 1765. There's even a drawer that's been stuck shut since then, and no one knows what the contents are. Isn't that fascinating? They are unable to open it because it's in a supporting wall, and any effort to pry it open may cause the entire side of the building to collapse. Hardly a comforting thought, as the man just said."

"Oh." Maura shrugged. "So we were all wrong."

"I never said that. They moved from their present location from the store's second shop. It was on a small street called Crane Lane."

She was silent, and he continued. "The current shop has been there since 1765, just two years before our dream, or whatever it is."

"And clearly the thing with Andrew and the dog happened well before that—in childhood." This did not seem possible. "Donal, are you sure you had no idea about the locations of the shop?"

"Why on earth would I know such a thing? I do not make it a habit to learn the lineage of all the shops in Dublin. And Maura, don't forget I've been in Germany for ten years, so my time in Dublin was limited to summer visits with my parents and my years at UCD. How many university students do you know of who research their own surroundings?"

"Of course. I'm sorry, I was just trying to figure out some logical explanation."

She came to him, her arms about his waist as he held her gently. It seemed right and natural, as if they had always been together, as if they had never battled or argued.

"Maura, there is something else."

"What's that?"

"I believe I left something at that shop."

"When you were a student?"

"No. Not me, then. Fitzwilliam. As I was speaking to that clerk, I remember placing an order that was never picked up."

"Odd."

"It's the same way in the dream I had. The background information was sketched for me, so swiftly that it was just there. Never was I aware of having the knowledge instilled. That's what happened on the telephone."

"I wonder why Fitz never picked it up?"

"Maybe because it's in the drawer that's stuck. And before he could retrieve it, well . . ."

"He died."

Donal nodded.

"I wonder—" she began, then stopped.

"Wonder what?"

"I wonder who we really are. I mean, what is reality, and what is a dream?"

Each was lost in thought, swirling notions that

seemed absurd, even insane, yet kept proving to be true.

"This sounds like class discussion in a freshman philosophy course," he said at last.

"Or conversation after a few beers after the freshman philosophy course," she added.

"I'm only certain of one thing."

She glanced up at him, eyes questioning.

"I am certain that I love you. And I mean me, Donal Byrne, not someone from centuries long gone."

"Oh, Donal. I think I love you, too."

"What do you mean think?"

"Well, I am almost certain that I love you, but it somehow gets all tangled up with Fitz and Kitty."

"I suppose that will have to do." He sighed. "Perhaps if we set them to rest, we can see about ourselves."

"Donal?"

"Yes?"

"Do you believe in ghosts yet?"

"I'm not sure, but I'll tell you one thing."

"What's that?"

"I'm beginning to believe in something. I'm just not sure what the hell it is at the moment."

Chapter 18

❦

Donal's apartment wasn't at all what Maura had expected.

She'd imagined a Euro-chic, sprawling place with track lighting and Scandinavian furniture, all blond wood and pale leather and chrome. Instead, his home was rather small, on the second floor of an old brick building on the other side of the River Liffey. The furniture was plain, almost suburban, but the touches were warm and homey. A three-legged iron pot served as a planter. The quilt thrown over the sofa was worn and stitched by hand. In the center of the living room was a worn chair, a hideous shade of burnt orange and avacado green. A drawing over the small mantel was of faces, some laughing, some pensive, others in conversation or alone.

"I drew that when I was first in Germany," he said when he saw her interest.

"You're kidding. You did this?"

"One of my many talents." He grimaced. "It's supposed to be—" He paused. "No, you tell me. Does it remind you of anything?"

"A pub," she replied without hesitation. "Not just any pub, though. It reminds me of Nesbitt's."

"That's exactly what I had in mind. It seemed too disturbing for the Germans who came to my flat in Munich, so I hid it away until I returned home. My wish had been to recall Ireland, not to torment others with a sea of Celtic faces. Can you give me a hand with this?"

In his arms was a large cardboard box so filled with papers that the top would not close. Donal kept the flap closed with his chin.

"Here." She took a corner, and together they lowered the box to the floor.

"All of my mother's notes on Connolly." Bending down, he placed his hand on the lid. "Years of work are in this box."

"Have you ever gone through these?"

"No. There was no reason, really. Until now, of course. And also . . ." his voice trailed off.

"Also what?"

"It was too painful. I remember her working on this book, going along with her on research trips. This was such a happy time, so many good memories, that to sift through her thoughts would be too difficult now that she's gone."

She folded her hand over his. "Maybe we should just forget this. Whatever information she had she probably used in the book anyway. There may be no point."

"No. There were a lot of ideas she was unable to

use, shreds of material that she was unable to pursue because of dead ends or her editor. Besides"—he opened the box fully—"I believe she would want me to go through them. Why else didn't she just get rid of all this? Here, you take this pile."

Handing her a stack of papers, he smiled. "Coffee?"

"No thanks. Maybe later."

And together they spent the better part of the day immersed in the life of Fitzwilliam Connolly.

At one time there had been solid proof of Andrew Connolly's plot to kidnap Katherine Burbridge. It had been widely reported in newspapers of the day, simply because Andrew had openly solicited help by advertising in Mr. Lynch's newspaper in Kilkenny.

"I wonder," Donal mused, pushing aside the remains of a sandwich. "Do you suppose copies of those solicitations would be in existence?"

"Nope." Maura reached her hands over her head in a stretch. "Your mother already thought of that, but the 1922 fire at the Four Courts here in Dublin destroyed most of the county's public records. And she checked in Kilkenny—no luck there."

"I remember that trip. We had a picnic on a hill, and I got stung by a bee."

She glanced up and smiled. "Poor thing."

"It was rather sad. Wait a minute." Straightening, he held a scrap of paper. "She made a stack of notes about Kitty and Andrew's unhappy marriage. Apparently there was no shortage of references to their discord."

"Of course, it was unhappy. Fitz was dead, she was forced into a marriage with a man she hated, and she was literally dying. Can you imagine how she loathed Andrew? That alone probably would have killed her. Where are the notes?"

"Damn. This paper was apparently clipped to the top. They must be here someplace."

But they were unable to find the papers. As Donal continued skimming the notes, she paused over a small notebook. Curious, she began reading.

"Maura, could you pass me that pen over there?"

She did not respond.

"Maura?"

Again, she remained motionless except for the intense turning of a page every few moments.

"Donal?"

She did not see the exasperated look he gave her as he stepped over the box to retrieve the pen.

"Your mother sensed him, too."

"Excuse me?"

"Here in this notebook. Your mother felt his presence while she was working, and it disturbed her a great deal."

"That happens to all biographers. I read about it once—when you're so intimately involved in someone else's life, you can't help but fall in love with them a little. That's why if I ever write a biography, I'm skipping Henry VIII and Adolf Hitler and jumping straight to Jean Harlow or Ava Gardner."

Slowly she lowered the book. "Your mother saw him."

"Henry VIII?"

"No. Fitzwilliam Connolly."

Donal chuckled. "Maura, you didn't hear what I

just said. All biographers seem to go a little crazy and become completely wrapped up in their subject."

"She was disturbed because he seemed to focus on you."

"What are you talking about?"

"Do you remember the nightmares you had as a child?"

"Every child has nightmares."

"While your mother was writing this book, she tucked you in one night, and thought she saw something out of the corner of her eye. Not long after that you woke up screaming that your brother was killing you."

"That would indeed be a nightmare, since I didn't have a brother. But as an only child, I'm afraid it loses it's effectiveness."

Maura was undeterred, her eyes fixed on the notebook as she continued. "So your mother came into the room, and you told her that you had the proof. Patrick had given it to you."

The smile faded from his face. "I said the name Patrick?"

She nodded. "And you put it in the yellow parlor."

"Maura . . ."

"I know. The yellow parlor on Merrion Square."

"What did she do? My mother, I mean."

"First off, she woke you up. But even awake you kept talking about Andrew and Patrick. Do you remember any of this?"

"No. But perhaps I was just aware of her work."

"That's the thing. She says she specifically kept her

work away from you, simply because she felt the story would be too disturbing."

"What about the research trips?"

"That came later, when it was already too late and you seemed to know more about the topic than she did. Part of her wanted to hear everything you had to say, the other part didn't want you to get so intimately involved."

"All I remember is being very interested." He rubbed his neck.

"You also told her that the proof was under the wallpaper in the yellow parlor."

"Now that makes no sense."

"Yes, it does. The first night I saw Fitz, when he was haunting the house, he was looking for something. He was searching the walls behind the yellow parlor."

"I wonder why my mother didn't check there?"

"She tried. But the cantankerous owner of the house, Delbert Finnegan, wouldn't allow her—or anyone else for that matter—to enter the house."

"I wonder why?"

"He was afraid."

"Of what?"

"Of losing his right to live there. You see, I don't believe old Delbert or I, for that matter, bear any relationship to Fitzwilliam Connolly."

"This makes no sense."

Finally she lowered the notebook. "I think I am a direct descendant of his housekeeper, Mrs. Finnegan."

"This makes no sense," he repeated. "Where did my mother find that out?"

"She didn't. I just know."

"Oh, Maura." He dropped the papers in his hand. "What are we doing?"

"I assume that's a rhetorical question."

"Absolutely not." Abruptly he stood, backing away from the box. "This is absurd. We've been sucked into a murder mystery that can have no possible impact on our lives. What will it prove? The main characters have already been dead for centuries. It doesn't matter."

"Yes, it does!" Her voice was more emphatic than she had intended. "Don't you see? With all of this unsettled, we'll never be able to find happiness."

He simply stared at her, then crossed his arms. "Who will never be able to find happiness?"

"We." When he didn't respond, she began to twirl a piece of hair.

"I'm wondering, do you mean you and me?"

"Of course? Who else could I mean?"

"I'm not certain. But I don't believe I'm in this equation. I don't believe I am a factor at all."

"What . . ."

"I'll take you home now." His mood had grown somber, and she saw him shake his head just slightly as he piled the stray papers back into the box.

"Are you ready?"

"Donal, I have no idea what's come over you. We seemed to be working toward a common end, and then all of a sudden you freaked out."

"I did not freak out."

"Then explain this. Why am I suddenly getting the bum's rush?"

"Lovely phrase, that. I must remember it. 'Bum's rush' did you say?"

"Please, Donal."

"Here's your purse."

She refused to accept it until finally he just slipped it over her shoulder.

"Tell me." She refused to budge.

Opening the front door to his apartment, he paused. "You see, Maura, I believe you are quite mistaken."

"About what?"

"About the happiness you crave. I don't believe it's between you and me, not at all."

She merely frowned, but he did not see her expression. His stared at his own hand hand clutching the doorknob. "You are seeking happiness in the past."

"No, you're wrong."

"Then tell me, Maura." Finally he looked directly into her eyes, searching. "How can I convince you to live in the present?"

There was nobody for her to turn to, not anymore. She had ruined her relationship with Donal, with none but herself to blame. Until she stepped alone into her hallway, she hadn't realized how much she had grown to depend on him, on his wit and humor and common sense.

Once again Maura had managed to sabotage a potentially wonderful relationship. This time she had really done a number, really screwed up her life in a way she had only toyed with in the past. All by herself, with no outside help, she had alienated the most brilliant and caring man she had met in years. No, ever. He was the most wonderful man she had ever met.

If only he could come back. If only he would walk through the door . . .

There was a loud knock.

It was him! It had to be Donal.

She ran to the door, and it was . . .

"Patrick! Please, do come in!"

He was covered with mud and muck from a long ride.

"Kitty." He stepped inside quickly, glancing behind once before closing the door. "How fare you?"

"Well, thank you. Did Fitz tell you?"

"He did, indeed. Of course, I will stand up for him and deem it a high honor to be his witness."

"You were always to be with us, Patrick. We are just shifting the ceremony ahead a few weeks."

"And not a moment too soon. I just came from Kilkenny."

"Please, come in." She allowed him to pass ahead. "May I take your coat? Mrs. Finnegan can remove the speckles on your cloak."

"Oh, thank you. I rode the horse Fitzwilliam has given to you."

"Did you now?" She pulled the silk cord just inside of the parlor, summoning Mrs. Finnegan. "How did you like her?"

"A fine bit of flesh, Kitty. She'll speed you anyplace you desire."

Mrs. Finnegan entered the room and curtsied, gently removing his cloak.

"You are a wonder, Mrs. Finnegan." He smiled.

"And don't I know it, sir. Worth my weight in gold, I am."

She shook her head and clucked over the spotted cloak as she left the room.

"I will be direct," he said the moment she had left. "I have here more newspapers, featuring Andrew's cryptic solicitation for aid in abducting you. And there is no sign of him. He seems to be hiding out amongst friends we know not of." He reached into his waistcoat and withdrew the papers. "There are also some mentions of the Annie Delany matter."

"Were you able to tell a constable?"

"Nay. They know already or at least suspect his role in the death of the Delany girl. I pray I did the right thing, but I notified no officials, simply because once the law becomes involved, the issue is no longer a private one. Who he is or family connections make no difference. English law is rule here, and as such, Andrew could easily pay with his life, should he carry through his scheme. It is a felony to abduct anyone against their will. He could hang for it unless we can stop it ourselves."

"Poor Andrew." She sighed.

"Poor Andrew my foot! It's poor Fitzwilliam, poor Kitty and—need I add—poor Patrick. Andrew has been quite successful in pulling together a fine band of ruffians. The sooner you are safely wed, the better. Where shall we put these for safekeeping?"

"I did have an idea. Fitz is having the upstairs parlor done in yellow paper, and we will just paste it behind the new paper, between the two windows, under that dreadful landscape he seems so strangely attached to."

"Brilliant, absolutely brilliant. And so we will carry forth tonight?"

She nodded. "All will remain calm here, as if nothing at all is wrong. Fitz is over on Maiden Lane, I will stay here and do some sort of useless womanly task."

"You should not be left alone. What if Andrew should arrive and hasten his plans?"

"I doubt that. And don't forget, I am far from alone here, with Aunt Sarah and Mrs. Finnegan and Edward, the stable boy. I believe the four of us, not to mention Fitz, could thwart any silly plot of Andrew or his drunken companions."

"It is not a silly plot. For your sake, you must realize how serious his intentions are. Should he kidnap you and succeed in finding a priest—and mark my words, I have no doubt he has procured a couple-begger for this purpose—you will be legally wed to Andrew. As your husband, he will be entitled to all you possess, including—forgive me—you."

She closed her eyes. "I know. God help me, I know. I only wish . . ."

"Only wish what?"

"I only wish Andrew would be gone, perhaps to America. How can we live together after the wedding under one roof, knowing what his intentions had been? There can be no happiness for Fitz and me, not with Andrew casting a shadow. How can Fitz trust his brother?"

Patrick placed his hand under her elbow. "He does not trust his brother. Indeed, he . . . no. I am not at liberty to continue."

"Please, tell me."

"Fitzwilliam was going to tell you this evening, but he has changed his will, drafting a new one that leaves all of his worldly property to you, should anything happen to him."

"I can't even think of that," she breathed. "He has skipped over Andrew in my favor? What if Andrew marries me yet? Will he not yet accomplish his purpose?"

He shook his head no. "The stipulation is that you are to receive all and in trust of your children with Fitzwilliam, unless you are married to Andrew. In that case the property skips to the next person."

"And who is that?"

"God forbid it is necessary, the property—everything—will be entrusted to me."

"But does that not then place you in danger of Andrew's plots? I would be secure, for marriage would not be a possibility for what he desires. But you—after you, it would all be his."

Now Patrick smiled. "No. Tell no one, but in the rare event that you and I are gone, and should you have no heirs, the heiress will be . . . well, I hear her now."

Mrs. Finnegan bustled into the room, the cloak now spot free. "Here we go, sir." She smiled. Then she looked at their faces, the grin on Patrick's, the gradual delight on Kitty's. "Now what is it with the two of ye?"

"Nothing, Mrs. Finnegan." Kitty handed the cloak to Patrick. "Just thank you, thank you for everything."

"Will you be requiring me for anything else, ma'am?"

"No. Thank you."

The older woman curtsied and hastened from the room.

"And, Patrick"—she extended her hand—"Thank you for being such a fine friend to both myself and Fitzwilliam."

He bowed over her hand. "It is always an honor, my dear Kitty." Straightening, he slipped the cloak over his shoulders. "I will see you ere the day is over. Oh, and Kitty?"

"Yes?"

"The dreadful landscape between the two windows upstairs? Fitz painted it." He put his tricorn on. "Good afternoon."

With that, he left.

There was a knock on the door.

Maura rose to open it, still drowsy with sleep. Hadn't she just answered the door?

"Charles," she said when she saw who it was.

"Maura, we need to talk." There was an unusual seriousness to him, an urgency she had never before seen.

"Are you feeling well?"

"No. I feel quite ill, in fact. Would you have a drop of the creature about to settle my nerves?"

"The creature?" Did he know about Fitz? Then she realized he meant liquor. "No, Charles. I'm afraid the best I can do is tea or milk."

"Never mind then. This has to do with your Roger."

"He's not my Roger."

"Forgive me, then. But he seems intent on stirring

up trouble, more than trouble. Did you know he has secured ownership of this town house and your business over in America?"

"How? How can he? He has no right!"

"Did you sign over Finnegan's Freeze-Dried to him several months ago?"

"No. He just signed on as a consultant. He said he would help me turn the company around, but once he got a good look at the books and how much money we were losing, he vanished."

"I'm afraid he did not vanish, Maura. A gentleman by the name of Peter Jones just telephoned me. He's gone over the books at your company back in Wisconsin, and it seems to have been turned over to Roger Parker, who has secured a buyer . . ."

"Wait a moment—this is impossible. Why didn't Peter call me first instead of you?"

"He wanted to find out the status of your holdings here in Dublin before he spoke to you."

"I think I could also use a drop of the creature . . ." Her voice faltered.

"Maura, my dear. I do hate to bring this up, but did you not read any of the papers you've signed over the past six months? I myself watched you scribble your name on the sale papers for the factory without reading them. It's a very bad habit."

"Oh, Charles, what can we do?"

"I do know one person who can help."

"Who?"

"Donal Byrne. Now don't make that face, Maura. The man has an enormous firm behind him, plus he seems to have a record of pulling off all sorts of impossible business stunts. Look at what he has done here, managing to convince a German drug company to invest in an Irish furniture factory. If that doesn't demonstrate some fancy financial footwork and some brilliant number crunching, I don't know what does."

"I can't ask him, Charles. I just can't."

"Is it your pride?" Is that what is standing in your way?"

At first she shook her head, then, grudgingly, she nodded.

"Pride. It's such a small thing to ruin so many people's lives. Did I ever tell you about my ex-wife? Well, the reason she's my ex-wife is because I was convinced she was seeing another man. By the time I found out I had been mistaken, I had already moved out of our flat and made a scene in the middle of a rather posh dinner party. Seems the gentleman I accused her of seeing was an overly attentive waiter more interested in tips than in anything else. But I was too embarrassed to admit I was wrong, and so I am alone today and likely to remain so for the rest of my life."

"I'm sorry, but this thing with Donal is so different, so complicated. I mean, you have no idea."

"No. No, I don't, and that's the truth. If you don't contact him for your own sake, think of the employees back in Wisconsin or what Mr. Parker intends to do with your house on Merrion Square."

"What is that?"

"He wants to turn it into a combination museum and amusement arcade, called The Oscar Wilde Kingdom. It will have video games, a laser show, all sorts of things."

Roger. Of course that is what he would do—a man

of action whose idea of high culture was subscribing to a premium cable channel. Now she had no choice but to contact Donal. "I'll call him soon . . . just give me a few moments."

Charles nodded. "Grand. I'll be off now . . ."

Before Charles could leave, the telephone rang.

"Maura?"

It was Donal.

"I just remembered what the order left at Read's was."

"What was that?"

"It was a penknife—for cutting quills into pens. It was to be a gift for Patrick for standing up with me at the wedding. It had his initials and the date engraved."

"Oh." She really wasn't certain what that would prove. Before she could ask, he answered.

"I think that's what Andrew used on his brother, the knife he used to—"

"Stop." She couldn't let him continue, to say the words "to kill Fitzwilliam," although she knew exactly what he meant. "Please don't say it. I understand. But what can we do about it?"

"You said that Connolly's wedding outfit changed from blue to black. You changed that, Maura. Do you suppose we could change this, too?"

"Could you come right over?"

"No, not right now. I need to think, to figure this thing out. I'll ring you a little later if I come up with anything. Let me know if you have any ideas." His voice sounded tired.

"Are you okay?"

"I don't know. This whole thing is insane. I'm just wondering if I am, too. And, Maura?"

"Yes?"

"I'm sorry about this afternoon." Then he hung up before saying good-bye.

Charles smiled as she opened the door for him. "I don't have a single doubt that the two of you can settle this whole thing."

"Oh. Sure."

"Good luck."

"Thank you."

She was so distracted when she let him through the door, she never saw Roger Parker across the street, leaning against a fence, staring at the house with unsettling intensity.

CHAPTER 19

It was a relief to walk through his door, the threshold that represented safety both corporally and spiritually. And at last it was done in the antechamber of a small chapel on the other side of the park. She was his wife and nothing else could harm them.

"Fitz, I . . . what are you doing?"

Before she could protest, he had scooped her into his arms and carried her into the hallway.

"You are now my bride," he whispered into her ear. "And this is your home, always and forever."

She laughed, wrapping one arm around his shoulder and placing her other hand against his cheek. "And you are my husband and an utter buffoon. Should you stumble and we fall, 'twould serve us both right."

Patrick was not far behind. "Is no one to carry me?"

Fitz gently lowered Kitty to her feet. "So you wish

to be carried? Very well." He began to remove his jacket, the simple, elegant black suit that had been stitched up in haste for the wedding. Tossing it on the banister, he loosened his cravat and took an appraising look at Patrick.

"Nah," he said, dismissing his friend with a wave of his hand. "Kitty, he's your burden. You may carry him if you wish. I refuse."

The three friends laughed together, a moment of relief and joy. With a sobering nod, Fitzwilliam placed his arm around his wife and looked at Patrick. "Truly, my friend, I know not how to thank you for all you have done. I have something for you, for being in every way my best man."

Reaching over to a small round table, he picked up a package wrapped in light green cloth. Patrick took a deep breath.

"I do not need a reward. Everything I did was from friendship."

"And that is how this token is offered, in friendship."

Patrick smiled and opened the package. "A penknife! And a very handsome one indeed. See my initials, Kitty."

"That will help you sign all the important documents you will no doubt be called upon to attend. You do have a marvelous hand."

"Thank you. Both of you. It was my privilege. I only hope that this incident has not irreparably strained the fabric of your relationship with Andrew."

"Ah, my dear brother Andrew." He sighed. "There is naught amiss with the lad that a good year or two aboard one of my vessels will not cure."

"Is that what you're going to do? Does he know of your plan?" Kitty asked.

"Not yet, but he will soon enough. I have been too soft on the lad, all in the name of protecting him. It has been an error, as I see now. I believe his problem has been seeing too many performances of *The Beggar's Opera.* That must be where he garnered the notion of abducting Kitty. Idleness has been his demon. He is a good boy, he just needs to be guided, a task at which I failed."

Patrick and Kitty exchanged glances before Patrick spoke. "Fitzwilliam, you know there is more amiss than a simple lack of guidance."

"And what would that be?"

"My love," she began gently, "I thought you realized this already. He is not just an aimless youth. In truth, he has far too much ambition and direction. He knows exactly what he wants, and he will get it, no matter what the means or who suffers in the end."

"Fitzwilliam, I have heard unsavory tales of your brother's escapades. He is known both here in Dublin and in the counties west as a ruffian and a bully, using your name and position to gain whatever he desires at the moment."

"As much as I value your opinions, I know him best of all. He is my younger brother, and as such, he is a ripe target for such gossip. Surely, he cannot be blamed for bearing the Connolly name, any more than I am to blame for being the eldest son. Now, shall I call Mrs. Finnegan for a round of wine? We need to toast our happiness."

"Does the name Annie Delany sound familiar?" Patrick asked.

"Annie Delany? Nay, it does not. Should it?"

"I am not surprised. She is an unfortunate girl from Kilkenny who was brutally assaulted last autumn after the Rotunda Ball. It is said that your brother was responsible."

Fitzwilliam shook his head. "Again Andrew is a target. No doubt some clever squireen was attempting to extort a sum of money from me. The fact that I never heard of the unhappy girl's name is proof that Andrew had nothing to do with the incident."

"The girl died before she could make a statement," Patrick said flatly. "The only reason you did not hear of the event is because you were on a voyage at the time. Had you but read the papers I have given you, the facts would have been all too clear."

"The papers are in the place we agreed upon already. I had not the heart to read them but made my legal decisions based on the few pages I skimmed." Then he crossed his arms. "If Andrew is truly suspected of harming the Delany girl, then why have the Dublin Castle authorities not even paid me a call? And then why have her parents not come forth to press blame?"

"They are afraid." Kitty reached for her husband's hand. "Andrew has threatened them with ruin, using both your name and power as his shield. You are well respected, my love, and the Delany's suffered their daughter's loss in silence, for fear you would withdraw your support of the Catholic landowners."

Fitzwilliam stood in bewildered silence. "I would never do that, never even think of using such a cruel device."

"You must understand," Patrick began softly.

"There are many in the west as well as in nearby counties who are indebted to you for all you have done. Yet by holding their property in your name, protecting all they possess from the anti-Catholic laws, they are virtually beholden to you for their very livelihoods. All they own is under your name simply because you are of the Protestant faith and legally entitled to hold property. Your goodness alone stands between them and destitution, and they know it thoroughly and unequivocally."

Kitty sighed. "As Catholics they have no rights, cannot own a horse valued at more than five pounds, cannot hold land or a house or enter public office, even joining the military is forbidden."

"You need not list the injustices, Kitty. I know them all too well, as did my father. That is why I hold these titles and deeds. But it is ownership in name only, a technicality to protect them."

"But your brother has been using that technical ownership to his own ends for years," Patrick shouted, then calmed his voice. "God's blood, Fitz-william, how can you be so blind? I thought you understood. Andrew enjoys his journeys west because he is out of your reach, and no one dares to question his authority. They all believe his commands come straight from you, and who is to contradict his claim? Not me, surely. Not Kitty, although now that she is your wife her voice may be heard in some quarters . . ."

Fitzwilliam's entire posture changed from defiance and disbelief to a sinking defeat. "I need to sit down," he murmured. "I need to think," he said after he had settled in a chair.

He did not say a word for a long while, only glancing up at the other two with an expression of increasing helplessness and distress, a look that was disturbingly incongruous with features of such strength. Several times he began to speak, and then, as if he already had the answers but had been afraid to recognize them, he would stop himself and drop his head. Finally he spoke, his voice broken.

"Now it makes sense, terrible sense. I have only addressed the situation in half measures. My God, how could I have let this happen?"

"Do not blame yourself, Fitz. Andrew has always been thus, and you cannot be faulted." She sat beside him.

"When I last rode west, I did sense a strange sort of reluctance on everyone's part to entertain me. 'Tis a small thing, I know, but in the past I would return to Dublin exhausted by their lavish hospitality. And do you know what I foolishly thought was the cause of their distance? You, Kitty. I was self-centered enough to attribute their aloofness to our announced engagement. I had been told by so many that I was quite the catch, quite the bachelor prize."

"Well, that was true. And now your head is swollen beyond all reason, and you are conceited to the point of offensiveness." She kissed his cheek, but he did not seem to notice. "You are my prize, and I have won you. And as I am the victor, you are my spoils."

He sighed and looked first at Kitty, then at his friend. "Can you fetch me the papers I have so long denied?"

"I shall be more than willing to retrieve them."

"Thank you. You see, only then can I be sure, to satisfy my own mind."

Patrick nodded. "I am indeed sorry, my friend, to give you this news on this happy day." He bowed once to Fitzwilliam, then to Kitty and he left the room.

Kitty smiled sadly. "I am so sorry. To hear this today, after our wedding, I fear will bring us ill luck."

"Kitty." He closed his eyes, rubbing a weary hand over his forehead.

Together they awaited the return of Patrick.

And in the next room, Andrew, who had heard all that transpired, clenched his fists in fury.

She awoke, the room hazy in darkness, not wishing to fully rouse herself. It was too comfortable, too delicious not to enjoy a private rest after a day of such excitement, of such emotional turmoil.

All would be calm soon, and then they could embrace the happiness they deserved. All would be calm soon.

He entered the room with such stealth, she did not even sigh in her sleep.

It was difficult not to congratulate himself on his own cleverness. He had outfoxed them, all of them, and now she would be his. All of his life he had been pushed aside, simply because of the misfortune of his birth. Such a small thing, really.

Once she had been taken with him, smitten and loving. That he knew. She was a woman of means from a family of considerable fortune. Until the other had turned her head, she had been his, all his.

It churned his stomach to think of them together. It

was no longer the money now, although that had been the original reason he had sought her out.

The money was secondary.

Because the most vital thing to him now was to win her heart, to get beyond those fools who sought to protect her. When he had her heart, he could thumb his nose at the rest of the world, all those who said he was a good-for-nothing and lazy, because with her heart came the money.

Of course he should have acted sooner, he should not have let things get so far. But his triumph would be all the greater because it was grasped so late. He had given the lesser man a head start, so to speak. It had been an honorable move, and all who spoke of him would grant him that.

The way she simpered and smiled with that man would soon be a distant, retreating memory to everyone, including the lady herself. She did not know yet that she was in love with him, and it galled him to see them together, cooing like deranged lovebirds.

Soon she would coo at him, soon she would forget the other man, for he would be nothing.

She rolled over in her sleep, and he remained motionless. It would not do to wake her now. Not after all of the planning he had done.

And there were those who had scorned him, said he would amount to nothing. How they would line up to praise him now!

Almost over her bed, the only illumination was the full moon. Even the moon had been in his plans, for he had known tonight would be full, with blue beams streaming through the window.

Was there a noise downstairs?

No. It didn't matter anyway. He would be silent, and she would be silent as well. He would offer her no choice. He would be the master, and tonight would be just the beginning.

Slowly he pressed his lips against hers. She responded fully, deeply, stretching against him like a wanton feline. Then she pulled back. But before she could scream he placed his hands about her neck. He had not intended to do that, but she had forced him. How could he continue if she called out?

With his hands about her neck, his thumbs pressing down on her throat, he again put his mouth over hers. But it wasn't as pleasant. She kicked and bucked, so he put his body over hers, and she made unappealing sounds, grunts and moans so great as to almost squelch his desire.

Almost, but not quite.

For beneath his body he could feel the soft outline of her breasts and the furious pounding of her heart. That was her desire, he knew. She wanted him, too. Never had she desired the other one.

He lessened his grip on her throat, and she gasped, her chest heaving. No other sound came.

His hands searched below. He would take her now, for he was ready. He would take her now . . .

"Help!"

How had she cried out?

His hand clamped over her mouth. She would not ruin it, not even in her passion. For that is what her cry meant.

And then the door burst open, like a thousand splintering thunderclaps. . . .

* * *

All over her.

He had her pinned in her own bed, and by the time she was fully awake he had already tightened his hands on her throat.

Was she alone? She could not remember. She tried to cry out but was not sure how loud her voice had been.

Now she could feel it, her life ebbing away. Perhaps it would be better this way, far better than to be taken by him. Perhaps she should stop the struggle, just give in and let fate take its course.

There was a commotion, shouts and calls and footsteps on the steps.

And that was the last she remembered.

"Maura! Open your eyes, please."

Cradled in his arms, she opened her eyes. Donal looked down.

"Thank God." He held her close. There was a cut on his face, and it was bleeding, but she couldn't think clearly.

"What happened?" Her voice was a croak.

Someone else was in the room. "The gardai will be here in two shakes."

"Charles?"

"You're safe now, Maura. Thank God, you're safe now," Donal murmured into her hair.

She closed her eyes, just for a moment, to keep the room from spinning so.

"You're safe now," repeated the voice. But it was a slightly different voice. And the smells were different, she smelled horses on the man who held her.

"Fitz?"

"Forgive me," he whispered. "Had I not heard you, I cannot think of what might have happened. Andrew is below with Patrick . . ."

The voices overlapped.

"Roger is below with Charles . . ."

They blended into one, and when she opened her eyes she saw Donal, yet over his form, like a vague superimposition, was Fitz. Their words and expressions mirrored with such precision, they acted as one.

And then he faded. At first she could not see which one was fading, and she feared they both would.

"Please come back," she cried.

"I will never leave you . . ."

The other, his voice growing distant, as if he walked through a narrowing tunnel. "I must leave. She waits. She waits . . ."

"No!"

One voice now. "I will never leave you." He held her more tightly. And then she herself seemed to fade out.

Charles and Donal sat downstairs at the Merrion Square town house, both shaken, both clutching glasses of whiskey, provided by a compassionate garda while their statements were being taken. The whiskey remained untouched for a long while as each man mulled his own thoughts.

"She'll be fine, Donal. The doctor said all she needs is sleep."

"It's my fault." He finally took a sip. "I didn't take Roger seriously."

"I can't believe what I did. Me, Charlie MacGuire,

the easy target of every bully from the time I could walk, actually injured another man."

"I have to thank you, Charles. Had you not decided to come over when you did, well . . . I would have been too late."

"I don't know what came over me." Charles stared down into his glass. "I never really thought about coming here again, I just did. And when I saw him attacking Maura, I grabbed the first thing I could reach—that old penknife."

Donal said nothing, but he, too, had seen the knife when the ambulance worker removed it from Roger's shoulder. It was an antique, with the initials P.K. elegantly scrawled on the hilt.

"The man is insane," Charles muttered.

"Of course, he is. I can only hope he is defended by an incompetent barrister. No offense."

"None taken, my lad." Charles drained the contents of his glass in a single swallow. "More of the creature?"

Donal shook his head. "Something strange has been happening," he stated.

"I know. You have barely touched your drink."

"Besides that. Have you felt it, Charles? Have you felt something odd in the air?"

"I would be lying if I said no." He poured another generous splash into his glass. "In truth, it's herself that brought it on." He tilted his head up toward the bedroom on the third floor where Maura was asleep.

"When did you first feel it?"

"The moment I showed her this house. She began to act differently when she walked through the door, as if she had an altogether different purpose than just a Yankee collecting an inheritance."

"It was as if she belonged."

"That was part of it," Charles admitted. "But there was something else as well. I can't put my finger on it exactly, but it was almost as if she carried with her a sort of spell, and all of us were under that spell while we were with her."

Donal nodded. "I thank you, my friend, for your help. All you have done . . ."

The solicitor scoffed. "I did nothing, nothing at all." He seemed to grow more pensive. "But I have had some peculiar dreams."

"Have you now?"

"More than dreams, more powerful. In it I was a man by the name of Patrick."

Donal kept his expression blank. "A common enough name, especially here in Dublin."

"It must have been my own sense of fancy, but I imagined myself a friend of Fitzwilliam Connolly. And the dream would not go away altogether. It was always there, hanging like a mist just waiting to be addressed, waiting patiently to be recognized."

"Do you feel the dream now?"

He thought for a moment, swirling the whiskey in the glass as he considered the question. "No. It's gone, at least for now. But I have a feeling it is indeed gone forever. It's like a book—I've finished it, and never again will I read it for the first time. I know the story. I can recall it whenever I wish, but it is over for me."

Donal took a deep breath. He was about to tell Charles his part of the dream, but something in

Charles's expression caused him to hesitate, then abandon the idea entirely. It would be too disturbing for Charles. He had already done more than his fair share, an unwilling participant. The less he knew about what had happened, the sooner he could return to his world of deeds and wills and everyday things.

"Well, Donal. I'll be off, if you don't mind. Will the two of you be well here?"

"Thank you, Charles. We'll be fine. Oh, and I'll come by tomorrow on my way to the factory."

"Yes. Yes, indeed, there are some lose ends to be tidied up."

He stood, took one quick gulp of the drink, and reached for his jacket.

"To Nesbitt's?" Donal raised an eyebrow.

Charles nodded in bright conformation. "To Nesbitt's. I'm meeting Evie there."

"Your ex-wife?"

"The very one. It is the most peculiar thing, Donal, but ever since Maura came into town, Evie and I have, well . . . things have been different between us. Better, I mean. She says I'm the man she hoped I would become, whatever that is supposed to mean. In other words, she fancies me again." He grinned and walked to the doorway with a distinct bounce to his step.

"That's grand, Charles. Do you think the two of you will get married again?"

"Married again? Why, there would be no need."

"Why is that?"

"Because, dear lad, we were never divorced. Good evening, Donal, and I'll see you in the morning."

He tipped an imaginary hat and left, the sound of his jaunty whistling heard clearly through the closed door.

Donal chuckled and latched the lock.

And, his back toward the staircase, he knew someone was behind him. Instinctively he knew it was not Maura. She would have spoken. She would have felt differently, not like this, not causing his spine to be traced with an icy finger.

Slowly he turned. At first he saw nothing. Then, as his eyes remained still, he saw a slow swirl of what seemed to be smoke on the staircase.

The swirling began to speed up, becoming swifter and thicker with every twirl, faster and faster it spun, and like clay on a potter's wheel, a shape began to emerge from nothing.

It was tall and solid, the image swirling, and Donal held his breath.

Finally, on the steps stood the unmistakable, three-dimensional figure of Fitzwilliam Connolly.

Donal simply stared, unafraid of this long-dead figure, yet uncertain as to what he should do.

Connolly returned the gaze, taking in the form of Donal Byrne at the foot of the staircase.

Every aspect of the apparition was vivid and astonishing. His boots glinted in the light. His hair, thick and slightly unruly, cascaded over a broad shoulder. From the expression on his face, he too was appraising the man before him, noting every detail of Donal's appearance.

He felt as if he knew the specter. An understanding deeper than any he had ever experienced flowed between them, an intimate knowledge of each other that was not of any known world, but that was complete and natural and pure. More than that, Donal felt as if a part of him *was* the man, an invisible part that only he knew of, only he himself and perhaps Maura.

So Donal did the only thing that seemed right and natural. He smiled.

At that the other man cocked his head, a silent question, and offered a genuine, unforced smile in return. His arm reached for Donal, as if they could touch, or shake hands. Then the hand dropped in futility, an unspoken knowledge that touching would be impossible.

And then he did something extraordinary: He bowed. It wasn't just a simple nod, or a sketchy movement forward. It was a deep bow at his waist, a gesture that was at once archaic and utterly universal, a motion offering honor, perhaps friendship.

Donal did nothing for a few moments, and then he, too, bowed in a forgotten gesture of greeting and respect, paying homage to the man on the stairs. By the time he had straightened, the man was gone.

He knew, Donal did, that he would never see the image again.

For after two and a half centuries of unrest, he was finally at peace.

At last it was over.

Chapter 20

"So nothing's changed." Maura descended the steps slowly, observing every detail of the town house. The early morning sun beamed in blurred streaks through the dirty windows. The single bare lightbulb was hanging with dismal resignation where a brilliant crystal chandelier once sparkled.

Donal jumped to his feet, any last traces of slumber gone the moment he saw her. "How do you feel?"

"Tired," she admitted. "Were you here all night?"

"Of course. Here." He reached for her hand, and as his clasped hers, she paused.

"Nothing has changed." The urge to cry was almost unbearable.

"You're wrong. Everything's changed. I was up all night reading your books. They are all different now."

"Then why am I still here? Why didn't Fitz and Kitty's children get this place?"

"Come over here and sit down. I'll explain everything."

Wearily she followed his lead. "Did they both live a long and happy life together? Please tell me that first."

"No, I'm afraid not."

She sat beside him on the sofa. "Oh, Donal."

"It seems Kitty was, indeed, ill. She died in Fitz's arms less than a year after their marriage."

Her hand flew to her mouth, hoping that somehow Donal had been wrong. Yet she knew what he had said was the absolute truth. Part of her died with that knowledge, as if an empty, hollow core expanded within her.

"How awful," she breathed.

"Perhaps. But for that one year they were happy."

A wistfulness laced his voice, a softness that had not been there before. If it had, she hadn't noticed it until now. He seemed different somehow. The house was exactly the same, every chipped corner and scuffed inch of it.

But Donal, he had changed. What was it? His voice was unaltered, his movements as swift and sure as always.

Puzzled, she watched his features before she spoke. Perhaps the difference was right there on his face.

"Did Fitz remarry?" Her eyes narrowed as she scrutinized his reaction.

"No, Maura. He didn't have much of a chance. In 1770 his ship, the *Katherine,* went down somewhere in the Atlantic during a storm. He was on his way to America to start a new life."

Her tears began before he had finished speaking.

Once they started, she was unable to stop them from flowing. The thought of his early death, of the terror he must have felt as the ship rolled and shattered into pieces, of slipping into an angry sea, knowing he would not survive.

"Maybe he would have been better off without our intervention," she said as he handed her his handkerchief. "Maybe he would have been better off dying here on the steps."

"How can you possibly say that? Think of Kitty alone, that she didn't suffer his death. My God, he would have suffered far worse, and gladly, to have spared her his death. He always knew that perishing at sea was probably his fate, although he did not relish the thought and hoped to avoid it. And they did have that year together, at least they had the year. Most people don't even get that."

What a romantic notion for the pragmatic Donal Byrne. How very unlike the man. But he was so absolutely correct. At least they had a year, a rare and wonderful year.

"You're right." She wiped her eyes. "Of course, you're right. What about Andrew and Patrick?"

A vague smile traced his lips. "Well, Andrew recovered from his wounds, and his older brother promptly sent him to sea on one of the more miserable routes to South America and Australia."

"He deserved far worse," she whispered.

"Oh, not to worry. He got far worse than a lack of suitable tailors—his own men killed him."

"His own men?"

Donal nodded. "It seems he attempted to go against his brother's orders by gathering slaves. The ship would not hold additional passengers, and the details are sketchy, but it seems a first mate shot him. There was a very brief investigation, but all in all everyone seemed relieved by his death. Don't forget that Kitty and Fitzwilliam were dead by then, so there was no one to mourn. And Patrick shipped himself off to America."

"Patrick did? Where did he settle?"

"Well, you can read any of his biographies if you want more details. All I know is that he was a signer of the Declaration of Independence and lived to a ripe old age on a Virginia plantation."

"That's wonderful." For the first time she smiled. "He deserved to be happy. Did he ever get married?"

"Late in life he did marry the widow of a friend. He didn't have any children, though, so when he died this house and the factory were left to the heirs of Mrs. Finnegan—the housekeeper—and yours and ol' Delbert's ancestors."

They sat in silence for long moments, each pondering the fates of four people who lived and loved and laughed and sorrowed over two centuries before. It hardly seemed possible that they were gone.

"Well," she began haltingly. "I guess that just about wraps things up."

"And what about us?" His voice was barely audible, layered with doubt, yet she knew what he had said.

"I don't know."

It had reached his eyes now. Always Donal's eyes had been spectacular. Now there was something else there, a depth and kindness and warmth that had been either missing or simply invisible.

"But I do know, Maura. I loved you before, yet after what happened last night . . ." He did not complete the sentence. There was no need.

"Donal, we have so many problems between us."

"I don't see it that way. We're both alive, we're both right here, right now. What else could possibly matter?"

"The factory. What are we to do about that?"

"While you were still sleeping, I gave that matter some thought."

"I thought you spent all night reading."

"I'm a fast reader. So after I had finished reading, I began thinking about the factory. And I realized what a shame it would be to change the basics of the place after so many years."

"Something has to be done," she argued. "It can't last much longer losing money at this rate."

"You're right. The problem is in the expense of the raw materials as well as the labor. If we use less expensive wood and more modern machinery for the primary steps, saving the hand labor for finishing, we would cut the costs and increase production."

"No. I don't think using cheap materials is the answer."

"I didn't say cheap. I said less expensive. There's a difference. Look, at the moment we are producing very fine reproductions of antique furniture. Other companies can do it just as well and more efficiently."

"I realize that, but . . ."

"Maura, have you ever seen some of the real Irish country furniture, pieces from farmhouses?"

"Not really."

"It's splendid, absolutely beautiful. It's made mostly from pine, less expensive than oak and the other woods. In design, the pieces are simple and basic, yet there is a true artistry in the purity of the lines, in the finishing touches."

His enthusiasm was infectious. "Go on," she urged.

"Every single man already employed has the skills. They have just not had the occasion to use them. We can get a few new pieces of equipment, hire a few recent university grads, and go from there."

"Perhaps we could have the finishing work, the more interesting stuff, done in the front room, so people touring the place could see how it's done."

"Maybe. No period costumes, though, or shoes with funny buckles or pots of gold with fake rainbows."

"No costumes," she agreed. "No rainbows or anything else that can be found on a cereal box. This will be real Irish artistry. And each piece can be unique, one of a kind. The basic designs will be the same, but the men can add their own touches, a carving here, perhaps stencil work there."

"Brilliant, absolutely brilliant!"

She was stunned. "I thought you said I wasn't a good businesswoman."

"Did I say that?" The smile left his face, and he leaned back, resting his elbow on the arm of the sofa.

"You most certainly did. More than once you've brought up the failure of Finnegan's Freeze-Dried, and my mishandling of almost any situation that comes my way."

This was not what she had intended to say, but she

couldn't help herself. Everything he had said about her failings still bothered her more than she had realized. With a few cutting remarks, he had managed to undermine her confidence.

How could she ever be happy with someone who would constantly criticize everything she did?

"You must think me a wretched article indeed," he whispered.

She blinked. This was not the reaction she had expected, not at all.

Closing his eyes, he continued. "I did say those things. Now I believe I know why—I wanted to hurt you, to bruise and harm you."

"But why? I never did anything to hurt you."

"Ah, but you did." He opened his eyes, and there was such sparkle and life in the glorious blue that she very nearly gasped. "You made me feel again. And with that feeling came hurt and pain and fear, everything I had been escaping from for so long. I knew you were fragile, and I instinctively knew where to aim. I couldn't target anything else about you, so I targeted the one thing that was not your fault, and that was the faltering of your father's company."

"But it was my fault." She swallowed, unable to turn away from his compelling eyes.

"See what a good job I made of it? I am ashamed, Maura. For in truth, I believe the problem with Finnegan's Freeze-Dried has nothing to do with you and everything to do with the product. The wonder is that a company producing nothing but freeze-dried cabbage could survive at all."

She remained silent, part of her wanting to defend her father's idea, the other stunned that she hadn't thought of that before. As if reading her thoughts, he went on.

"Maura, nobody really needs freeze-dried cabbage. People around the world do not express desperate longing for it. God knows fresh cabbage is bad enough. Do we really need it on hand for every occasion?"

With supreme tenderness he placed his arm about her shoulder, pulling her toward him. "But you did an amazing thing. You came up with clever ideas to make people think they needed the cabbage. Can you imagine what you could do with a good product? Why"—he kissed her hair—"you could be amazing. You already are."

"Oh, Donal. How on earth did you just do that?"

"Just do what?"

"You've just admitted to saying terrible things to me, but made me grateful that you did by turning all of your rotten words into something incredibly sweet."

"It's you, my love. You see, you proved me wrong on several counts, something I was quite unused to. But one item in particular has caused me to see everything in a whole new light."

"What was that?"

"You proved that we do have souls. Not only do we have souls but they touch and mingle and adore. Otherwise, how could you have such complete command over mine?"

The first kiss was as light and sweet as an air-spun confection. And then it changed, as sweetness gave way to longing, and at last passion, sharp and deep, became simply need.

And sometime before noon, they both agreed that it would be sheer folly to ever again deny that need.

They stood in the yellow parlor before a faded patch of wallpaper between the two windows.

"I wonder what we'll find," Maura murmured. There was a sense of awe, of wonder. Finally they would uncover papers hidden for two centuries.

"I already know what we'll find—the papers proving Andrew's nasty intentions. I'll bet there will be old newspapers and such, maybe all sorts of letters he wrote."

"We'll soon find out." Donal handed her a damp sponge. "Shall you do the honors?"

"I'm not sure. Is this place all mine again?"

"That's what Charles said. Roger's bid on the house was as fraudulent as his background."

"And his teeth," she added.

Donal grinned. "And his teeth," he confirmed.

"Well, here goes. Let's discover what secret papers Fitzwilliam Connolly hid in his own house."

They worked slowly, deliberately, to do as little damage as possible to the delicate wallpaper. She dampened the paper just enough for Donal to pull strips of it away.

"There is nothing," she said after they had been painstakingly laying the fragile paper on wax paper so they would be able to replace it later.

"Wait a second. What's that?"

A small corner of a piece of paper became evident.

They looked at each other, realizing that whatever they had just uncovered could very well unlock a mystery from the past. Was it proof of Andrew's attempt to kidnap Kitty? Perhaps the false papers he wrote to frame Patrick? Maybe even a confession of some sort.

"Careful," Donal said to himself as he eased the paper out.

"What the devil?" He stared at the document, holding it so Maura could see it as well.

"What on earth is this?"

He laughed. "It's a receipt."

"What for?"

"For some unspecified item from Thomas Read's Silver Shop."

"But the penknife was already picked up."

"This is for something else. Wait a moment, there's a note on the back."

Maura recognized the handwriting immediately. It was written in the distinctive hand of Fitzwilliam Connolly.

Patrick, Again, my friend, you come to my aid when I need it most. I trust this signifies you and Kitty and the child are well, and for that I am grateful. I also trust that I am merely at sea and not engaged in a voyage of a more permanent nature. Whatever the cause of my absence, convey to her my everlasting love. Yrs, Connolly.

"Okay, now I'm completely confused," she said, rereading the letter. "Whose child?"

"I haven't the faintest notion," he admitted. "At least, I'm not exactly sure."

"What do you mean? You have an idea what all of this might be about?"

"Maura, how would you like to fetch a stroll over to the good Mr. Read's shop? I believe we have neglected to pick up an item for far too long."

"Sounds swell by me." She took his arm. "You don't suppose we'll owe any money on this, whatever it is."

"Nah. The receipt says it's all been paid for."

"Cool."

"Very cool indeed," he agreed, and they set out in a fine, soft Dublin day to find out what Fitzwilliam Connolly ordered in the spring of 1768.

The clerk at Read's did not seem at all surprised. It was as if it were the most normal thing in the world to have an order picked up two and a half centuries late.

"Ah, so you forgot all about it, did you now?" The young man commented with a wink as he looked over the receipt.

"We did," Donal said. "What with all the recent commotion and all."

"The commotion?" The clerk looked up for a moment.

"The world wars, the founding of the United States, the Napoleonic Wars, a moonwalk or two, not to mention our own troubles here with the famine and all." He shrugged. "We were sidetracked."

"Ah, yes. I can see as to how that would happen. I myself find it hard to pull away from reruns of *Dynasty.* You know, I think I'm certain the very parcel this is. Lucky for you it's not in the stuck drawer. 'Twould be lost forever then. Ah, here we go now."

From beneath a counter he pulled a large, oblong package.

"Are you sure?" Maura asked dubiously.

"Of course I am. Look—the numbers match."

He was right—the numbers matched.

The clerk then produced a leather-bound ledger. Touching the tip of his finger to his tongue, he paged through the signatures. She saw a flash of dates, most from the last century. "Do you mind signing for the parcel?"

"No. Not at all," she said.

He scribbled the number of the package, then handed her the pen.

She turned to him. "Donal, would you rather sign?"

"No, Maura. This is all yours."

She smiled, then leaned over to write her name. When she straightened the clerk stamped it "Received."

"There we go." He passed the package into her hands.

"Do you have any idea what it is?" She couldn't help but ask.

"No," the clerk replied. "But whatever it is, the person who ordered it had no need of it. That's the way it is with most of the unclaimed orders here. The person simply had no need, for whatever reason. And that's where the stories are."

The package wasn't particularly heavy. "I don't know if I can wait until we get home. Do you mind if I open it here?"

The clerk raised his eyebrows. "I was hoping you would. I myself am overwhelmed with a desperate curiosity."

Maura set it back on the counter. "Scissors?"

"Take your pick," the clerk offered, sweeping his hand along a display case filled with hundreds of scissors, in gold and silver, some engraved and etched, others plain and functional. She chose a funny-shaped pair with a vine entwined along the blade.

"Ah, a fine example of Victorian grape shears. Lovely, isn't it?"

She cut the string and pulled the brown paper wrapping from the package. Beneath the wrapping was a plain wooden box with brass hinges and fixtures.

"Donal, it's beautiful."

"Open it," he urged.

Slowly she opened the box. And inside, embedded in plush green velvet, was a complete set of silver baby dishes and utensils. Engraved on each piece were tiny gold birds.

"Will you look at that?" The clerk whistled. "The workmanship. It's lovely. And what is that?" He pointed to a small round disk with a wooden lever protruding from the center.

Maura turned to ask Donal what he thought it was, but he had suddenly become pale. "Are you all right?"

He nodded once. "It's a pacifier. I need to step outside. Excuse me."

She turned to the clerk. "I'll be right back." The clerk didn't look up from the box, pulling out rounded spoons and a little cup, all with the delicate bird on the handles.

Donal was on the winding street next to a rusty black bicycle, leaning his arm against the grayish bricks of an old building, his head down.

"Donal?"

He did not respond immediately. Finally he looked up, his eyes damp with tears. "He ordered that to be ready, in case she should ever have a child when he was away. He hid the receipt, for he never wanted Kitty to know how he longed for a child of theirs. And when he realized how ill she was, that a child was out of the question, he was all the more relieved that he had never told her about this. He never wanted her to see the receipt, never. Only Patrick knew."

"But then he left the country. Perhaps he forgot about it," she said.

"No. He didn't forget. And all of the papers about Andrew were kept by Patrick, just in case. Apparently they were never needed. Andrew died ignobly enough on his own. But the clerk inside was right."

"About what?"

"The reason it was never picked up. There was no longer any use for it. But maybe . . ."

"Maybe what?" She bit her lip, thinking of all the hopes and dreams shared by a long-ago pair of lovers. They wanted only the simplest of things from their lives: each other and a family and a home. Yet they had been denied such things.

"Maybe we can use the dishes, you and I. Perhaps that's why all of this has happened." He turned her toward him, staring down into her face. "I want to marry you, Maura, as soon as possible. I don't believe we should wait to know each other, for we know each other better than we could in a hundred lifetimes."

All she could do is nod, knowing how right he was and how very right they were together.

"Is that a yes?"

Again she nodded.

"And will you always be this obedient to your husband?"

With her mouth still opened in mute surprise, her expression still one of shock, she shook her head.

"Good! Now, let's go back and claim the baby's things. We have a wedding to plan."

Later at a pub in the Temple Bar district, the clerk was finishing his second pint and ordered a third when a cluster of his friends entered.

"Have I a tale to tell to you boy-os." He wiped the foam from his upper lip. "It's about an American, an Irishman, and how they were brought together by a two-hundred-year-old baby set handed to them by yours truly . . ."

EPILOGUE

Jimmy O'Neil looked both ways before crossing the street to the Merrion Square house. Clutched against his black jacket was a bottle, the outline clearly visible even beneath the crumpled brown paper bag wrapping. A young woman walked past with a small terrier without glancing at him.

"And what are you looking at, young miss, and you with a poky little dog like that?"

The young woman kept walking at a brisker pace, uncertain what the strange little man had just said, but certain that his tone was accusatory in nature.

He paused behind a green cylinder mailbox, peeking out when he felt the coast was satisfactorily clear. Just as he was about to make his final break, a cluster of children led by a nun passed.

A few stragglers didn't move fast enough for his pleasure. Raising his hand to the smallest one, he hissed, "Get on with ye, little snapper! And mind you, don't you be looking at my bottle!"

The child burst into tears and ran ahead to catch up with his class.

Content at last, he raced to the gate of number eighty-nine and a half, one of the most splendid homes on the block. They had fixed it up grand, they had, with the garden and the polished brass and the red door. Herself had done most of the work while himself spent time at the factory, making it again a pride to enter altogether.

Now the orders were coming in from all over, from Europe and America, even from Japan, although Jimmy couldn't imagine what anyone from Japan would do with a great Irish cupboard, or a scumble-painted chest-on-chest, and they with no shoes at all and tiny cups that would fall through the slats.

Just last week they began making Waterford car beds, snug domed beds that resembled gypsy caravans. Americans were wild for them, especially with the quilts the ladies were making.

All in all, the past eighteen months had been grand. Maiden Works had never seen higher profits, and now that the Byrnes had managed to buy out the Germans, times had never been better. Even Kermit MacGee had missed but one day of work in well over a year, and that had been because of a boil on his back. Shame.

Jimmy climbed up the steps, admiring the fine bootscrape, and a little pot of mums on either side of the door. Those pots had been another of herself's ideas, little flower pots painted by local children.

They couldn't make them fast enough at the factory, that was for sure.

The doorbell had a fine ring to it. The Byrnes had restored the original chimes, taking away the electronic buzz that had been there before. He was about to ring again when the door flew open.

"Jimmy! Come on in!" Donal Byrne held the door wide open.

A fine-looking lad, Jimmy thought as he entered, glancing up at the chandelier. He could recall the first time they met, a serious young man with no joy whatsoever. It seemed impossible that this was the same man, a lad with a quick smile and easy charm. It was indeed an honor to work with such a man.

"I brought you a little something in honor of the occasion." Jimmy handed him the bottle.

Donal pulled down a corner of the bag. "Thank you. Let's see, a scotch bottle, filled with a clear speckled liquid, with a gin bottle top. Jimmy! You shouldn't have—this is your best poteen!"

"It's that indeed. The finest I have yet to make. Stay away from that rat poison MacGee brews up. That's why it's illegal entirely, inferior stuff like that. Do you remember old Maddie Bowen?"

"The blind woman with the limp?"

"She had neither until she took a single swallow of MacGee's poteen. Deadly stuff, that. I gag at the notion."

"Well, thank you, Jimmy. I'm sure Maura and I will enjoy this." Donal watched as a clump of an unidentifiable substance swirled from the bottom of the bottle, then settled heavily against the side.

"And how is herself?"

"She's grand, Jimmy. Just grand. She was a real trouper—it was sixteen hours, you know."

"Bless her altogether. And the little one? What's its name?"

"Katherine. But we're calling her Kitty. She looks just like her mother, absolutely lovely."

"Is she fair or dark?"

"Fair, I think. There's so little hair on her head at the moment, it's hard to judge."

"A drop of this"—Jimmy tapped the bottle—"and she'll have enough hair to wrap about the cradle twice in no time."

"I'll keep that in mind. And Jimmy, tell the boys that the cradle is brilliant. I've never seen a baby sleep so well."

"A drop or two of this"—again he tapped the bottle, nodding sagely—"and we will all sleep like innocent babes. I'm back to work now. Twelve more orders this morning, Mr. Byrne. One was for a dozen dressers in all styles, Galway, Ulster, Wexford—imagine! Oh, and a store in California, America, wants to carry nothing but items from Maiden Works. Pity, he seemed such a nice fellow on the telephone, and he living in a place about to break into the ocean altogether with the next earthquake. Well, give herself my best."

Before Donal could invite Jimmy in for a taste of the poteen, he was gone, hobbling down the street, his fine head of hair gleaming white.

He closed the door, giving the bottle another look. The rumor in the factory was that Jimmy used rats in his poteen barrel for flavor and to speed up the fermentation process.

One of the men from work had filled the holy water dishes in his house with the poteen, frantic to get rid of the telltale bottle before his wife could find it, but unable to pour a drop of it down the drain. His wife had dipped her fingers into one of the dishes, and, after making the sign of the cross and noticing the peculiar aroma, proclaimed the event a miracle.

Donal smiled and put the bottle on a table. Upstairs in the third floor bedroom, his own miracle was waiting for him.

Picking up the flower arrangement that had just arrived, he made sure she would be able to read the card. It was from the entire staff of Finnegan's Freeze-Dried, the company she had sold just over a year ago. Peter Jones was now the head of it, and with the addition of dried fruits and a line of health drinks, the company was expanding with such speed, it had been featured in a *Business Week* cover story.

Nobody had been more thrilled at their success than Maura. Although some of the ideas that had propelled them to such success had been hers, vetoed by her father years before, she refused to accept any credit. Never had she complained or bemoaned that the company was no longer hers.

"This is where my life is now," she had said. "This is where my present and future are, here in Ireland with you, not back in Wisconsin."

She was indeed a wonder, his Maura.

He entered their bedroom softly, watching her as she slept. Somehow he couldn't watch her enough, as if he was never able to get his fill of her, of the mere sight of his wife. In her sleep she stirred, and he leaned over and brushed a strand of hair from her face. She stretched her arms over her head and opened her eyes, and Donal simply watched her movements with pure joy.

"Was that Jimmy O'Neil?"

"It was, indeed. And here are some flowers from Peter Jones and company. May I sit on the bed?"

"Of course." She patted the spot next to her. "They're beautiful, aren't they?" She inhaled the fragrance of the bouquet as he set them on the table next to her.

In a single movement he settled on the bed and leaned down to kiss her. Her hand cupped his shoulder, and she sighed.

"How are you feeling?" he asked. All of her color had returned, her cheeks bright with health.

"Wonderful." She smiled, propping herself up on one elbow. "And how are you feeling?"

"I'm not the one who just had a child. Is she still asleep?"

"Mmm. She's really so good, Donal. Other babies fret and cry, but Kitty is an absolute wonder. Look over at her—she even smiles in her sleep."

"Biddy Macguillicuddy said it's gas."

"And what does she know?" Maura giggled.

He glanced over at the cradle where the infant slept, her mouth moving in a content sucking motion even in her slumber. "Isn't she amazing," he whispered.

Maura just stared at her husband, at the expression of love on his face. Never in her wildest dreams could she have imagined such happiness. There were moments when she literally shook herself, wondering if Donal was real or just a blissful dream, a fantasy conjured in her mind and heart.

But he took her hand, his heart filled with such warmth. His hands had become hardened with the work at the factory—he had insisted on learning how to make the furniture himself. And he was good. Jimmy O'Neil himself had said he would hire Donal, had Donal not been his boss.

"Are you baking bread?" She only just noticed the fragrance of Donal's soda bread.

He nodded, still staring at his daughter.

"How wonderful that she'll grow up eating homemade bread." Maura raised his hand to her lips and kissed his palm.

Slowly he turned to face her. "My love." His voice was low. "I never imagined life could hold such joy. You have given me so much."

Again their lips met, and she slipped her hand behind his head to draw him closer to her. She always wanted him closer, ever closer.

He pulled away. "I believe I am in the middle of burning two perfectly fine loaves of bread." He grinned.

She sniffed, then returned the smile. "I've always loved burned bread. Sort of Cajun—blackened soda bread."

"I'll have to give Nino the recipe."

"I'm sure he already has it," she replied.

Donal stood. "I'll be right back. Where was that fire extinguisher again?"

"Behind the kitchen door—right where you put it after the last time." He began to leave. "Donal?"

Pausing at the door, he turned. "Yes?" Even in that single word, he managed to infuse a bounty of love. For a moment she simply blinked, relishing the very presence of him.

"Do you think we'll ever see them again?"

He did not need to ask who she was talking about. "Why? Do you miss them?"

"Not exactly." Sitting up fully, she began to twirl a piece of hair. "I just want to know how they are, what they are feeling. But you didn't answer my question. Do you think Kitty and Fitz will ever come back?"

He leaned against the frame of the door. "Well, I don't know if they have ever really left us."

"Have you seen them?"

"No. But I feel them, every day I feel them. It's a softness, like a gentle rain that is more of a mist—hardly noticeable, but there just the same."

"I feel them as well sometimes. Not Patrick or Andrew, not them. But at times I look at you, and I see Fitz in your eyes."

He took a deep breath. "Once that thought angered me. I wasn't sure if you loved me or a ghost. And now I realize that somehow I see Kitty in you. Not all the time, just certain moments. And it feels right, as if that is how it should be."

"Perhaps they have given us the happiness they longed for. Do you think that is possible?"

"Absolutely." He was about to continue when he frowned. "Do you smell smoke?"

"The bread!"

"Christ! I forgot!" Before he turned to rescue the bread, he stopped. "Oh, are you up to having Charles and Evie drop by this evening?"

"Fine, great—Donal, the bread . . ." and Donal darted down the stairs.

Maura leaned against the down pillows and closed her eyes, marveling how on earth she could have ever thought Ireland was anything less than magical.

Prologue

Richmond, Virginia
August 1865

The heat was almost unbearable. Constance Lloyd dabbed at her temples with a handkerchief, worn and frayed, but freshly laundered and pressed. About her wrist was a small drawstring bag containing the last few Union dollars in her possession. She dare not leave it behind at the Smithers sisters' boardinghouse, even for the brief walk to the post office. Sweet as the elderly women were, and as respectable as the other boarders seemed to be, Constance was not foolhardy enough to leave her worldly goods unprotected. Had she been so reckless, she never would have survived the past four years.

A cart rolled by on the unpaved street, the dust rising in a dry swirl, causing her to pause and close her eyes.

Had it ever been so hot in Richmond?

"Good day, Miss Lloyd."

Constance opened her eyes to see Mr. Bryce, his features sharp and haggard, tip his hat. Although he was of an age with her own father, he had just returned from active duty in the Confederate army. It had taken him months to walk back to Richmond after the war had ended.

"Good day, Mr. Bryce," she smiled, remembering him years ago, a stout man who would always slip her a licorice whip when he came visiting at the Lloyd plantation.

"Is it hot enough for you?" Mr. Bryce's face was mottled in the heat, the sparse gray hair dampened against his scalp.

"Not quite, Mr. Bryce," she replied sincerely. "That's why I'm heading further south today, toward the post office. I'm hoping there will be less of a chill down there."

Mr. Bryce laughed, more of a brittle cackle, and the laugh became a cough. She politely ignored the cough, and he tipped his hat once more, saluted her with two fingers, and continued on his way.

How strange the encounters were with people she had always known. Now they seemed to be strangers, separated by the very ordeal that should have drawn them together. At first the defeat of the Confederacy did unite them. As the weeks became months, blame and mistrust and simple fear of the future seemed to overtake everyone. Even the simplest of facts became distorted in the mundane discomfort of daily life. Instead of patriotic songs and speeches, the survivors engaged in finger-pointing and accusing every neighbor of harboring sympathetic thoughts toward the Yankees. Instead of going forward with their lives, most seemed to dwell in the past, playing games of what might have been if only so-and-so had done such-and-such. The only ones to escape suspicion were the fallen heroes. They alone were at peace.

Constance glanced up at two of the intact structures remaining in Richmond, the State House and the Confederate Executive Mansion. Both stood solid and proud as always, surrounded by half walls and empty shells of spectral ruins, skeletal remains of the city that once was Richmond. Planted firmly above both roofs were large American flags, waving in the blistering August heat. How strange those flags still seemed to her eyes.

Had it ever been this hot in Richmond?

The post office was just ahead. Constance did not acknowledge the trio of Union soldiers who stepped aside for her to pass, all three mumbling a greeting. Her failure to recognize the men had nothing to do with the Union victory or any latent hostility. She had no more energy for that sort of thing. Instead it was an admission of how things had changed. Not everyone in Richmond was a friend.

Not so long ago she would have been chastised for walking on the street without an escort. Had Wade Cowen seen her stroll down a public street alone, he would have been furious. But Wade, her fiancé, was dead these four months.

Although they had not seen each other for over two years, in a furious, impassioned exchange of letters they had agreed to marry when the war ended. She had wondered of late if Wade, whom she had known since childhood, had truly loved her as a woman and not just as a childhood sweetheart. It didn't matter now, not really. The day after peace had been declared, Wade—who had never been much of a horseman—had been killed leading a charge against a group of picnicking Federal soldiers.

He was given a hero's burial, the last of the fallen Confederates, it said on his tombstone. Constance had been told the truth by one of Wade's fellow officers: poor Wade had simply lost control of his horse. When he realized he was riding toward a cluster of stunned Feds, he probably went through his choices and decided it was better to die a hero than to live a fool. So at the last moment, struggling with the reins, he pulled out his sword and waved it, more in an effort to regain balance than as a threat.

The Feds shouted at him to stop, and when he could not, they shot him once through the forehead. Just once. The officer who shot Wade had written Constance a note about her fiancé's bravery, and everyone agreed he felt terrible about the shooting.

The line at the post office was long, as Constance knew it would be. Everyone was hoping that some distant relation up north would mail them money. Virginians who had previously declared to have no connections whatsoever with the Union were now writing frantic letters, asking for loans, reminding cousins by marriage in New York and Ohio and Vermont of the binding thickness of blood.

The line snaked forward as the single clerk shook his head at requests for free postage, inquiries concerning a parcel an individual knew, just knew would be arriving any day now.

"Poor Miss Lloyd."

It had not been a greeting. Someone behind her had simply issued a statement.

"Poor Miss Lloyd, indeed." Another woman echoed her companion's opinion.

Constance did not even blink. She was used to it by now, the murmurs and gentle tisking of acquaintances who pitied her. It seemed absurd that after four years of violent death and disease, of moral destruction, of tragedy such as the world has seldom seen, the plight of eighteen-year-old Constance Lloyd seemed to wring condolences from even the hardest of hearts.

True, her father had perished of the

mumps shortly after enlisting in the Confederate army. Soon after that, her mother died of what seemed to have been little more than a bad cold. By the time the main house of the plantation erupted in fire, there were too few servants, or slaves, as the Feds called them, to do much more than watch the conflagration.

Wade's death had been the final blow, although by then she was too numb to feel much of a loss. Everyone had suffered during the war, not a single person was left unscathed. But Constance, whose path to maturity was marked by each devastation, seemed to evoke pity in everyone.

It was absolutely intolerable. There was no place for her to escape the down-turned mouths and sad eyes of sympathy.

". . . and then her beloved fiancé Wade Cowen . . ."

She clutched the drawstring bag so tightly her knuckles turned white.

". . . and her mother. Don't forget her mother. I was at her coming out, and never was there such a belle in all of Virginia. She was English, you know, from England."

The women's voices rose as they discussed Constance, the marble columned mansion where she grew up, the paragon that was her father, the perfection that was her mother, her poverty, the mended tear in the skirt of her dress.

Constance stifled the urge to scream. How delightful it would be to turn around and face the old hens, to hit them over the head with her purse, or to tell Mrs. Witherspoon that her beloved son had sold the family silver for Union whiskey.

Instead, she moved ahead with the line.

"Miss Lloyd," said the clerk when at last she reached the window. "There is a letter for you."

The clerk seemed relieved to finally have something to give to someone. He bobbed behind the shelves and emerged holding a battered envelope. "It's from England," he announced in a loud voice. A quivering hush fell over the post office as she took the letter in her bare hands—when had she last worn gloves?—and stepped away from the window.

Her hands were trembling. "Please, God," she whispered, aware that she had not prayed for a very long time.

With her thumb she gently loosened a

flap, pausing only once. "Please," she repeated.

This was it. She had written her mother's cousins, asking if they knew of a position as a governess among their friends in England. It had been a last resort, a final attempt to regain control of her life. Should this fail, she had no place to turn.

She stepped to a corner of the post office for privacy she knew would elude her, but she couldn't possibly wait until she reached her tiny room at the Smithers sisters' house. She held her future in her hands.

Taking a deep breath, she slid the letter from the envelope and tilted the first of what seemed to be many pages toward the light.

"My dear Cousin Constance, We are delighted to inform you that there is, indeed, a position for you here in England. Come as soon as possible. Enclosed is a one-way passage . . ."

That was all she could read before her vision misted with tears. Clamping her hand over her mouth, she was unable to stop the gasp that escaped.

She was saved.

The gasp was followed by another, and before she could leave the post office she was weeping with relief, loud, wrenching sounds, tears rolling freely from her eyes.

She had not cried in years. But it didn't matter, nothing mattered.

She was saved.

"Poor Miss Lloyd. More bad news, no doubt," said Mrs. Witherspoon as Constance ran from the building, bumping into a brass spittoon and begging its forgiveness in her haste. "Was there ever a more wretched, unfortunate girl on the face of this earth?"